ROGUE MERCENARY

By John R. Monteith

BRAVESHIP BOOKS

CHAPTER 1

Jake Slate wrapped Terry Cahill in a bearhug. "Welcome to married life."

"Easy, mate. I'm not made of steel, like you."

Releasing the groom, Jake considered his age. "I'm pretty sure this is the strongest I'll ever be. I once read that thirty-nine years old is the peak of a man's strength, which I thought was really cool until it passed me by. Now that I'm forty, it's all downhill."

"Are you trying to depress me?"

"Hell, no! You got a great wife. And I'm not just saying that because I'm afraid of her."

"She's fifty kilos of fury I'd never tangle with."

"And, she'll be keeping your testicles in a jar from now on, I imagine?"

"She already does, and no complaints from this happy husband."

Eyeing the banquet hall, Jake found it ascetic for the occasion of his fellow submarine commander's wedding. He assumed Israeli toughness guided the décor's theme, noting that Cahill's wife's Aman intelligence service colleagues wore their military dress uniforms. "She didn't want a traditional Jewish wedding?"

"She's not very religious. Neither am I, mate. Sorry."

After a year in biblical studies that intensified his beliefs, Jake took no offense. "My friends don't need to share my faith. I just noticed that your ceremony seemed awfully non-Jewish."

"It's a secular trend among Israelis."

Across the room, a stranger caught Jake's eye.

She was taller than average and seemed built of shapely iron. Above pronounced cheeks, her dark eyes absorbed light, leaving a veneer of camouflage over mysterious thoughts, and her posture suggested innate defiance.

Jake noticed his colleague taking interest in her. "Check out the Russian bear. He's not doing so bad."

Cahill risked the glance. "Dmitry's got a hard on."

"I hope not. If he does, he's got equipment issues."

"Not his pants, mate. Look at his face. I think he's in love."

"He just met her. We all just met her. I still don't understand why Pierre insisted on bringing a stranger to your wedding."

"He said he'd explain later and that it would all make sense. I think he's on one of his dramatic attempts to earn an academy award."

Jake considered the Frenchman's flair for intrigue an overused but tolerable trait. Over the years, it had become less impactful but more endearing of the fleet's aging patriarch. "I'm sure of it, given how Pierre behaves. But he'd better hurry before Dmitry swallows her. I've never seen him so giddy."

"True, mate. But Dmitry's no idiot. See how he's staying an arm's length away."

"Has he been watching the videos of Ariella schooling you in Krav Maga?"

"I don't think this new lady's a hand-to-hand fighter. She doesn't have that look."

Jake frowned. "And Ariella does?"

"Right. Good point. Can't always tell whose hands are lethal weapons. Maybe we should rescue him before he gets himself punched."

"Yeah. Let's go."

As Cahill stepped towards the Russian, Jake trailed him, placed his hand on the groom's shoulder, and whispered. "You want to bet who she is?"

"Nah, mate. I'm afraid I'll be right."

As they reached the conversation, Dmitry Volkov aimed his peppered beard at the Australian. "Terry! You enjoy married life?"

"No complaints."

"This Danielle."

Cahill waved. "Yeah. We met briefly already."

Danielle nodded. "Congratulations. It's been an honor to attend."

"Thanks, and married life's great so far. Speaking of which, has anyone seen Her Majesty?"

Jake scanned the room for a white gown. "Lieutenant Colonel Dahan is speaking with her brothers, it appears."

"Ah, me beloved bride and the new in-laws. Well, if you'll excuse me. Can't help it, but I miss her already, and we have lots of hands to shake." Cahill departed.

Jake eyed Volkov. "Your English is getting pretty good."

"I try hard, you know."

The unexpected female guest wore a conservative blue dress that covered all but her neckline. The inflections in her voice were like icepicks pelting steel but somehow feminine. "He's trying really hard."

"How's he doing?"

Her smile was rote, her eyelids closing as she tried to hide her disdain for small talk. "Not bad. I appreciate the effort."

Jake put his friend on the spot. "I think he's trying to flirt."

She eyed the Russian. "And I appreciate that effort, too. There's no harm in a little flattery, and he seems friendly enough."

Volkov smiled. "You see, Jake? Almost two years I study English. Now I can talk to beautiful lady. Hard work pays off!"

Danielle Sutton smirked. "I didn't say your flirting was working."

Volkov blushed. "I must try harder?"

"No, please don't! But we should get to know each other."

"*Da*! That's what I hoping!"

Jake intervened. "That's what I was hoping as well, although for more professional reasons."

Volkov protested. "I am professional!"

"I'm not arguing that." Recognizing his colleague's helplessness in front of the stranger, Jake worked with it. He shifted his tone and bragged on the Russian's behalf. "Dmitry saved my life more times than I can count."

Danielle gave another polite but dismissive smile. "I'm sure you can count that high."

Snorting, Jake countered. "Yeah, but he's really that good. I'm sure there are times he saved my life that I don't know about!"

"*Da*! I am that good. I sound proud, but I am true."

She showed her first signs of warmth to Jake. "I can't argue with that. He looks true to me."

"You mean 'it' is true, Dmitry. You are correct because 'it' is true. And you are the best. Crap, I just admitted it out loud. Humility comes with age, I guess. But I tip my hat to you, buddy. You're a stud."

Volkov frowned. "I don't understand all you say. Should I get translator?"

"No, don't bother. I said you are as good as me. Maybe better."

The stranger played along with pandering to the Russian. "Hmm. A stud, huh? This crowd doesn't disappoint." She shifted her attention to Jake. "I hear that you and Terry are studs, too, although less accomplished in submarines forcibly removed from battle. That is how you guys compare yourselves against each other, isn't it?"

Jake fell silent, eyed her, and wondered if she knew too much. He wanted to disengage. "Well, Dmitry seems to have mastered English enough to keep you entertained-"

A man with a French accent interrupted. "You're not leaving the conversation now, are you, Jake?"

Dressed in a tuxedo, Pierre Renard approached with a confused and wifeless Cahill beside him.

Jake greeted his colleagues, "The man of the hour. Or should I say 'men'?"

Renard waved a dismissive palm. "It's Terry's night. Actually, it's Ariella's night, and I stole her husband away while she floats about the room. It's wonderful to see her so happy. But I owe my commanding officers an explanation about Miss Sutton's presence. So, here we are."

Jake admitted his curiosity. "Yeah, Pierre. I'm dying to know."

"Danielle Sutton is formerly 'Commander Sutton' of the United Kingdom's Royal Navy, and the former commanding officer of the *Duke*-class frigate, *Westminster*."

Jake saw her with new understanding. The military connection made sense, adding a piece of circumstantial evidence to his theory of her presence. "Impressive. And as long as we're talking about her like she's not here, I assume you've got some big news about why you invited her to join us tonight?"

"Of course, I do." Renard paused to create anticipation among his audience. "She will be the commanding officer of a *Goliath*-class submersible transport ship."

As the words circled in his mind, Jake aligned them with the news he'd expected. As he digested their meaning, the Frenchman's insights seemed predictable in retrospect but nonetheless exciting. "Keep talking."

Renard giggled. "I can't believe I did this. I'm giddy like a schoolgirl. It's my wedding gift to Terry."

Cahill interrupted. "You already paid for my entire wedding. What more could I want?"

"That was just a gift of money. Danielle is part of the gift of a growing family, one of which you are a senior sibling, so to speak."

Jake prodded for more. "That sounds great, but you're still holding back juicy details. And would you wipe that smile off your face? You're turning red."

"It took three and half years, but it's complete. I'm actually impressed with myself now that it's done."

Jake sighed. "Just spit it out, Pierre."

"To lighten the burden on the *Goliath*, to allow a greater reach of our fleet, or both, depending on the circumstances, I've built a sister ship for the *Goliath*. It's called the *Xerses*, and Danielle will be its commander." The Frenchman held his breath, awaiting his audience's shock.

But the drama fizzled.

Scowling, Jake undermined his boss' flair. "You promised a sister ship to the *Goliath* a long time ago."

Dismayed, the Frenchman needed a moment to recover. "Really? Hold on." He cast his eyes downward. "Perhaps I'm getting old and losing my memory."

"You mentioned it on the mountain during one of our team-building climbs, but then you never mentioned it again."

"Oh shit, I did mention this once before, didn't I?"

"Yeah. Like over a year ago. And I think you're actually late in delivering it. I was wondering when you'd finish it, but I didn't want to pry."

"You're draining me of every shred of pride, man."

Jake shrugged. "Pride's overrated. Confidence counts."

Renard attempted to recover a semblance of intrigue. "Aren't you at least impressed that I found a commanding officer?"

Folding her arms, Danielle Sutton eyed her new colleagues' buffoonery while smirking.

After checking that she hadn't fled the merry band of idiots, Jake answered. "Of course. You can't have a... was it the *Xerses*?"

Renard flicked his hand. "Yes."

"By the way, I personally like the ongoing biblical references. Real nice touch. Anyway, you can't have a *Xerses* without a commanding officer. We're just getting to know her."

"You're not taken aback that she's a female commander? It isn't... 'a thing' for you gentlemen?"

Jake considered Volkov and Cahill. "We all had women in our combat fleets, except for Dmitry, and the way he's acting, I'm not sure he's even seen a woman before, period. You may want to keep an eye on him."

The Russian protested. "I not sure what you say, but don't mind."

Cahill further deflated Renard's drama. "Liam's skipper on the *Perth* was female, and he turned out alright."

Renard lobbed his final theatrical grenade. "Well, she's a surface warfare officer without a second of service on a submarine. I'm taking a really big risk here. Surely that must stir some emotions."

Jake chuckled. "Wait. You're trying to negotiate against yourself. You're trying to make hiring Danielle look like an impossible win that you somehow magically pulled off with your infinite wisdom and heroic insight. I'm sorry to disappoint you, but at first blush, she fits right in."

Renard pouted. "I feel so transparent."

Danielle's face turned red as she bit her lip and applied every facial muscle to limiting the width and height of her smile.

With the Frenchman recoiling, Cahill continued the onslaught. "Liam's been a gem on the *Goliath*, and I always trust him to command it in my stead. He never worked under water before joining us, but not all surface sailors are complete bunglers, much as we enjoy mocking them."

Relaxing her folded arms, the new arrival gave a glimpse of her moxie. "Thank God my bungling was always incomplete."

Jake snorted. "Sorry, Danielle. Terry's delirious with nuptial joy. And Pierre? We're still trying to explain his behavior, but we are slowly getting used to him. We all saw this coming."

"I feel violated."

Jake chuckled. "It's okay. We still love you. And it's awesome that we're going to have another combat transport ship."

"Oh, don't patronize me."

Jake dealt the deathblow. "Does somebody need a hug."

The fleet's patriarch sighed and then stepped away. "Raincheck on that. Let me escape with what shred of dignity I still have."

CHAPTER 2

Commander Ozan Dogan checked the aging Turkish submarine's location. The chart showed the *Preveze* ninety miles south of Cyprus, drifting with the Mediterranean Sea's currents.

"Captain?"

Dogan rested his eyes by looking into the cramped confines' farthest distance. Grateful that the *Type-209/1400* hull design allowed him to see its innards fore to aft, he allowed himself a moment of intentional breathing while rubbing his forehead. "What's on your mind, master chief?"

The tiny man with soft eyes and a strong stance leaned into Dogan's ear. "The men are restless, sir. They know something unusual is happening, and they wish to know our mission in detail."

Dogan stood straight and met the master chief's stare. "The men wish to know, or you wish to know?"

The small man nodded. "I am among the men who wish to know. I've never seen such secrecy in all my twenty-one years of service."

After reflecting, Dogan conceded. It was time to divulge the full picture. "Very well. Bring them together in the crew's dining area tomorrow morning after breakfast, and I'll explain everything."

The master chief hesitated.

"What's wrong?"

"Sir, I've never seen them this anxious."

"Seriously?"

The short man nodded.

"Alright then. Round them up and get me when you're ready."

"Thank you, captain. I'll see to it." The master chief walked away.

Dogan stopped him. "Master chief?"

The tiny man turned. "Sir?"

"Have someone draw all coastlines within five hundred nautical miles of our position on the whiteboard. I'll add a few doodles of my own when I tell my story."

"Yes, sir."

As the master chief departed, the *Preveze's* commander craned his neck towards the man of average build who hunched over two seated sonar technicians. "Exec!"

The man strode to his captain. "Sir."

"I'm going to inform the crew of our mission parameters."

The lieutenant commander in his young thirties grunted. "Yes, sir. I mean, if you think they're ready."

"Ready or not, they need to hear it. The master chief was giving me a read on their pulse. The worry's getting out of hand."

"Understood, sir. We trained for months to monitor Greek naval activity, and now, all of a sudden, we're here. But the men are professionals and should be able to adapt quickly."

Dogan disagreed. "That's wishful thinking. Never underestimate the capacity of confused men to become desperate in their thirst for knowledge."

"Ah. You make a good point, sir. Would you like me to take the deck and the conn?"

"That's a good idea. Do so, and I'll take a break to prepare my thoughts."

"Any special orders while I'm running the ship?"

"Yeah. Don't shoot any weapons, don't break anything, and don't get us killed. You have the deck and the conn."

Thirty minutes later, Dogan was seated in his quarters reflecting upon his mission. He inhaled the scent of stale dust hiding beyond the reach of cleaning rags within the twenty-five-year-old submarine.

His perspective was broad, earned from his education at the University of Chicago's Harris School of Public Policy, the world's second-best college of government behind that of Harvard. After a poor childhood of disadvantage and abuse, Dogan exuded gratitude for his Navy.

From the depths of victimhood, which included sexual abuse by a disturbed uncle, he'd fought through the psychological agony of having been reduced to a carnal toy by a trusted person with the help of a caring mother.

With her support, he'd evolved from a victim to an overachiever, excelling in his schooling. But as his adulthood had approached, he'd feared her effort wasted as privilege had fallen to wealthier children. Facing a lifetime of limits, he'd found liberation through his mother's relentless pleas to businessmen, politicians, and flag-rank military officers, which had born fruit when an empathetic admiral had considered his cause.

His mother's efforts had enabled his admission to the naval academy in Istanbul, and Dogan had excelled, graduating in the top ten percent of his class. Then the submarine fleet had taught him tactics, leadership, and, after his executive officer tour, national strategies by placing him at the Harris School.

And the school had taught him much.

Wise, sane, and compassionate people could commit mass killings for rational reasons. Only a single autocrat was required to kickstart atrocities, forcing nations to kill preemptively or retaliatorily for self-preservation.

He ruminated over history's examples. He believed that every dead German citizen in World War II could be traced to Hitler's evil and every dead Japanese national to Tojo's greed. Dresden, Nagasaki, and Hiroshima served as knockout blows to regimes of death, forcing them to surrender in hopes of sparing a greater body count from continued warring.

Dogan pondered this as he faced a decision.

Could he kill thousands, if ordered?

The unshakeable anxiety lingering from his abusive childhood compounded his doubt in his resolve to pull the trigger. He expected orders to come from fleet headquarters in Ankara, but history had taught him that commanders at sea often bore the burden of harsh command decisions.

And missing an opportunity to strike thousands–repeats of the World War II knockout blows–could beget chain reactions killing tens of thousands.

Action killed.

Inaction killed.

And Ozan Dogan might bear the burden of strike, and possibly the decision to attack.

He picked up a sound-powered phone from the wall and dialed the corpsman, the only other person aboard the *Preveze* who enjoyed private quarters.

The medical professional's voice was deep. "Corpsman."

"Corpsman, captain. Bring medication."

"I'll be right there, sir."

"Thank you." Dogan hung up the phone, stood, and paced. Listening for footsteps, he heard them approaching and then opened his door before the corpsman could knock. "Get in here."

The corpsman darted into his commander's stateroom and sat in the guest chair without being asked.

He had that leeway.

Dogan was indebted to him for delaying his retirement to render personal support that only a trusted companion with proper training could give.

Two years ago, when he'd taken command of the *Preveze*, Dogan had suffered a panic attack during a simple exercise. Refusing to show weakness, he'd delegated his role to his executive officer as a surprise training opportunity. He'd then made a hasty exit and had turned to the only safe person–the corpsman.

And Senior Chief Asker had given him a compassionate ear. Concerned for Dogan, he'd devoured everything he could about the psychology of childhood sexual abuse to assist his captain through rudimentary therapies.

As Asker had helped Dogan manage his nerves, he'd shown a deeper compassion than that of a man concerned with his own interests. He'd acted as if rescuing another human from suffering, and Dogan noted it.

As the therapeutic techniques helped, he'd grown fond of Asker, and he appreciated his discretion. The Turkish Navy knew nothing of Dogan's childhood and its lingering effects, and it never would.

Asker extended the pill and a cup of water. "I can't imagine the stress, sir."

Dogan gulped the Valium. "I hate talking about it, but I imagine you're going to make me?"

"Isn't that why I'm the only enlisted man who knows what we're doing out here?"

"Yeah, but–"

The only man with unwritten permission to interrupt his commander did so.

"No, 'buts', sir. I'm always safe for you. No pressure to talk unless you want, but you really should."

"Well, I don't want to."

"Fine. I just heard about your upcoming brief. You'll get all the therapy you need when you update the crew."

"Oh, great. Should I do deep breathing, yoga, or singing exercises while I talk to them?"

"None of the above. You've been through worse. With all the crap you've been through, you're braver and stronger than you think. You'll be fine." The corpsman extended another plastic cup that Dogan had assumed was his colleague's drink. "Will you hold this?"

"Uh, sure." It felt cold, and Dogan examined the crushed ice. "What trick's this?"

"The game is, you balance that cup in your palm–no fair gripping it–without spilling it while we walk to the crew's dining space." Asker stood.

Dogan watched his cup of ice. "They're ready?"

"Yeah. I checked on my way here. Nobody suspects that I'm your medical crutch. At the moment, I'm just the messenger asking you to join the crew. They're ready and waiting."

As Dogan followed his companion out the door, his palm felt cold. "I don't mean to be an ass, but this game is stupid."

"I know. But it'll be a show of strength when you arrive with it still in your hand."

"Based upon that statement, I'm afraid you're the lunatic. Not me."

"You're not a lunatic. You're in permanent recovery from trauma."

The ice almost tumbled, but Dogan rebalanced it. "Quiet! Or people will hear."

"Who will hear? Everyone's on watch or waiting for you."

"Fine. I still think this is silly." He used most of his focus to keep the ice from falling while following the corpsman down the short passageway. He reached the cramped dining area that held two dozen eager pairs of eyes facing one whiteboard.

As Dogan examined the dry-erase artwork, the cup fell from his palm and splattered on the deck.

Asker called to the nearest petty officer. "Grab your captain a new cup of ice and a refill. Diet Pepsi, right, sir?"

Confused, Dogan nodded. "Yeah. Diet Pepsi. Thanks."

Asker knelt beside him and whispered. "You dropped the cup."

"I got klutzy there, but I was distracted by that nice drawing of Cyprus and the sea's southeastern coasts."

"Yeah, that was good detail by whoever drew it."

"What was this ice cup trick all about? All I did was create a slip hazard."

"I'll pick it up while you brief the crew."

"What was the point of this ice?"

"How much did you worry about this lecture between the time I handed you the cup and arriving here?"

Dogan realized his focus on the ice had deflated his anxiety. "You crafty bastard."

"Flattery will get you nowhere. Go talk to your crew."

Dogan stood and strode to the whiteboard.

Feeling forty-eight eyes upon him, he grabbed a marker–a

comfort toy as much as a writing instrument–and addressed his sailors. "I hear that you all have questions about what's happening."

The senior quartermaster barked a question over the rising ruckus. "Yes, sir. You let the quartermasters share the ship's location with the rest of the crew, and I think everyone's concerned about how far south we are."

"Understood."

The murmurs and side conversations died as the senior quartermaster continued. "I mean no disrespect, sir–"

Showing his quiet strength, the master chief intervened. "If you mean no disrespect, tread carefully as you finish that sentence."

"Of course, master chief. It's natural for men to speculate. Some of us are guessing that we're being sent as an insurance policy for possible hostilities against Israel. Some are guessing Egypt."

The master chief eyed Dogan to transfer the conversation to him.

Dogan launched his explanation. "We are farther south than we've been in a long time. And I'll spare you wasted words and doubletalk. You're correct to think that we're an insurance policy. We are exactly that, but you've all guessed the wrong country."

Emboldened, the senior quartermaster eyed his captain. "Can you tell us which country, sir?"

"I can, at my discretion." He scanned his sailors and saw the expected courage underneath veneers of uncertainty. They were ready. He inhaled slowly and then shared his secret in a strong voice. "We're one of three submarines being prepositioned against possible interference by an American aircraft carrier battle group."

A pallor fell over the room.

Seeming to have prepared for this moment with insider knowledge, Asker rescued his commander. "The fleet wouldn't send us on a desperate mission, would it, sir? There must be some logic behind this."

Dogan jumped on the opening. "Of course, not. Why would they waste this perfectly good submarine when there are even older ones they'd sacrifice first?"

Nervous chuckles deflated some of the tension.

"Depending how the tides of war go, the Americans may never come. And even if they do come, depending where they go, we may end up doing nothing. It'll be a matter for diplomats to decide."

The master chief spoke next. "Do we have any idea where the American carriers are?"

"Good question. That's why I wanted the map on the white-board. By the way, who drew this?"

A young petty officer answered. "That was me, sir."

"Not bad. I could navigate by it." He drew X's in an arc across the dry-erase marker map of the Mediterranean Sea. "These seven points mark locations during the last twenty-four hours where our air forces have encountered American combat air patrols. The presence of air patrols suggests the presence of an American carrier behind a wide screen."

Raising his voice, the master chief verbalized Dogan's concern. "Sir, that's farther east than we've seen American carriers in years."

"Exactly. That's why we're out here."

The master chief continued. "Why would the Americans push so far east unless provoked?"

Dogan revealed his final surprise. "To maintain a working relationship with the Americans, President Erdoğan informed President Trump that we're preparing for a largescale military campaign. He didn't ask—he informed. And he did so days ago, earlier than the international press will reveal. That was a calculated risk, the downside of which was giving the Americans a reason to move their carriers into positions, if they choose to interfere."

As Dogan thought the weight of the news would silence his audience, the master chief proved him wrong. "Aren't we at least pretending to be allies with the Americans? We're all part of NATO, such as it is."

"That's true. This is political jockeying with the intent of averting hostilities between us and the United States. There is real risk, but we can all relax and breathe easy, since this will probably flair out before it ever happens."

Iron-willed, the master chief continued his probing. "Still, sir, treaties and handshakes are the products of politicians. They can say we're all friends today, but when you position adversarial warships near each other, bad things can happen."

"That burden lies on my shoulders and that of the fleet." The tension in the room remained above a healthy level, and Dogan added more commentary. "I didn't come out here to die any more than you did, gents. You all know I have a fiancée back home that I'd really like to see again."

Nervous chuckles told Dogan his crew accepted their mission's gravity, except for the master chief, who dug deeper. "You mentioned the tides of war, sir. Can you tell us which war? We were at peace when we deployed last week."

"True. But you all get to learn something today that the rest of the world will learn in due time."

"What's that, sir?"

"We're invading Syria."

CHAPTER 3

Wearing the first female version of the mercenary fleet's uniform, Danielle Sutton tucked her white collared shirt into her beige slacks. The *Goliath's* domed bridge was cramped compared to the British surface combatants upon which she'd served, and she gazed at deck plates while swallowing saliva.

Liam Walker caught the gesture. "It's alright. I had the willies during me first dive. These submarine bubbleheads like Terry take it for granted, but we sane surface warriors know it's unnatural to be under water."

Refusing to show weakness, she eyed the *Goliath's* executive officer. "I'll keep that in mind, but I'm here to learn how to handle the *Xerses*, above and below the water."

Walker continued his uninvited coaching. "Terry's been helpful getting me used to it. It's good to have a surface warrior and a bubblehead teamed up as the commander and the exec. I understand you've selected an executive officer with submarine experience?"

Wary of men's rampant penises seeking her sexual wares, she eyed Walker's hand, and his wedding ring relaxed her. After the injustices she'd endured in the Royal Navy, she'd remain slow to trust men.

She already had a dozen female British veterans pegged as recruits to staff the *Xerses*, but she needed to trust her male colleagues as well. The thought of her future executive officer comforted her. "I could've picked a female submarine officer, but Mike's been a good friend since the academy. He's commanding an *Astute*-class now, but he's retiring in four months."

"Given Pierre's generous pay scale, I imagine he'll be here in five months, then?"

She snorted. "More like four months and a day. He was going to try a sales job to supplement his retirement, but three years in Renard's fleet will have him enjoying lobster and truffles for life."

Seated behind her with a tan from his honeymoon, Cahill stood, glanced through the domed windows at the Pakistani patrol craft off the *Goliath's* port beam, and then at the communications ship off the starboard quarter. A final look at the chart preceded his announcement. "It's time. Are you ready, Miss Sutton?"

Having grilled Cahill on the quality of his crew, she was ready to test the *Goliath* for seaworthiness after its latest upgrades and repairs. Upgrades, she liked. Repairs to damage from combat gave her the creeps, complicating her restlessness before her first submergence below the waves.

Reaching within herself, she found her confidence. There were surfaced maneuvers to experience with the beautiful beast before submerging it, and she hoped to gain trust in the *Goliath* before taking it under the water. "I'm ready."

Cahill lifted a microphone to his mouth. "This is Terry Cahill, commanding officer of the *Goliath*. We'll be conducting our first high-speed maneuvers and test dive since getting our proper port bow section. During this evolution, Danielle Sutton will have the deck and the conn under my instruction for training. Recognize her voice and obey her commands until Liam or I say otherwise. Carry on."

Although wondering whose voice hers might be confused with on the male-dominated ship, she appreciated Cahill's gesture.

He muted the microphone and handed to her. "Introduce yourself and let them know that you have the deck and the conn."

She accepted the microphone. "This is Danielle Sutton. I have the deck and the conn."

Cahill coached her. "You'll get used to keeping one eye on the sea and one on the panels, but Liam and I will watch the ship's status for you. Just drive it like you stole it and leave the buttons and icons to us."

She found the Australians' levity warming. "Thanks, Terry."

"Take it for a spin. Try ahead standard, which is fifteen knots."

Ahead standard. Fifteen knots.

These were the first terms anchoring Danielle in naval reality since setting foot aboard the maritime world's most infamous aberration. Until that moment, the submersible combat ship with a bizarre design allowing it to carry two submarines on its back stymied her. She'd experienced nothing like it during her twenty-two years of officer training and naval service.

Although the United States had multi-hulled blue-water combat ships, the British fleet had none, and nothing else compared to the *Goliath's* bizarre twin-submarine-hull catamaran design with destroyer keels and bows. Per her logic, a naval vessel shouldn't have a port hull and a starboard hull with a tiny tunnel connecting them.

The idea of using that tunnel under the water freaked her out.

One shock at a time, she thought.

But with details of the ship's design chasing each other in circles throughout her mind, the shocks kept coming.

A poor excuse for a destroyer, the *Goliath* had railguns–one per hull–offering a weak proxy of naval gunfire defense against incoming missiles. The familiar Goalkeeper close-in weapon system on the port bow provided a respectable last-ditch defense, but a true destroyer knocked down missiles with missiles.

The jack-of-all-trades *Goliath* was a master of none.

Renard had swayed her to believe the ship could escape below incoming weapons, and she'd found the concept attractive. Any destroyer captain would like that option, she'd admitted. But once submerged, the mediocre destroyer became a terrible submarine.

Although she'd never been in a naval submarine, she hesitated to grant the *Goliath* that moniker. It lacked main ballast tanks, relying instead on its propulsion, high-speed pumps, and shallow operating depths to surface during flooding casualties. From her studies, a submarine without high-pressure gas to create an explosive expulsion of water from its ballast tanks was handicapped.

Lacking that ability defined the *Goliath* as a weak submarine, even before considering its other shortcomings.

It had no active sonar system.

It had no torpedo tube reloads.

It had no bow-mounted sonar system.

It had no hope in a battle against a true submarine, and from what Renard had stated, its best asset against an undersea adversary was running away.

These faults had sounded excusable when the Frenchman had tempted her during her weak moments after the unfair poisoning of her Royal Navy career. She would've accepted salvation from anyone back then. But after months of healing, she questioned her decision to join Renard's Mercenary Fleet.

Get it together, she thought. The bridged dome reminded her of her decision's finality. "To whom do I give the order?"

Walker's smile was relaxing. "I'll take your orders, ma'am. We don't usually prefix our orders by calling to a person by name, rank, title. It's usually just me and Terry up here. It took us a few missions to settle on the semi-formal routine, but it's working."

"Alright, then. All ahead standard."

Finally, something normal happened.

The deck undulated under her feet as the rakish bows sliced the waves. Aqua spray shot over the forecastles, arcing into twinkling white prisms that spewed the sun's refracted rays before falling back into the blue water.

Cahill interrupted her moment. "How do you like the ride?"

She answered truthfully. "It's smoother than I expected."

Walker clarified her experience. "If you're like me, you're used to riding much higher on the bridge. Down here, close to the water, it's much more stable, and there's hardly any rolling with the catamaran design. But your horizon's so bloody low that you can't see half the proper distance ahead of you. It's just weird for us surface warriors."

Accepting her sensory overload, she nodded.

Cahill brought her back to her task. "We normally try some tight turns about now."

Perking up, she had an idea. "Let's do some man-overboard maneuvering. We'll hit an Anderson turn to the right and then reverse it with a Williamson turn to the left."

The ship's proper commander became meek. "Um, which one's the reciprocal bearing one, and which one's the roundy-roundy one? I don't recall the names."

She gave him a sideways glance.

"Hey, I'm a bubblehead! People don't fall off submarines as much as destroyers, I imagine."

Walker spoke. "She's got a good idea, Terry. Let her run with it."

Danielle shared her first accepting glace with the former *ANZAC*-class sailor.

Seeming to warm to the bonding, Walker continued. "Finally, Pierre was smart enough to let a surface warrior command one of his damned ships."

Cahill turned cynical. "I can put you on half rations, you know."

Walker feigned obedience. "Oh, but where are me manners? I meant no offense, mate." He paused and added under his breath. "Bubbleheads are so sensitive."

"How many times has this bubblehead saved your happy arse?"

"Oh, more times than I can count, mate. Please don't put me on half rations. What with all the gourmet food Pierre feeds us, I'm not sure I could handle gaining only three kilos around me waistline per week instead of the standard six."

Danielle studied the liquid crystal displays while trying to swallow her smile. A radar blip caught her attention, and she looked through the windows and spied the target. "I'd like to make the turn before we impale that fishing ship off our port bow."

Cahill regained his composure. "Sorry. Right. Uh, let's warn our Pakistani pals to get out of the way. Liam?"

"On it, sir." Tapping to a new circuit and then lifting a microphone, Walker exchanged quick words with the escort ships. "They're moving. Give them a minute or two."

Through the window, Danielle watched the escorts drift behind her and escape off her port quarter.

Cahill deemed it safe. "Go ahead. Give it a go with the Anderson, Williamson, or Walker turn, if you want to name it after Liam."

"Right full rudder, no course given, belay your head."

Walker tapped keys. "The rudder is left full, ma'am. No course given."

Danielle realized the ship's executive officer was the lowest ranking person to handle the menial task of touching the computers. Royal Navy ships had similar automations but inserted an enlisted human brain into the process as a sanity check and to free officers from the distraction of data entry.

Without dedicated stations for technicians, the *Goliath's* domed bridge boasted a stark efficiency. As Danielle pondered it, she grasped her concern. The efficiency allowed for a smaller ship's staffing, which meant lower operating costs.

But when deployed, commanding officers liked large crews for one simple reason.

Damage control.

When walls and containment vessels ruptured, letting water, fire, or toxic gases into unwelcomed spaces, human hands and courageous hearts were necessary for repairs.

Per her reckoning, the *Goliath* and *Xerses* must suck at damage control for lack of people, and seeing the executive officer handle the rudder and engine order telegraph with his fingertips made that concern tangible.

But she sought the other side of the story. By tapping the buttons, an officer had to think twice before committing to an order, running it through the brain and then confirming the brain's decision with tactile response.

John R. Monteith

As the *Goliath* turned, she thought it might be okay to touch the buttons herself after learning them, and she kept an open mind.

Her concerns dissipated as the ship's speed and smooth handling argued in favor of its claim as a destroyer. After several turns, she accelerated the vessel to twenty, and then to twenty-five knots.

Immersed in the familiar task of ship handling, Danielle pushed the *Goliath* through its paces. Her Australian colleagues were accommodating as both coaches and peers, explaining the quirks of the abomination that was a square peg in the round hole of her past naval experiences.

The abomination became a beast beneath her, obeying her will with a muted grace that fell short of the precision she'd seen on the British fleet's frigates and destroyers. But despite its sluggish turning and acceleration compared to the world's best combatants, it claimed a peculiar and endearing grace.

She knew she only borrowed the *Goliath* from Cahill, but an ocean away, the *Xerses* was waiting. As she ordered an all-out sprint, she treated the behemoth under her feet like a cherished cousin of her future command.

Walker interrupted her romanticizing. "We're steady at thirty-four knots. Wow. This is our best speed ever, with all the propulsion tweaks and a very clean hull."

Danielle ignored him, but her subconscious mind picked up and voiced an irregularity. "I can't smell the water... I can't feel the atmospheric pressure... I can't hear the wind."

Walker nodded. "Bloody hell. You're right. I'd never put it into words. I've always focused on submerging as the source of me willies, but even surfaced, this bridge is a nasty dome of sensory deprivation."

Cahill chuckled. "For you surface skimmers, maybe. But I see it the other way. Having a window is sensory overload for us prairie dog submariners. I just want to hide under water."

A comment slipped from Danielle's lips. "This is a mindfuck."

Cahill stepped beside her. "I like a lady who isn't afraid to swear. In fact, I just had a honeymoon with one. But did you just call me baby ugly?"

"I'm sorry, Terry. I didn't mean it."

"You didn't, huh? In this fleet, we have no secrets. Truth?"

"Okay, it's a real mindfuck. But that doesn't mean I don't like it."

"No offense taken. You'd better fall in love fast, since you've got this baby's twin waiting for you in Taiwan. But let's get to our dive. Much as I'd like to impress you with a crash dive, I'll restrain meself. Let's test an emergency backing bell and slow to ten knots before we submerge."

Excitement drained from her bones as she braced for the moment she'd dreaded, although she had a final fun activity before diving, the crash stop backing bell. "Is there a code phrase for strapping in before we hit the brakes?"

"You could say it just like that."

"Okay." She lifted the microphone and keyed it. "All hands prepare for excessive maneuvering. The next order will be an emergency backing bell. All hands strap in before I hit the brakes."

"Perfect."

"Will you let me know when they're strapped in?"

Cahill shrugged. "They've all been strapped in ever since you took the conn."

"Your confidence is overwhelming."

"Sorry. It only takes a couple errant taps to set the ship into dangerous accelerations."

Danielle wasn't sure how much offense to take. "Why not just lock out all the screens within my reach?"

Walker buried his face in his hands, turned away, and chuckled.

"Oh, you sons of bitches."

"Hey, don't blame me. It was Terry's idea."

Cahill shot daggers into Walker. "Nice loyalty to your chain of command, mate."

"It's okay, guys. I probably would've done the same thing. You don't want the new kid screwing it up."

"With that attitude, you might just fit in here." Cahill's tone grew serious. "Now you might want to brace yourself on the handrail or strap into a seat, if you'd prefer."

"I'll stand."

"Me, too, mate." Walker gripped the rail.

Cahill found a seat against the aft bulkhead. "Okay. I'll sit, then. Fewer bodies to bang against each other." His seatbelt clicked. "Miss Sutton, you have permission to order an emergency backing bell."

After giving the order, she felt her body's weight pressing against the railing. Her sixty daily push-ups paid off as she held strong.

While the twin screws pulled the sterns downward, they lifted the forecastles and lessened the bow wakes.

Identifying a little gift from the *Goliath*, she made a mental note. She'd never watched her own bow wake from a profile view, but with the port hull almost within reach through the window, she saw one of the ship's bow wakes recede.

Finally, she had something new, unusual, and useful in a world of sensory deprivation.

Beside her, Walker aimed his face at a screen. "Twenty-five knots. Twenty. Seventeen. I recommend easing–"

She wasn't waiting for an invitation. "All-back one-third."

"Slowing to all-back one third, ma'am." Walker entered the command into the system. "We're at all-back one third, making turns for four-point-two knots sternward. Steerageway is unreliable. I recommend giving no course until steerageway is more reliable."

Envisioning the hydrodynamics undermined her enjoyment of the high-speed maneuvers, and she appreciated Walker's white lie.

Two screws shooting reversed water underneath two hulls against the ship's forward momentum created odd behaviors. Her ability to overpower the ship's inertia with the rudder was a complex matter, but it remained intact, despite Walker's steerageway comment.

But facing her first dive, she didn't care which way her ship pointed while steeling herself against the pending shock. She believed Walker had understood this when declaring steerageway unreliable, and she took the easy option of letting the abnormal ship aim itself where it wanted. "Steerage way is unreliable, aye. We'll coast."

The *ANZAC*-class veteran continued sharing data. "Speed is twelve knots forward and slowing."

"Very well."

"Eleven knots."

"Belay your head." *Damn it*, she thought. *That was an unnecessary order.*

Unblinking, Walker rolled with her order. "Belay my head, aye, ma'am."

When the *Goliath* slowed to ten knots forward, she acted. "All stop."

"The ship is at all stop."

"All-ahead two-thirds, make turns for ten knots."

"The ship is at all-ahead two thirds, making turns for ten knots."

Unclicking his belt, Cahill stood. "Not bad. I've got only a few pointers to cover later. Are you ready to dive?"

She feigned bravery. "I can't wait."

"Good. Describe the next steps for me."

Recalling her studies, she welcomed the test. "We'll shift propulsion to all six MESMA systems, shut down the gas turbines, and flood water into our trim tanks. The ship will accept a descent rate that Liam enters into the system and it will steady itself at a depth of thirty meters, as measured at our keel. Or our 'keels', however we talk about 'the keel'."

"We call it 'the keel' unless we need to specify between port and starboard. That pretty much goes for everything that we have two of—the keel, the bow, the stern. And your explanation was perfect. Routine-wise, you need to only order the shifting of propulsion and then order the ship to dive. The rest of the

John R. Monteith

parameters are standard. Other than that, sit back and enjoy the plunge."

"May I shift propulsion and submerge the ship?"

"You may shift propulsion to the MESMA units, secure the gas turbines, and then submerge the ship. And keep giving orders to Liam. No need to announce it to everyone."

"Shift propulsion to the MESMA units."

Walker responded while tapping fewer icons than Danielle had expected. "I'm shifting propulsion to the MESMA units, ma'am. It takes a couple seconds... the system's updating... and propulsion is shifted to the MESMA units."

"Secure the gas turbines."

Walker obeyed, the rumbling subsided, and Danielle assumed a sea monster had reached from the depths and silently extracted the *Goliath's* twin hearts. Her world became freakishly quiet, like a morgue. No wind, no spray, no turbines. Expecting the speed to taper off, she stared in disbelief at the port hull's bow wake, which held firm as the ship maintained ten knots.

Something this big was supposed to make more noise when it moved at ten knots, but the MESMA systems–the French version of air-independent submarine propulsion systems–were quiet.

Walker announced the obvious. "The gas turbines are secured." He prompted her next order. "The ship is ready to dive."

"Very well. Submerge the ship."

"I am submerging the ship."

After Walker hit icons, the seas crawled up the ship's sides. Gentle waves lapped the windows, and Danielle's hands became vice grips on the railing while water rose over the dome.

Translucent fluid filtered the sunlight above, turned into blue, and then yielded to blackness. As the sun became a memory, the bridge's artificial lights illuminated the room.

Walker broke a silence Danielle found paralyzing.

"The ship is submerged, passing ten meters."

Danielle froze.

"Fifteen meters."

Again, she said nothing, and a dark form shot over the dome.

30

She whispered before she could think. "Oh, fuck."

Walker calmed her. "It's just a shark, or a really big fish. Maybe a tuna. We'll have it for dinner when we get back, okay?"

She remained tense but remembered how to speak English. "Thanks, Liam."

Cahill offered a dose of compassion. "It's alright. I grew up on submarines, but none of them had windows. If you weren't trembling a bit, I'd be worried, especially since you've never gone down in a submarine."

She looked at her tapping foot, thought about steadying it, but allowed herself the ongoing distraction. Taking courage from her calm companions, she uttered something coherent. "It's frightening, but it's beautiful."

Cahill nodded. "I can't argue that. How many people get to–"

An explosion echoed.

Before Danielle could register a thought, Cahill pulled her from the panel, and she became a spectator to a crisis, trapped under the water, staring at a shallow but infinite abyss.

As reports shot from loudspeakers, she digested the damage.

The starboard railgun had become a cataclysm of fire, smoke, and carnage.

But not flooding.

Somehow, as Cahill and Walker transformed themselves into an orchestra of effective brilliance, the ship steadied at thirty meters, and in a world where normal was impossible, everything seemed normal–except for a dead man in the starboard weapons bay.

"You have the bridge, Liam. Hold depth but slow to seven knots. I'm heading aft." Cahill became the commander Danielle hoped to become as he cleared his mind to focus on her. "Are you okay?"

"Yeah. Yeah, I'm fine."

"Okay. Keep Liam company up here. I need to head aft and see about the damage."

She blurted her knee-jerk reaction. "Isn't that an exec's job?"

"Yeah, normally. But when I recruit a man to his death, I'd like to see for meself what I did wrong. And the crisis is over, at least for now." He moved towards the stairs.

"Terry?"

"Yeah?"

"I'm not okay."

Cahill scowled but stopped to listen. "What's wrong?"

"Holy Jesus! What's wrong? We're on a routine shakedown, and we took an explosion, lost a main cannon, and had to put out a Class-D fire of burning metal. And a man just died. And we, I mean you and Liam, just handled it all without surfacing. How?"

He knelt, revealing the pounding veins in his neck. "We have enemies, and you learn quickly that shifting from surfaced to submerged operations, or vice versa, might sucker you into a trap. For all we know, a dozen Harpoon missiles are flying above us and timed to arrive right now if we surface. Staying cool, staying quiet, and changing nothing is good."

Danielle heard Dmitry Volkov's voice over the acoustic-powered underwater communications network–the underwater phone for lack of a better moniker. Leading the *Wraith* in a patrol against undersea interference, Volkov frantically sought answers.

And somehow, with impossible reserve, Cahill refused to respond. He seemed to read her question. "Dmitry will stop asking soon. He can hear everything he needs. Down here, we take a lot of value from a little information. Dmitry heard the explosion, but he also doesn't hear us losing depth or taking flood waters into our ship. He knows we're okay for now."

On cue, Volkov shifted from worry to acceptance. His voice rang from the loudspeaker, randomly garbled at certain points as processing circuits compensated for the water's interference. "I see you have depth control. I await your report."

"Why didn't you answer him?"

"Dmitry's good, but he's only human. Someone could've slipped through his nets and be listening to us. I don't want to give away information to a possible adversary."

She looked away. Then she met Cahill's gaze. "You're making it impossible to think I can do this."

"Did you pee your pants?"

She scowled. "No."

"Alright, then. Good enough for now. Welcome to Renard's Mercenary Fleet. Now, if you'll excuse me, I have some unpleasant business."

CHAPTER 4

Jake hurried to keep pace. "Pierre, what's wrong?"

"Speak French, please."

The American traitor shifted to his second language. "Okay. What's the hurry for? You're not acting like yourself."

Keeping his brisk pace along the hallway within the Naval Group facility in Toulon, Renard answered. "I'll tell you after we pass the appropriate security barrier."

Knowing when to shut up, Jake let mixed emotions swirl within him. Two civilian guards and two French marines examined his passport while ushering him through security imaging.

A rigid man handed Jake a magnetic card. The 'Naval Group' moniker atop the plastic reflected the current name of an old company. Jake recalled it as DCNS, which had employed Renard two decades ago during his delivery of *Agosta*-class submarines to Pakistan.

Switching his brain to swearing in French, Jake called to Pierre. "Now can you tell me what the whore is going on?"

Pierre shook his head and marched down the hallway.

Another pair of guards watched Renard's every move as the aging Frenchman tapped a memorized code into a security door.

Jake's head buzzed with speculation as he and his boss presented badges to the guards.

Renard snapped Jake out of his thoughts. "I said I'm ready to talk. We're in the inner sanctum. Are you listening?"

"Yeah. Sorry. You were saying?" Again, Jake tuned out as he examined the military command center, with rows of consoles and a mancave-sized frontal display screen.

"...sabotage on the *Goliath*."

Jake hoped he'd misheard his boss. "Sorry. It's been a while since I've been this immersed in French."

Renard sighed. "I'll explain later why you must speak, read, write, and listen in French. For now, please trust me."

"Of course. But this is still weird."

"Did you hear me when I said that someone placed an explosive device on the *Goliath's* starboard railgun?"

Jake still digested the news. "Yeah. I guess."

"One man is dead." Renard slid into a seat at the room's front.

"Crap. A friend of Terry's, I imagine?"

As his fingers brought his screen to life, the Frenchman exhaled. "This is terrible, Jake. I vowed before even meeting you to create no more widows. Now, at this point, I've lost count."

Jake found the Frenchman's verbalized vulnerability overdone for one lost crewman among many, and he remained alert for a deeper reason behind his boss' unease. "Is there anything I can do?"

The gesture helped, as Renard released a tense laugh through his nostrils. "You've done much already by being here." The Frenchman aimed hurting eyes of steel blue at Jake. "I draw strength from our friendship."

Jake patted him on the shoulder. "Don't get weepy on me. We've got a job to do, whatever it is. You didn't bring me here to hug you."

"Right. To work." Renard transformed himself into the sly fox the American respected. "Miss McDonald has helped trace the explosive device to an Indian national who bribed a Pakistani technician to plant it on the *Goliath*."

"Shit."

"Shit, indeed. But that's more innocuous than it seems. The death seems unintentional, given that Mister Radcliffe suffered his injuries only because he was hunched over the gun during detonation. He lost his life as collateral damage from an attack on the weapon."

"Okay. So, a poor soul named Radcliffe got unlucky. But you're not worried about this sabotage?"

As the screen before invoked a map of the Mediterranean Sea, Renard shook his head. "Miss McDonald moved into black ops since our last dealings, but her power within the CIA proper is still growing. She's had our situation analyzed and believes it was a message–not an attack."

Jake grunted. "I suppose a real attack on the *Goliath* would've needed bigger bombs, or more of them."

"Indeed."

"So, what's the message?"

"Leave Pakistan and don't come back."

"That's it, then. All those years you helped them with those *Agostas*, and now Admiral Khan can't protect us anymore."

"He's an old friend but an even older man. He's been retired too long, and I failed to see his waning power. Karachi was never truly a homeport, but I had been considering it."

Jake reflected upon the region. "I hate it, but I can't blame India. Would you want our fleet parked in your enemy's dry docks next door?"

"Apparently not."

"So, where's the fleet. Where's my *Specter*? It was still docked in Karachi when this happened."

"If you'll excuse the command decision, I had Terry take command of your ship with as much of a crew as I could scrounge. He'll board the *Goliath's* cargo bed at sea, and then Dmitry will use the *Wraith* to escort the *Goliath-Specter* tandem."

"Understandable. Then Terry moves back to the *Goliath*, and I'll take the *Specter* to our new home port, wherever that is."

"We'll address that later. There's still more to tell."

The deflective comment alarmed Jake. "This story gets worse?"

"The irony is the timing. Before Miss McDonald finished helping me trace the saboteur, she offered me a mission."

"Offered or ordered?"

"Is there a difference with her?"

"Shit, Pierre. I wouldn't put it beyond her to have ordered that sabotage attack on us, just to remind us who she thinks she is. She's that shrewd."

"I'd considered that, but even so, it wouldn't matter."

Jake let the comment linger unanswered while pondering its cryptic magnitude.

"Why don't I let her explain it herself. She's awaiting our call. Pull up a chair."

As Jake obeyed, Olivia McDonald's face appeared on the display. She retained her core beauty, but lines of age, stress, and substance abuse cut across her face.

Surprising Jake, she spoke French, recalling the time she'd ensnared him in Avignon while he'd hidden from the law. "Can you hear me?"

"Indeed, we can, young lady. We can see you, too. Can you see and hear us?"

She was cold, ignoring Jake's presence. "Yes."

Renard continued the conversation. "Olivia, can you update our status and include a little backstory for Jake's benefit?"

"This mission is the big one. It's the reason I let you exist."

Apparently, even Renard had limits on his tolerance of the conceit spewing from their CIA connection. "Will you excuse us a moment, Olivia?" He muted her, rolled his chair from the web camera's view, and leaned into Jake. "Did you ever truly love this she-demon?"

"I thought I did, but that was over ten years ago, and I was in a bad place."

"Beware of any lingering compassion you feel for her. Be pleasant and kind, but never trust her. When you develop plans with her, remember to develop an anti-plan that addresses her turning against you."

"That's why you're here, Pierre. I'll take cues from you."

Ignoring Jake's comment, Renard returned his unmuted attention to the CIA officer. "Understood. I gave Jake a bit of backstory."

Jake noted how easily Renard lied to her and assumed she did the same to the Frenchman. The relationship seemed impossible, but the shady mercenary and Olivia had maintained a loose and abusive father-daughter rapport.

She shared her intelligence. "The *Lincoln* battle group is moving east in the Med, close enough to launch twenty-four-hour airstrikes against Syria and southern Turkey."

The news disturbed Jake. "Turkey? A NATO ally?"

"That's the point. It's time for you and Pierre to step up. Turkey informed us that they're invading Syria."

With Renard remaining oddly silent, Jake answered. "Isn't that good? Let them stomp out whatever's left of ISIS."

"The Kurds are already in Syria. It's not about ISIS. For the Kurds, it's a land grab. You should know that better than anyone."

Jake recalled his wife's family having fled to Kurdish-controlled Irbil, Iraq. The Kurds were heroes against ISIS, but as the evil scourge had retreated to Syria, the Kurds had become thieves, stealing from the people they'd protected. "They're no saints."

Cynicism dripped from her tongue. "Well, it could be Tony the Tiger fighting the Cookie Monster for all I care. What's important is that Turkish surface combatants are deployed in littoral waters to prevent American maritime support, and Turkish submarines are deployed to dissuade carrier battle groups from interfering."

Jake drew conclusions aloud. "Let me guess. The Americans don't need protection from the Turks, but they need protection from themselves–to avoid crushing Turkey and risking worldwide escalation."

"You're getting it."

"That's where we come in. We... what? We dissuade Turkey? We attack Turkey? And since we're mercenaries with tight lips, everyone will know you made us do it, but nobody can prove it. America gets plausible denial."

"I knew you weren't stupid. You'll remove the Turkish submarines, you'll position the *Goliath* to attack Turkish land troops with the railguns, and then you'll await my orders."

Jake pondered the situation before answering. "I imagine we

can get a new railgun onto the *Goliath* during its transit to the Med, and we can get through the Suez with some big bribes. It's an unpleasant scenario, but it's what we're in business for."

Olivia aimed harsh eyes at Renard. "He doesn't know, Pierre. Stop bullshitting and tell him." She signed off, and the map of the Mediterranean Sea returned to the Frenchman's screen.

"I'm sorry, Jake."

"For what? What is she talking about?"

"I must go to Washington and submit myself to house arrest."

Processing the gravity, Jake felt upside down. "Because we'll be close to many American ships, they don't want to risk us turning tail and attacking them."

"Correct. I go willingly."

Realization hit Jake. "I'm not commanding the *Specter*, am I?"

Renard was despondent, his strength failing. "Danielle will command the *Goliath*, and Terry will command the *Specter*. I've sent two translators with him in case the crew forgets their English during times of stress."

"Terry's brain's been wrapped around the *Goliath* for years, and he's hardly set foot on a *Scorpène*-class."

"I know, Jake. But remember that Henri practically commanded an attack against Chinese ships himself."

"And he made a mistake."

"We recovered."

Jake sighed. "Okay. I work for you. You need me here in charge of your fleet. That's why you have me speaking French. I get it. The support team speaks French, and it gets worse. I'll be alone without reliable communications with you."

"Correct."

"Anything you could tell me after you leave this room will be monitored by the Americans. While you're under house arrest, I'll do what Olivia says, but I'll have to watch for her betrayal."

"Correct again. It's too much pressure on you, too soon. I didn't think you were ready yet, but unfortunately, you must be."

Jake felt unbalanced. "Wow. It's a lot to deal with, but I can get my head around it."

Renard inhaled and then sighed. "I'm going to call a CIA officer in Washington now, and what you're going to see will be difficult. Before you fly into a rage, I must point out that Ariella is involved, and I've spoken to trusted people in the Israeli military who know of her captivity. If Ariella were to disappear, Aman would know, although I can't guarantee that they'd act."

Nerves chewed at Jake's stomach. "You're scaring me."

"We should all be scared. This situation is highly unusual." Renard tapped keys and brought up the face of an unfamiliar woman in a dark blazer. He switched to English and exchanged a brief salutation. Then he switched back to French. "Jake, our position may feel hopeless, but we have some power. As I hand the reigns to you, you have power."

"Spit it out."

"They have our families. Mine, Terry's, yours, and even Dmitry's parents."

Decades of anger, which Jake had fought into dormancy, roared to life. "Linda!"

"I'm sorry."

"If anyone hurts her, I'll kill them and leave a trail of dead bodies until I get to Olivia. If it takes the rest of my life, I swear it."

Renard seemed at ease with his colleague's anger, having used it to recruit him into treason long ago. "They're all together in a luxury hotel in Washington, but they cannot leave."

Jake knew to slow his rage and let it simmer while awaiting a proper time for revenge. "If I do something Olivia doesn't like, she'll execute our families. She's that batshit crazy."

"Keep your speculative horrors in check. There are many ways this works out to everyone's mutual benefit."

"And there are many ways people die, including my wife and all our families."

"Would you like to speak to Linda? I've just called up a conference call with her in the hotel."

Jake rolled his boss from the console and stooped over it. His wife looked forlorn but strong. He switched to English. "Linda?"

She smiled upon seeing Jake. "I miss you!"

"Are you okay?"

"I won't lie. It's been hard."

Knowing that a tyrant's malice caused his wife's suffering transformed Jake. Ancient victimhood had gifted him the rage to lash out and steal the USS *Colorado*. But he'd never wanted to hurt anyone, except those who'd hurt him.

Now, in an instant, he was reborn as a new species, the demon he needed to become to challenge Olivia's despotism.

Everything he'd learned during his biblical studies crashed to the ground. His intellectual beliefs remained, but a diamond-hard barrier crystalized between his heart and his god, as pure anger made him incapable of feeling.

Dignity, valor, and virtue drained from him, and his mind's eye drew harsh lines of division. Everyone on the wrong side of the 'us' line was a 'them'.

His wife, his fleet, and their families were 'us'. The Earth's other seven billion living souls were 'them'.

In a shocking moment of self-awareness, he feared himself for seeing 'them' as nonhumans. Then he released the fear, realizing there was no more 'self' to fear.

Jake Slate was gone.

When he'd lashed out in rage as a twenty-six-year old victim, he was a vengeful human.

Now, no longer human, but a demon.

A demon named Vengeance.

CHAPTER 5

Jake hushed his wife in Aramaic, the language she'd been teaching him for years. He wondered how many Iraqi neo-Chaldean Aramaic translators the CIA had available for monitoring an American citizen in Washington DC hotel room.

Few, he hoped.

Burdening the CIA's resources with language obfuscation offered him some leverage against his new American enemy. But his mastery of it was choppy. "Aramaic possible and to speak slow."

For her husband's sake, Linda oversimplified her native words. "I taught to say things but not other things. Aramaic is okay, since easier for me. They let me. I am okay."

"Good. I married a smart woman."

"Marie here with her kids but don't see much."

"Good. She strong, married to Pierre."

"Old Russian couple here doesn't speak English. There's a translator. Say are Dmitry's parents, but actors maybe."

"Doubt is good. Continue." Jake looked to Pierre and switched to French. "Can we insert our own translator? I don't want the risk of a CIA agent weakening our families' cohesion with lies and filters. They need to communicate amongst themselves as much as their babysitters will allow."

Pierre canted his head. "Good question. You saw a potential weakness and sought to convert it to strength."

"No time for groveling."

"Right. Bring it up with Olivia and be prepared to give something in return. Also be prepared to back off and choose another battle. And keep up the foreign language. You're making Olivia squirm since I'm sure that Aramaic translators are busy with

Iraqi affairs. Well done."

"Then why isn't she forcing us to use English?"

Renard grunted. "I'm sure she'd like to, but she would consider herself weak if she did. This is an example where her arrogance works in our favor."

Jake found Renard's world enveloping him, but he also surprised himself with his ability to adapt.

Linda continued. "Ariella's been a sweetheart."

A klaxon alarmed in Jake's belly. He wanted to interview the military intelligence officer. "Get her here."

"Okay." Linda looked away and shouted across a space that looked like a sprawling common room in a five-star hotel suite. "Can I have Ariella?"

Seconds later, a familiar-looking face appeared beside Linda.

A throaty Israeli accent laced the woman's English. "It's a compromised position, Jake. That's all I wish to say. Watch what you say, or we may lose our speaking privileges."

As time slowed with rising adrenaline, Jake found himself becoming a paranoid master of word choice. He dropped subliminal hints to the CIA about embracing his new power. "I understand we have limits on what we say. I am learning a lot while I have the world's twenty-first largest and most battle-tested fleet at my fingertips."

"Well said."

A doubt gnawed at Jake. "Prove that you're Ariella Dahan."

In the screen, he watched a pallor cover Linda's face before she stood and distanced herself from a potential Israeli imposter.

The woman who looked like Cahill's new bride responded. "Fair enough. That's a good question."

Jake felt an unsettling juxtaposition of his spiritual faith slamming against his anger and the power at his fingertips. "Stop kissing my ass, and let me be very clear. If anything happens to my wife, I'm sending big weapons right down the gut of the carrier battle group."

The woman claiming to be Ariella Dahan retained her composure. "Understood."

Impressed the channel remained open, Jake suspected he was free to say whatever he wanted. Although the captives were probably warned of subjects to avoid, a renown international madman on the other side of the Atlantic Ocean could rattle off threats and accusations all day. Anyone watching a video of Jake's verbal venom would ignore them as the rantings of a terrorist.

So, for the benefit of those who eavesdropped, he ranted.

Viciously.

"If I can't get to your carrier... No, let's give my target a tangible name. If I can't get to the *Abraham Lincoln*, prepare graves in Arlington for the crews of your surface ships, or God help them, your submarines. I know how you train them, and Dmitry alone can humiliate, terrorize, and crush any three of your best."

"It's me, Jake."

"Shut up. Until proven otherwise, you're Olivia's agent. As I was saying. Big weapons. Like heavyweight, no shit, crack-the-*Lincoln's*-keel Black Shark torpedoes. Hear how calmly I accept my responsibility of avenging my dead wife, if it comes to it. I am no American."

"Okay, Jake."

"I said shut up or I'll send my fleet back to Karachi and let you muddle through your mess with Turkey. You will not speak again until I ask you a question or tell you to. Do you feel me?"

"Yes."

"I've accepted the necessity of killing thousands of Americans to undermine your perceived control. For the agents who are listening, make some eggheads analyze the conviction in my voice, and then tremble. And I when I said 'torpedoes', I meant plural 'torpedoes', which Terry and Dmitry will pump into your sons and daughters. The lucky ones will be vaporized. The unfortunate ones will drown, choke, or burn to death. Do you feel me?"

"Yes."

"I mean 'torpedoes' because fuck Olivia and every CIA agent, American military officer, and politician who has the slightest hint that you're threatening my wife."

Jake continued with added flair and gamesmanship, having no idea where carriers stored their munitions. "And if I can't get a submarine close enough, I know where to place railgun rounds to recreate the *Forrestal* disaster times ten on the *Lincoln*. And don't think that my commanders–yes, my commanders while Pierre's in custody–will hesitate if I tell them, truthfully or not, that Americans have turned on them. Do you feel me?"

"Yes."

"My fleet historically spares lives by using limpet and slow-kill torpedoes, but you've forced me to reverse our loadout. I'll give Dmitry and Terry the limpets and slow-kills they need to place on Turkish submarines, and then I'm giving them each twenty crack-the-keel-and-vaporize-American-flesh heavyweight Black Sharks because fuck you, you have my wife. Do you feel me?"

"Yes."

"Repeat the numbers of heavyweights."

"Twenty heavyweights."

"What type of heavyweights are they?"

"Black Shark."

"Try again. I described them as I now see them."

"Crack-the-keel-and-vaporize-Americans..."

"Crack-the-keel-and-vaporize-American-flesh heavyweights. Repeat that with me until Olivia hears it in her nightmares."

The woman repeated the phrase three times.

"That's enough. Since my staff will be busy reviewing plans to blow up the *Lincoln*, I want the battle group's commanding officers flown in to personally stencil the names of their ships onto my heavyweights. Ten torpedoes on each of my submarines will be labeled 'Kiss your ass goodbye, Abraham Lincoln.' Do you feel me?"

"Jake, I don't think–"

"Then you kill the Turks." He hung up.

Expecting Renard to break the thick silence, the Frenchman gave him silent space.

As a request to reconnect appeared, Jake answered it, and the woman claiming to be Ariella reappeared. "You'll receive a call soon. I suggest you answer." The Israeli woman's face froze.

Seconds later, Olivia's hail chimed.

Jake answered. "Go."

The CIA rogue's image was an obfuscated grainy mix of weird pixilation, and her voice was the baritone demonic drone of a voice changer.

Her clandestine call encouraged Jake, suggesting he'd pushed his new enemy beyond her comfort zone. He feigned ignorance of her tactic. "You're coming in fuzzy."

"You hear and see what you need. I agree to the stencils, but not to using American military personnel to do it."

Driven by an unyielding but controlled anger, Jake cut her off.

After another minute of feeling his heart race, he answered another hail from the hotel room. The Israeli woman appeared again. "You should answer the next call."

Jake answered Olivia's hail "Speak."

Still hiding her identity with voice and video smokescreens, she negotiated. "I can request that the unit commanders witness the stencils over video. That's the best you'll get. I don't have the power to give orders to the Navy."

Jake lifted his finger to terminate the connection but realized he'd accomplished his goal. Whoever was in charge, whether Olivia or someone higher up, had heard his conviction and believed.

But an idea crossed his mind. "How many officers out there are academy grads? Include the air wings."

"I'll check." After a delay, she spoke again in her sinister voice scrambler. "Covering the three classes ahead and behind yours, there are fifty-eight Naval Academy graduates."

"Just my class."

"Seventeen, mostly aviators."

"Highest ranking. Commanding and executive officers."

"Graham Morrison commands the *Stockdale*."

Jake recalled a friendly man he wasn't close to. "Keep going."

"Robb Chadwick commands the *Bainbridge*."

"I slept across the hall from him for four years. He's a saint and would give anyone his kidney if he thought it would help. Ask him if I have the stones to kill him and his crew."

"I will check my contacts in the naval channels. I remind you that Commander Chadwick believes you're dead. You'll burden him with a state secret"

"No, you're burdening him. But he's tough. He'll cope, and I'm not done. After twenty weapons on my two submarines are stenciled for the *Lincoln*, the other twenty will say the same thing, except with the names of the battle group's escorts in place of the *Lincoln*. I want every ship in the battle group represented. Do you feel me?"

"Yes."

"Repeat my numbers."

"The twenty remaining weapons will have stenciled targets with the names of all the battle group's ships on them."

"I'll have the weapons flown from Toulon to Port Said for the weapons load, and you'll pay for the loading. I don't care how fast you get that done. I'll leave the panic to you on how desperately you want my fleet deployed. Do you feel me?"

"Yes. Port Said weapons offload and onload."

"The ones on the *Wraith* will be stenciled in Russian so that my friends can read along while they ruin your career and tie the deaths of thousands of Americans to your failure. Do you feel me?"

"Yes. Russian stenciling on the *Wraith*."

"Your narcissistic ambition would drive you insane if my fleet's actions end your career in pounding shame. Therefore, I know that my promises–not threats–are landing. Do you feel me?"

"Yes."

"Now, I want to talk to the woman who claims to be Ariella."

Olivia's fuzzy image disappeared.

The Israeli woman's face replaced that of the CIA despot. "Jake. Can you hear me? I believe we're back online."

"You're not done proving that you're Ariella Dahan. What do you know that nobody outside our fleet knows?"

She looked away in thought and then settled on an idea. "Vasily, who is Dmitry's dolphin manager, adopted two female Iranian dolphins after you rescued an American submarine."

"I'm sure Olivia was watching them rescue the dolphins through a drone the whole time. Do better."

"I don't think she'd know they were both female."

"That's a twenty-five percent chance of guessing, or she could've somehow overheard Vasily talking. God knows it's not hard to follow him for a day and hear him spew every thought in his mind. Not good enough."

"I know, Jake. I was just warming up. Here's your proof. Just this week, Vasily gave the female dolphins proper names. He waited to get to know them first. One of them is Shadi, which means 'joyful', and the other is Roshan, the 'bright one', because she learns quickly. Terry told me that on our honeymoon."

It was news to Jake. "I'm putting you on mute. Stay there until I get back." Sensing a pulse much calmer than he expected, he slid his chair to an adjacent console, brought it to life, and summoned the *Wraith*.

The Russian-staffed ship's bleary-eyed sonar ace appeared. Although the translator was absent, Anatoly's English was improving. "Hi, Jake. You need Dmitry?"

"No. Find Vasily and ask him the names of the Iranian dolphins."

Anatoly frowned. "Dolphin names? I no understand. You know Mikhail and Andrei."

"No. The new dolphins. From Iran."

"Oh. I understand. Wait please." Two minutes later, the *Wraith's* sonar expert reappeared. He spoke while reading from a notepad. "He say names are Shadi and Roshan. I maybe get it wrong. I get Vasily?"

"No, Anatoly. That was good. Thank you. Good night."

"It actually early morning–"

Jake shut off the connection and returned to the woman he'd verified as Cahill's wife. "Your story checks out, Ariella."

The Israeli warrior shifted into ally-mode. "Keep your strong stance. Don't apologize. Not to me. Not to your wife. Not to anyone. You must act as God now."

"Wasn't planning on going soft. My resolve will grow stronger every minute."

"We're in this together."

Appreciating a warrior's presence with his wife, Jake softened to her. "Thank you."

"A God doesn't thank people."

"Good point."

"Do you want Linda back here?"

"Yeah. I need to calm her down."

Linda appeared next to Cahill's wife. "You're scaring me, Jake."

"Good. Be scared but healthy scared. Ariella will protect you. She knows what to do. I love you honey. Look after her, Ariella, and I'll do the same for Terry." He cut the connection and turned to Pierre. "I guess this is goodbye."

Renard glared at him. "I recant my statement about doubting you. I'm leaving my fleet in capable hands."

"We need to warn Danielle. Can you contact her?"

Renard smirked. "Done hours ago. Her sister and parents are seeking refuge in my personal bunker outside Avignon."

"At least we have one uncompromised commander."

Renard leaned into Jake's ear. "Don't look now, but if you use the leftmost console and enter Marie's birthday as eight digits, you'll have a secure connection to my bunker. I expect that Olivia doesn't even know to monitor it."

"Good to know."

"You'll also find a complete rundown of the upgrades to the *Goliath* in an encrypted file in the documents folder. It has the same password as the connection to the bunker."

"I'll read it in detail."

"There's a complete section of that console's hard drive that is encrypted behind that password. It's running a Linux server, and you can unplug and plug it in again to the Internet as needed, just in case you need it."

"Damn. That's good thinking."

"I've also asked key crew members to send their loved ones on vacations under false names and with daily relocation. Children are out of school. Jobs are on hold, and they rightly trust me to compensate them for financial difficulties. But now I regret that I must leave you and place our fleet in your hands."

"God willing, we can get through this." Jake hugged his friend, released him, and then watched a willing prisoner walk out the door.

CHAPTER 6

Dmitry Volkov's head spun.

Days after learning his parents had landed in their American hotel jail, he steadied the *Wraith* at fifty meters, leaving ten meters below his keel. The rapid and shallow dive reflected the paranoia of his former colleague and new boss, Jake Slate, who'd ordered immediate submergence.

Although calmer than his American colleague, Volkov admitted his anger.

During his childhood, his parents had recognized his attraction to logic, math, and science, and they'd nurtured him into a capable student. While raising him in the suburban environs of St Petersburg, where he'd found refuge from frozen winters inside books, they'd guided him into the Russian Navy.

As he'd excelled in the submarine fleet, he'd sent them money to assure their comfort. After his scapegoat expulsion from the fleet, he'd then applied his gargantuan mercenary paychecks to assuring their luxury, with gifts of fine clothing, jewelry, cars, and other gestures of gratitude.

But after learning of their detention, he felt responsible for their mortal danger, and he needed a clear mind to follow Jake's orders and save them. So, he swallowed his anger and prayed it would stay at bay while he averted American-Turkish hostilities.

During his last video call with Jake, he'd seen deep seas of rage behind the American's eyes. Until this mission-at-gunpoint, he'd only heard stories of his colleague's past anger. Now, he saw surges of that frightful power, and he feared it.

With Cahill on the *Specter* patrolling less dangerous waters, and with Sutton still looking for the toilet on the *Goliath*,

Volkov saw himself as the fleet's only chance.

He needed to remove the Turkish threat, and counting on the others was irresponsible. His colleagues were outside their elements, and Volkov bore the weight of his fleet's success on his shoulders.

They had his parents.

Any *Type-209* submarine unfortunate enough to cross his path would suffer a fearful fate. Volkov wondered if he could keep his judgment unclouded to mete out appropriate destinies and avoid excessive force.

Compounding his predicament, he viewed taking orders from an American like enduring constipation. It was annoying but tolerable, depending how long it lasted.

His most disconcerting issue was his fluttering heart, and he sought a confidant to whom he could confess–the dolphin trainer.

Lacking his executive officer, who'd boarded the *Goliath* to be its only submarine-trained officer, Volkov called to his sonar expert. "Anatoly?"

Seated at his console, the sonar ace looked up. "Yes?"

"Get the team searching for *Type-209* submarines. Then I'll want you to take the deck and the conn."

"I'll get the search started for *Type-209* submarines. They're grabbing some chow first, though."

Despite a clock ticking away his parents' safety, Volkov demanded as much patience from himself as he could muster. "No hurry. We have all week to hunt bad guys."

"Isn't our homeland supporting Turkey in this... whatever they're about to do?"

Casting his voice across the control room, Volkov answered the question for multiple listeners. "We're not in the Russian Navy anymore. We're a mercenary ship without a homeland. Your paycheck should remind you of that, if hearing orders from our American commodore doesn't."

"Sorry, Dmitry. It's just strange attacking Turkey."

"We've attacked NATO allies before, when they deserved it."

He reflected upon a mission against Greece and then corrected himself. "Well, maybe even if they didn't deserve it. I'm no diplomat. But we have our mission nonetheless."

Anatoly sighed. "I suppose you're right. I'd be a hypocrite to cash my paychecks and then wiggle out of my duty."

Picking up on a subtlety, Volkov lowered his voice. "You don't seem convinced of that."

Anatoly answered in a near-whisper. "Pierre made me send my wife and sister on a vacation to avoid capture, like your parents. He said only the families of key players were targeted by the CIA. I don't know whether to be flattered or outraged that he chose to protect my loved ones."

Volkov scoffed. "Both, I guess. At least your loved ones are free. Not so for some of us."

"I can't imagine, although I tried to imagine the horror until I learned that my family was okay. They must have only wanted the commanders' families."

Remembering his need for clear thought, Volkov swallowed his anger about the incarcerated loved ones. "It's compromising. But there are ways out of this. So, if you can find a *Type-209* today..."

Anatoly raised his voice. "I promise you a *Type-209*. Maybe two, if you give me time."

After patting his colleague's back, Volkov moved to the room's central charting table. He expanded the capacitive touchscreen's scale to include the eastern end of the Mediterranean Sea. He then grabbed a stylus and drew a vertical line from Turkey's southern coast to the island of Cyprus, and then he added a forty-five-degree line from Cyprus to Lebanon.

Expecting one Turkish submarine to the north of Cyprus and two to the south, Volkov noted an icon representing the *Goliath-Specter* tandem heading above the sea's third largest island. Weaker at anti-submarine combat for his lack of practice, Cahill would tangle with only one adversary, and he'd have the *Goliath's* help.

The hard work rested with the fleet's best submarine–the

Wraith.

During his tenure with the mercenaries, Volkov had struggled with his identity and the acceptance of his brilliance. But after proving himself in difficult battles and receiving accolades from his colleagues, his resistance relented.

He was better than anyone.

Better than any rival nation's commander, from his immersion in real-world combat. Smarter commanders might exist, but simulators and training scenarios limited their development. The rigor of combat in Renard's fleet had gifted the Russian commander the world's sharpest combat skills.

He was even better than the legend he'd faced in the Black Sea when he commanded the Russian *Krasnodar*. After overcoming Jake's best punches, with Cahill assisting, Volkov had turned an ambush and a certain loss into a stalemate.

That display had cost him his job as a political scapegoat, but it had brought him into the Frenchman's fleet.

His challenge was to forget his anger, overcome his giddiness for the new British commander, and embrace his tactical confidence while remaining humble. Unsure whether to shake or stir that mix of emotions, he flagged his mind to alarm if it recognized one huge pitfall.

Overconfidence.

He needed to avoid mistakes of hubris.

Volkov glanced at the speed vector emanating from the icon representing the *Wraith*. It showed the submarine moving at eight knots, north by northwest, towards two expected Turkish targets.

"Dmitry?"

"Yes?"

Anatoly strode behind the backs of sonar technicians seated at Subtics tactical system consoles. "We've staffed the full section, and we've begun the search for *Type-209* submarines. I'm ready to relieve you of the deck and the conn."

"You have the deck and the conn." Volkov departed, and while strolling to the torpedo room, he gauged his emotional state, which remained dynamic and fluid since meeting the Royal Navy's most recent scapegoat. His inner workings seemed foreign and distant, but nothing wreaking of arrogance stuck out.

As he reached the weapons, he distracted himself by looking outward, and the harsh stenciling struck him with their cruelty. Heavyweight torpedoes dominated the racks, and the violent verbiage over their warhead sections riveted the risk of the undesired mission into his mind.

At the room's front, the dolphin trainer stooped over the tank holding his two weaponized cetacean babies. Vasily looked up as his commanding officer approached. "Dmitry, I don't like this. The anger is so thick among these weapons." He slid a compassionate hand over the nearest dolphin's back. "Mikhail is beside himself."

"Of course. Mikhail the complainer and Andrei the stoic. I suppose Mikhail only complains because he's so sensitive."

"You understand him."

Volkov tried to talk through the wild emotions raging through men and dolphins. "Pierre once told me that Jake's anger is the reason why we have a fleet. It's the engine that drove him, but now I fear it's the devil that consumes him."

"I know! It was before our time, but at the last dinner party, Henri told me Jake went wild killing North Koreans while they rescued that South Korean submarine. I fear Jake will never be okay."

Volkov pondered his accidental boss. "Jake must've gotten furious when he learned of the detainment, but his anger has already benefited us." He glanced at the nearest weapon's stenciling, which addressed the warhead to a *Kaiser*-class replenishment oiler in the *Lincoln* battle group.

Vasily frowned and pointed. "You consider this a benefit?"

Recalling the shuffling of weapons throughout his torpedo room in Port Said, Volkov admired Jake for making American battle group commanders view a short video of the stenciling. After having each warhead filmed with its threat, he'd sent the video to Jake, who'd then demanded reciprocal footage of

American officers watching the menacing footage.

A compromise had limited the audience to seven American officers gathered in one briefing room, but Volkov agreed with Jake in the audience's sufficiency. Seeing high-ranking seven faces ogle, cringe, and scowl at the mercenary fleet's written conviction told Volkov two things.

First, the Americans would think twice before meddling with Renard's Mercenary Fleet.

Second, if they meddled, it would be decisive–without quarter or remorse.

Volkov considered Jake's stenciling demand shrewd. It kept the Americans away, and it kept the mercenary commanders afraid of the Americans. If the forces collided, each side would attack with zeal, beyond any hope of political damage control.

And it would get someone's attention–the attention needed to free the captive loved ones, even if each ship in the mercenary fleet rested on the seafloor.

"The stenciling was a smart idea. The Americans had considered us an afterthought until then. Now, our fleets understand one another. I also believe seeing these messages reminds us of our commitment."

"Yes. Maybe. But this is a nightmare. Our missions until now have been proper... even noble. But this is desperate."

Volkov sighed. "I may be a better commander than Jake, but perhaps he's perfect as Pierre's replacement. His anger came from desperation. Maybe it can get us out."

"If he can keep it controlled."

"Time will tell." Volkov verified his solitude with his friend and shifted his tone. "Vasily?"

"Yes?"

"May we talk about something other than killing?"

"Sure."

Volkov swallowed and then exposed his soul. "I think I'm in love with Danielle."

Joyous surprise caked the dolphin trainer's features. "Hah! Is that true? Love is wonderful!"

"No! Don't say that. I need to cure myself of this. It's a terrible danger that could weaken my judgment."

"You want to cure love? Did you hear yourself?"

"Oh, I don't expect you to understand. Not completely, you know. Given how you... experience love."

Vasily scowled. "What do you mean?"

"I don't know. Maybe it's all the same. Ignore me. I'm over-thinking it."

"You're overthinking something. Why not tell me?"

Fearing his friend's judgment of his pending observation, Volkov's skin crawled. "I consider you a friend, and if you're homosexual, it's your business and it's nothing between us."

Hurting eyes burned Volkov's, and the *Wraith's* commander felt like a chump.

Then, Vasily burst into laughter. "You think I'm homosexual?"

"I... assumed."

"Because I am sensitive? Because I'm not married?"

"Well, you're a bit effeminate, too."

A tear rolled down Vasily's chuckling face. "Oh! Oh! That's hilarious." He laid a hand on Volkov's shoulder while catching his breath. "Dmitry, these qualities attract the most beautiful women!"

Blushing, the *Wraith's* commander apologized. "I hadn't seen it that way. I'm sorry."

"Don't be! It's a trap for lovely ladies. They think I'm safe to approach because I am considerate, and they find out how kind and compassionate I am. Then I have many beautiful lady friends, and I can't help it if some of them find me sexy!"

"I've failed to give you credit. I failed miserably."

"Yes, but that's great news for you." The trainer stiffened his back for his announcement. "I will be your love coach."

"Yes! Please! No, wait. I can't be in love. That's the point!"

"You are quite confused. Lucky you found me."

"Oh, damn it. You're right, I suppose. I can't ignore it any-more."

"True. But I can help."

Sensing himself before an expert, Volkov forgot the dangers surrounding his ship. "Tell me what to do."

"We start by understanding the science of love. Within the first months of meeting someone special, your body goes through a chemical transformation, and it's like an addiction. You feel lost without the person's attention, and that's called infatuation, not love. Be careful to discern between the two."

"Really? That describes everything that's going on."

"Yes. It's very strange, but you can manage it if you focus on familiar things. Make frequent observations of yourself during your daily routine and be aware of the silly and frivolous thoughts that jump into mind. When they do, observe them, and then let them jump out again."

"Where'd you hear that?"

"A long time ago, on Oprah, I think."

"I feel like I've landed on another planet."

"It's this mission. It's hurting us all, and we haven't even reached our patrol area."

"Soon, my friend. I don't think the Turks are foolish enough to push too far forward and abandon a de facto choke point between Cyprus and Lebanon."

Vasily glanced at the dolphins, each sleeping with one eye open, per the self-preservation of their species. "Tell me when you need my babies, and they'll be ready."

"I will. Thank you." Equipped with a nugget of sage love advice, and relieved to have Vasily as his heart's coach, Volkov departed and then walked his submarine with a new perspective.

He was in his element again, seeking submerged targets staffed by commanders of inferior ability. Confident, he saw the translator stepping out of the crew's bathroom stall.

The linguist greeted him. "How are you, Dmitry?"

Knowing his sailors could read him, Volkov answered truthfully. "I'm still adjusting to this mission."

"I could tell you were worried. We all could. Everyone knows there are some bad secrets behind this one."

"We'll resolve everything in due time. I'm going to get some rest before we enter our hunting grounds. Tell Anatoly to send a messenger to wake me in four hours."

The *Wraith's* commander slid under the crisp covers of his small sleeping rack. Images, scenarios, and fantasies of Danielle Sutton danced in his mind. Unable to sleep, he reminded himself that sleepless rest was better than no rest.

After ninety minutes of failure to achieve slumber, he heard a soft knock at his door. Then the door opened without his approval, spiking his heart rate.

A young sonar technician appeared. "Anatoly urgently requests your presence in the control room."

"*Blyat!* What's wrong?"

"We found a *Type-209*."

CHAPTER 7

In the *Wraith's* control room, an excited Volkov stood beside his sonar ace and examined a Subtics screen showing raw sounds from the sea. "What do you have?"

"Reduction gears."

A vertical line on a display showed a crisp tone, and the lack of unclean noises from the same direction–the sounds merchant ships made without regard to quieting–suggested a contact built and operated for silence.

A warship, probably a submarine.

Volkov probed. "It's clean, I'll admit. What can you learn from the frequency?"

"We know the harmonics of *Type-209* reduction gears, and that's what we're hearing. But it's off a bit, probably due to Doppler. If it's really the reduction gear of a *Type-209*, then the contact must be doing at least eight and a half knots."

Volkov knew that his new target could be an innocent passerby, but his mission's pressures precluded him caring. "Until we learn otherwise, this contact is a *Type-209* submarine. Designate it as 'Type-209 Alpha' in the system. Assign tubes one and three Type-209 Alpha."

After delegating his commander's orders to a junior sonar technician, Anatoly risked a protest. "Dmitry, I must remind you that three nations operate *Type-209s* in the Mediterranean, and all of them patrol the waters we're in."

"You didn't see me assign a heavyweight, did you?"

"No. Assigning one limpet and one slow-kill is logical and humane, but people shoot heavyweights back at us, and any hostility against other nations will only complicate matters."

Volkov scoffed. "Matters are already complicated, and the

Americans are good at telling others to stay out of their way. Any Egyptian or Greek commander is fully aware that Turkish *Type-209s* are being hunted, and if they still test us, that's their decision."

"I'm glad you're making the decisions. I wouldn't know how I'd deal with it."

"Look around you, Anatoly. If I become incapacitated, who do you expect to take my place?"

A pallor overcame the sonar technician.

"Don't worry. I'm in great health." Volkov strode to the elevated conning platform, sat in his foldout captain's chair, and looked at the nearest monitor. He raised his voice. "Attention in the control room, we have detected a probable submerged contact, designated Type-209 Alpha. I intend to give chase and determine to whom this submarine belongs. I'm also still deciding which weapon to hit it with, if not both. Any questions?"

Several men within the room shook their heads while most remained unmoving.

"Very well. I will accelerate to give chase. I have the deck and the conn. Helm, all ahead standard, make turns for twelve knots. Left ten-degrees rudder, steady on course two-eight-five."

A man seated at a maneuvering console acknowledged the order, entered the commands into the system, and announced the new, shorter battery life at the higher speed. "Ninety-eight minutes remaining on the battery, sir."

After the deck rolled under Volkov's feet, the *Wraith* steadied.

Anatoly, who'd slipped headphones over his ears while sitting before a Subtics console, raised the alarm. "We're losing Type-209 Alpha, Dmitry."

Volkov responded. "Our increased flow noise is deafening you?"

The sonar ace nodded.

"But they'll get away if we don't give chase, based upon your Doppler assessment of their minimum speed?"

Anatoly nodded again.

"Then I must shoot now." A solid solution, with the target's distance, direction, and speed, was impossible. But under the water, Volkov embraced the impossible. Being the best involved trusting his honed instincts. "Give me a bearing rate."

"Right, zero-point-two degrees per minute. It's a tail chase."

"Status of tubes one and three?"

"Both tubes are flooded with the outer doors closed. I need ninety seconds to warm up their gyros, if you want to shoot."

"Open the outer doors to tubes one and three. Warm up tubes one and three and prepare to launch them at Type-209 Alpha. I will launch them in impulse-eject mode. Standard runs to enable, search speeds, and terminal speeds. Passive searches."

After receiving confirmation of his order, Volkov angled the *Wraith* off its targeted submarine's counterfire axis. "Helm, right standard rudder. Steady course north."

Time stopped and then evaporated as the *Wraith* obeyed its commander's will.

Anatoly updated Volkov. "Tubes one and three are ready."

"Shoot tube one."

The plummeting air pressure popped Volkov's ears as the ejected weapon inhaled air into the tube behind it.

A young sailor announced the status. "Tube one away, normal launch. I have wire connectivity."

"Very well. Shoot tube three."

Another pressure drop gave Volkov an ear ache.

A second sailor controlled the slow-kill weapon. "Tube three away, normal launch. I have wire connectivity."

"Very well." Flashes of geometric awareness consumed Volkov's mind. To finish the job, he needed to shorten the distance to his target to continue hearing it. "Helm, all-ahead full. Do not cavitate. Make turns for twenty knots."

The *Wraith* trembled while obeying.

Forcing himself to appear calm, Volkov avoided the temptation to hover about the central plotting table or over the shoulders of his seated team. Instead, he kept his buttocks planted in his chair while watching the action on his nearest monitor.

Anatoly's voice was firm, respecting his commander's quiet confidence. "We're clear of the counterfire cone."

"Very well, Anatoly. Helm, left five-degrees rudder. Steady on course two-eight-five."

The deck rolled and then steadied.

Careful to avoid undermining his captain's authority, Anatoly walked to the elevated conning platform and spoke loud enough for Volkov to hear. "We're deaf at this speed."

"I know."

"If they double back, we'll be a–"

"They won't."

"I trust you, Dmitry, but–"

"Then I'll finish that thought for you. You trust me to take risks. Do you think that any captain of a *Type-209* in these waters is suicidal enough to reverse course into two torpedoes?"

"Yes! Yes, Dmitry. That's the problem. We're no longer a secret navy. We are studied, and everyone knows that our first punch is always humane. They know those weapons coming at them are survivable, and they may risk absorbing them to hit us with a heavyweight."

"That takes more courage in reality than in conversation, and I believe this commander's on a mission that requires him to cover ground in a hurry."

"He's going for the *Lincoln* battle group?"

"One way or another. It could be simple intelligence gathering, but yes."

"Which is not so simple against a fully alerted carrier battle group." Anatoly sighed. "Therefore, I leave the tactics to you, as long as you're healthy enough."

"Why not get back to your station and trust me?"

The sonar expert smirked. "Because there's nothing to hear when you push water over our hydrophones at twenty knots."

As if mocking the statement, an excited sailor half-stood to announce information arriving from hydrophones moving twice that speed. "Passive contact, torpedo one!"

"Send it to the system." Volkov glared at the icon of his first torpedo and the line of bearing to his target.

The intersection of that line and the latest line his submarine had drawn to its target tightened the range. The hapless *Type-209* was six miles from the *Wraith*, three miles from the closest torpedo. As seconds ticked, a blunt estimate of the victim's course and speed showed it moving at twelve knots, away from Volkov's ship. "Perfect."

Still standing near his boss, Anatoly raised an eyebrow. "My God, Dmitry. Do you even understand the concept of failure? You have Type-209 Alpha in your grasp."

"Not yet. Recommend a steer to the second weapon. It's veering slightly away."

As the sonar ace returned to his monitor and obeyed, the second weapon heard its prey, whose location became precise. Putting one weapon, the other, or both on Type-209 Alpha was inevitable, and Volkov slowed his vessel to avoid attracting other warships. "Helm, all-ahead one-third, make turns for five knots."

Settling his mind towards a decision, Volkov sought more information about the targeted ship. "Anatoly, can you identify the nation to which our target belongs?"

"Not yet. They haven't accelerated yet. They don't hear our weapons."

"They will. I want to know which nation."

A sailor revealed an astonished face. "Dmitry! Anatoly! You must listen!"

Volkov snapped. "Play it on the speakers."

Moments later, a watery garbled voice repeated a message in English, in Russian, and in English again in infinite repetition. Between each message arrived a cryptic series of beeps. Volkov needed to hear the Russian version twice before understanding.

Someone–or something–was telling him to choose an encryption scheme for interpreting the beeps. "Play the following encrypted message though scheme November-two-seven-eight-six." Then came garbled digital beeps. Then in English.

"Play the following encrypted message though scheme November-two-seven-eight-six."

The lead radio operator offered a quizzical look. "That's yesterday's encryption scheme."

Volkov was shocked. "Yes. But for our fleet. Nobody else's. This shouldn't be happening, unless Jake…"

"Shall I run the message through yesterday's encryption?"

Volkov sensed grave danger. "Yes. Quickly. Send it privately to my console."

"Yes, sir. Sending now."

Volkov slid headphones over his ears and listened. Again, the message altered between English and Russian.

"Mercenary unit, turn back. You are entering restricted waters and will be prosecuted if you continue. Reverse course." Then he heard it clearly in his native tongue. "Mercenary unit, turn back. You are entering restricted waters and will be prosecuted if you continue. Reverse course."

He tossed the headphones aside. "Helm, right full rudder, make your course one-zero-five."

While the helmsman obeyed, Anatoly scowled. "Our weapons?"

"I need to know who owns that *Type-209* before I decide their fate." Volkov smirked. "While you figure that out, have someone prepare a communications buoy for Jake with the course and speed of Type-209 Alpha. Recommend that he share the data with the Americans and inform him of our encounter with the automated warning from the American sonobuoy. Give the buoy a fifteen-minute delay on the surface but send the message immediately without my further confirmation."

"That's a possible death sentence, Dmitry. God knows what the Americans will do to them."

"You're right, but I don't…" he caught himself. He did care. "At a minimum, I'll tag Type-209 Alpha with torpedo one."

"What about torpedo three? Slow-kills have proven fatal before."

"Disable its warheads but keep it seeking. Let the crew pee

their pants for their audacity."

"Torpedo three is disarmed."

"Very well."

A sonar operator yelled. "I hear another repeating message. It seems to be the same as the first we heard."

Volkov shared his understanding. "I believe the Americans have dropped sonobuoys in a perimeter around the *Lincoln* battle group for our benefit. Obviously, Jake felt comfortable sharing old encryption schemes to avoid unwanted encounters. This surprised us, but it may be a good thing."

Anatoly barked. "Type-209 Alpha is accelerating… launching countermeasures… torpedo in the water!"

"Listen for the counterfire weapon's bearing rate."

"It's already drawing left. It was a desperate shot. No danger."

"Very well." Volkov stood. "Can you identify whose submarine that is?"

"I think so…. Seven-bladed screw. Making turns for twenty-seven knots."

"And?"

"And… it's Egyptian!"

"Excellent. Add that note to the communications buoy, if you haven't launched it yet."

"I haven't yet. I'm adding it." Anatoly's fingers flew across a clicking keyboard. "I'm ready to launch."

"Launch our communications buoy."

"It's away. And I hear it rising… surfaced."

"Radio operator, inform me of satellite confirmation when it arrives."

"Of course, sir."

Time ticked away as the buoy's delay counted down and allowed the *Wraith* to distance itself from its transmission.

The radio operator stirred. "Dmitry, I have satellite receipt confirmation coming in over our floating wire antenna."

Confident the information he'd gleaned would reach people who needed it, Volkov waited for Jake's input. But his patience waned after two minutes. "Radio operator, did Jake acknowledge receipt?"

"Yes! Just now."

"Any orders to reengage?"

"No, sir. He thanks you for a good job."

"Wonderful. All that effort, and no Turkish submarines removed. I'll head back to my stateroom."

Anatoly challenged his commander's nonchalance. "Don't you want to know if your limpet weapon hits?"

Volkov declined the offer. "Let me know after it's done. Whether it hits or not, the Americans can thank Jake for the gift, and the Egyptians can thank me for their lives."

CHAPTER 8

Long hours of boredom had become days of monotony as Dogan kept the *Preveze* on station in the pseudo-chokepoint between Cyprus' southern edge and Lebanon.

The simple act of snorkeling to recharge his batteries and gulp fresh air was a welcomed escape from the drudgery. With one eye closed and the other pressed against the viewport's smelly rubber, he followed the red and white running lights of a merchant ship passing him in the starry night.

A man at the station controlling the old submarine's inner systems and exterior control planes called out. "The battery's at ninety percent, sir. I recommend to secure snorkeling."

Considering the extra time required to push electrons into an almost-charged battery, Dogan preferred to hide. Further exposure of his periscope and snorkel mast was a needless and avoidable danger. "Secure snorkeling."

"Securing snorkeling… snorkeling is secured, sir."

The rumble surrounding Dogan died. "Lower the snorkel mast."

"Lowering the snorkel mast."

An unseen metal cylinder's glide into the free-flood compartment above the control room begat a gentle hum.

"The snorkel mast is lowered, sir."

Dogan inhaled to announce the pending descent of his submarine, but another man's voice stopped him.

"Flash message traffic!"

Rivets of excitement peppered Dogan, and his arm hairs rose over goosebumps. "How long to download?"

"Two minutes and twenty seconds at this baud rate, sir."

"Raise the radio mast half a meter."

"Raising the radio mast half a meter."

The gentle click of a hydraulic valve cycled above Dogan's head as high-pressure oil lifted the mast. "How's the baud rate now?"

"Unchanged, sir. Two minutes to complete the download. We may be receiving some videos."

"Bah. Lower the radio mast to standard height."

"Lowering the radio mast to standard height, sir."

More clicks, and the commander of the *Preveze* let his mind run amok in anticipation of exciting news.

Silent questions pelted him.

Was the *Lincoln* battle group charging forward?

Did one of the other two forward-deployed Turkish submarines find a destroyer or cruiser escort ship?

Had aircraft–often the first assets to clash in a military conflict–exchanged deadly fire?

"Flash message traffic is downloaded, sir. Our queue is empty."

"Lower the radio mast." Dogan slammed the outer ring around the periscope counterclockwise, porting hydraulic fluid to drive the cylinder downward. "Bring the flash message to my stateroom under two-man control."

"Aye, captain."

Dogan strode to the solitude of his quarters, propped open the door, and sat at his foldout desk. He fired up his laptop computer, inserted the USB stick with his commanding officer's encryption schemes, and then typed a password.

Soft footsteps approached, and then two men appeared, each with a thumb and index finger holding another USB stick. Per the protocol of two-man control, four fingers and four eyes had tracked the flash message from its invocation within the secure radio operator's locked room to Dogan's possession.

The senior radio man declared the obvious. "Flash message, for your eyes only, sir."

"Bring it." Dogan extended his hand and pinched the end of the USB drive. "I have possession of flash message traffic."

"You have possession of flash message traffic, aye, sir."

"Dismissed. Close the door."

In quiet solitude, Dogan inserted his flash traffic into an open USB port and awaited the satiation of unbridled curiosity. He paged through a curt narrative of powerful information, murmuring as he read. "Damn them."

After reading the news, he played a video taken from a long-distance reconnaissance aircraft. In broad daylight, the scene unfolded, and an unwelcomed problem became reality in Dogan's mind.

The mercenary fleet had changed from an afterthought from his briefings of world navies into a thorn in his foot.

Unsure with whom to share the news first, he chose someone safe. He dialed the sound-powered phone and heard his friend's deep voice.

"Corpsman."

"My quarters, Asker."

"Anxiety?"

"Yeah. Well, no. It's a healthy anxiety."

"That's good to notice the difference. Do you need your pills?"

"Maybe. Bring them just in case." To reduce his rising concern, he joked. "But also bring a few pills for yourself. This is wild."

Thirty seconds later, the corpsman knocked, clicked open the door, and jutted his head into his commanding officer's quarters.

Dogan waved him to a guest chair. "Close the door."

Asker clicked the latch shut and sat. "What's going on?"

"Take a look." Dogan reran the video.

"What is that?"

"That's an Egyptian *Type-209* submarine being forced to surface by helicopters from the *Lincoln* battle group."

"Where is that?"

"Great question. Two hundred and eighty nautical miles west by southwest."

"Oh my."

"Yeah. The *Lincoln* is that close."

Asker grunted. "I see your point about healthy anxiety. Maybe I should have retired. We could really end up in battle."

"Yeah. And against the biggest, nastiest, and angriest class of warship in the history of naval combat. But it gets even more intense." Dogan pointed his fingernail at the screen. "Do you see these small bumps on the submarine's hull just above the water-line?"

"Yeah. Now that you point them out, I do."

"Our analysts believe that the submarine was heeled over in a high-speed turn while trying to evade a torpedo."

Asker's eyes widened. "A torpedo? For real?"

"You see why my heart rate's up a bit."

"Yeah. They must have evaded, I assume."

"If myths weren't true, I'd agree. But it seems the torpedo did its job. It was a limpet weapon from that mercenary fleet we watched the Greeks tangle with about a year and half ago. The limpets don't usually land that high, and we'd normally only see one or two of them above the water line. But the turn placed them higher up the hull and made our conclusions easy to draw. That's the work of that Frenchman's fleet."

"I'd heard rumors."

"They were a myth, then they appeared against the Greeks, and then they slipped back into legend–or at least into another ocean, which was good enough for me. But we learned something about them by watching the Greeks, and we heard secondary reports from the Egyptians confirming the same type behavior when they attacked the Israelis."

"What's that, sir?"

"This mercenary fleet tries to avoid killing its targets."

Asker raised an eyebrow. "Because they have a conscience?"

"Possibly. But they work for pay, and for them, today's enemy is tomorrow's customer. Best not to kill your future clients."

"That actually makes sense. So, what do those limpets do?"

"They're just incredibly loud noise-makers in frequencies that are easy to hear over normal oceanic noises."

"Fascinating."

"Okay, it's not all that mythical. I mean, we've watched their entire fleet transit the Suez back and forth a few times in recent months, but nobody thought they'd have the audacity to get involved between us and the Americans."

Asker frowned at the laptop. "What are those? They look like still-frame images."

Excited by the video of the Frenchman's fleet work on the Egyptian submarine, Dogan had missed them. "Let's see." He tapped icons to bring up pictures.

They were snapshots of the rogue mercenary fleet transitioning the Suez Canal. Considering the images little more than artifacts worthy of study, Dogan was tempted to file them away for future reference. Then he saw the timestamp on one of them, and his ire rose. "Damn you, Commodore Kaplan."

"What's wrong, sir?"

The mercenary fleet reached Port Said yesterday and then dived immediately when the bottom was deep enough.

"I'm not following, sir. I deal with the human body–not warfare."

"It means that someone knew that the world's two most combat-hardened crews dived three hundred nautical miles from us yesterday. For some reason, my boss, or someone above him, didn't find it worthy of note."

"That does seem odd."

"Odd, and dangerous."

"Heck, even I can see that."

"I need to call him."

Understanding his boss' mindset, Asker warned him. "A career-limiting call?"

Dogan grunted. "Thanks for that. It would've been exactly that without grounding myself."

"You know that the conversation will be heated if he won't or can't give you a good answer. Be ready."

"I will." Dogan shifted to tactical thoughts. "But I'm subject to limited emissions control."

"Meaning?"

"Meaning, I can't broadcast anything except low-power over ship-to-ship circuits."

"You can't call Squadron that way, can you?"

Dogan smirked. "Actually, I can. It just takes a little patience."

The corpsman became agitated. "Do we have time? That mercenary fleet could be anywhere."

"Not anywhere. I need to rethink my math, but they're not here yet, if they're even coming this way. Not all of them."

"I'll have to trust you on that, too."

Dogan ruminated over mental numbers and logistic details.

From their nation's airspace, Turkish reconnaissance aircraft had followed American helicopters as they'd bobbed up and down in altitude, deploying and redeploying their sonar suites around the Egyptian *Type-209*.

Aided by the limpets, they'd made quick work of the over-curious Egyptians, and Dogan's best guess placed a mercenary submarine within launch range of the tagged submarine an hour before its forced surfacing.

Since that surfacing happened three hours ago, Dogan scratched one errant *Scorpène*-class adversary off his mental checklist. Whether it was the *Wraith* or the *Specter*, it lacked the speed to reach the *Preveze* before he could contact Squadron.

And the bizarre combat transport vessel *Goliath* lacked the stealth to hunt him. If surfaced, it would be seen. If submerged, it would be heard, unless it crawled at five knots to prevent its countless jagged edges from announcing its location.

That left the Frenchman's third ship, the *Specter* or the *Wraith*, free to harass him. But Dogan knew how to defend himself from a single adversary, even while shallow and contacting his boss. "Trust me on this. I need to call him." He snatched the sound-powered receiver from its cradle on the bulkhead, dialed the control room, and whipped the call button.

His executive officer answered. "Control room. This is the executive officer."

"Executive officer, captain. Take the ship to periscope depth and find me a relay ship."

Apparently craving any interesting activity, the executive officer sounded enthusiastic about the order. "Take the ship to periscope depth and find you a relay ship, aye, sir!"

Dogan hung up.

"What's a relay ship?"

"Someone very smart thought of something very simple and put communication suites on merchant ships transiting in and out of Mersin. It's our busiest port, and any spies working against us expect the heavy traffic. So, when ships go from there to the Suez, they won't attract attention as they can't help but pass close to us."

Asker raised an eyebrow and nodded. "I like where this is going."

"We're putting plain-clothed military personnel on ships to guard and manage the communications equipment. When they reach Port Said, they bribe the Egyptian captains and take rides on tugboats to our other merchant ships heading back to Mersin. Then we have a steady flow of relays going both ways in the shipping lanes."

"Brilliant."

"It gets better. The relay ships are constantly broadcasting to help us find them. We need to only track them, maneuver close the shipping lane, and use the relay to call Squadron while the merchant vessel drives right by, and we keep its civilian crew protected from knowledge of the exchange."

"Wow."

"That's called using our local waters to our advantage. And it's time to take the advantage."

Thirty minutes later, Dogan sat in his foldout chair, watching his executive officer handle the periscope. "You've told the sonar team to search for a *Scorpène*-class submarine, right?"

"Yes, sir. That's the new primary threat."

"Good." Dogan glanced at the nearest tactical display showing lines of bearing to a relay ship approaching from the north. Since the lines failed to fan out, he knew the ship was distant. He shared his thoughts aloud. "I'll broadcast when the bearing rate reaches half a degree per minute."

Sparing him from an unanswered comment, the executive officer kept his eye against the optics while answering. "I concur, sir."

Ten minutes later, Dogan saw the bearing rate he wanted. "Radio operator, transmit a hail message on the bearing of the relay ship. Repeat it three times. Low power."

After obeying, the radio operator glanced up from his panel. "Hail acknowledged. Secure connection established. I have a staff member from Squadron."

"Over the loudspeakers."

A distant man's voice filled the compartment. "*Preveze*, this is Squadron. Receiving your relay hail. Please respond. *Preveze*, this is Squadron. Receiving your relay hail. Please respond."

Dogan stood and reached for the radio bolted above his head. "Am I lined up?"

The radio technician answered. "Yes, sir."

"Squadron, this is *Preveze*. Receipt acknowledged. Over."

"*Preveze*, Squadron. Understand you have a limited communication window. State your need. Over."

"I request a private talk with Commodore Kaplan. Over."

A silent pause preceded the response. The absence of background chatter within the squadron's command center revealed the staff member's muting of the conversation. Then he returned. "Keep the line open, *Preveze*. The commodore will be with you. Over."

"Keeping the line open. Over."

Dogan spoke to his radio operator. "Pipe this to my quarters. I'll use my phone in there."

Seated in his private stateroom, Dogan lifted the phone and selected the channel connecting him with his commodore. He placed it against his cheek. "Are you there, sir?"

The voice was a strong baritone. "I'm here. Let's be quick. It's already a risk that you're broadcasting, even with a relay ship."

"I know, sir." Dogan blurted out his concern. "I need to discuss the mercenary fleet."

"I forwarded the information about the surfaced Egyptian as soon as I could. What's wrong?"

"I understand need-to-know protocols, but why didn't I need to know about the mercenary fleet's passage through the Suez Canal yesterday?"

The commodore snorted. "You're correct. You didn't need to know. Now that they've announced their participation with the Americans, you need to know."

Unhappy with the explanation, Dogan recalled the corpsman's advice about keeping his career alive and moved on. "I understand, sir. But are you reconsidering my priorities? Now that I know where the mercenary fleet is, I need to remove them before I can maneuver freely against the Americans. That would remove their meddling and also send a message to the Americans about our resolve to kill."

"I'll consider that."

Dogan recognized his boss' comment as a polite 'no' and inhaled to calm himself. He tried a new argument. "Do we really need two submarines here? Can't Commander Reis handle this chokepoint with the *Sakarya* and free me to hunt our new enemies?"

"Yes. Damn it, he could. But those are not my orders. And if you keep questioning them, I'll relieve you of command the second you come home."

"I'm not questioning your orders. I'm merely–"

"Or you can 'merely' keep challenging me and force me to relieve you now, if you prefer."

Frustrated, Dogan called upon quiet wisdom and realized a need to retreat. But cynicism laced his words. "I serve at the commodore's pleasure."

"Damn it, Dogan! Don't patronize me. This is war, and you know better. You're my best, and I need you, but you know damned well that you see only a fraction of the full campaign."

Crushing thoughts ran through Dogan's mind. *Victim. Victim.*

Victim. Then he hushed his inner child. *Not a victim. Warrior. Submarine commander.* "You're right, sir. I'm better than cynicism."

"You're also better than my other commanders, which is why you still command the *Preveze.* But one more unprofessional challenge, and my next order will be for your exec's eyes only, putting you under arrest. Watch yourself. Squadron, out."

CHAPTER 9

Jake's stomach churned as he withheld silent threats against his former lover. "I understand that I haven't met any mission goals yet. I was merely pointing out that Dmitry's gift-wrapping of the Egyptian *Type-209* was a gesture of good faith. We took a risk on your behalf, and we deserve some credit."

Letting him continue uninterrupted, likely to leave herself with the final word, she kept quiet.

Angered, Jake embellished his resolve to kill his former countrymen to maintain leverage against her. "If I'd been in two-way communications with Dmitry, I would've let the Egyptian pass and see how it fared against an American escort or two. You know, maybe crack a destroyer in half and do some of my future dirty work for me."

Refusing to bait or agitate him, Olivia remained quiet.

Remembering his family's captivity, Jake shifted mental gears from threats to compliance. "But I wasn't in communication, and Dmitry did what Dmitry does to spare you from an unwanted distraction–and probably an international incident."

Declaring Jake's arguments complete, the CIA maverick smirked. "You're entertaining when you try to be a little Pierre."

"Why am I still talking to you?"

"Because I own you. And no, don't ask again about forcing your own translator into the hotel room, letting the families have more time together, or more frequent check-ins."

"I gave up on all that hours ago."

"And despite your little reminder about Dmitry's warm up routine, remember that you've accomplished nothing." In the liquid crystal display, she reached forward, and the screen went dark.

To vent and to test the French companion seated in the console beside him, Jake issued his cynicism in English. "I really wish I'd hidden in a country where she didn't speak the language."

The on-duty officer looked up from his display where he was losing a game of solitaire while monitoring the mercenary fleet's nonextant radio traffic. He answered in French "Excuse me? My English is terrible. Embarrassingly so."

The fleet's new de facto commodore switched to French. "She found me a long time ago... never mind."

"Okay. I'm here to help. Just ask."

Jake chided himself for thinking he could've learned a new language in the short months between escaping death on his stolen *Colorado* submarine and hiding in Avignon, France. He considered himself smart with math and science but mediocre at humanities. French had come only after years of rigorous learning.

But then he remembered the language training open to military personnel. The Defense Language Institute Foreign Language Center could make a hard-working student fluent in nine months. Facebook and LinkedIn revealed that several of his Naval Academy classmates had used it to enable new career assignments.

For most of his adult life, he'd been hiding from his classmates. His treason had made him fear burdening them with the knowledge of his existence, but in the scant encounters with his academy classmates, he'd found receptive ears.

A decade ago, a Navy SEAL classmate had helped him recapture a stolen Israeli submarine. Although the classmates hadn't met in person, the SEAL had met Renard, had heard Jake's voice on an underwater phone, and had credited his treasonous classmate for shutting down a torpedo aimed at him.

That was one classmate, sworn to abject silence about Jake's existence, but aware and appreciative of it. If he could reach that SEAL, who'd since entered the civilian population, he might find an ally. He flagged the man as someone to seek for help. But he could do better, and he recalled the most recent and most profound encounter.

He's just saved Commander Andy Causey's life and that of his *Virginia*-class submarine's crew.

Then he'd dined with Andy and several other officers in secret.

Apparently, time–and numerous acts of penance–could heal wounds, and slowly Jake sensed his nation forgiving him. And after learning of his family's imprisonment less than a day ago, he remembered having reached out his Naval Academy classmates, even when targeting them.

When he'd first threatened Olivia with retaliation against the *Lincoln* battle group, something deep within him had made him ask for his academy classmates–even as he wrestled within his soul to declare them his fleet's military victims.

A powerful network once closed, now open–even for a presumed-dead traitor who'd returned to life with a litany of redemptive missions. "I've been a fool."

"Excuse me?"

Suspecting everyone, Jake used his healthy mistrust to wave off the French watch officer, whose uniform identified him as a Commander Buisson. "I'd like some privacy. Give me fifteen minutes. I'll monitor fleet traffic."

"Of course. It's your mission. I'll be in the break room."

When alone, Jake fired up LinkedIn, sought his classmates, and thumbed through national law enforcement agencies looking for graduates from his class.

One popped up in the Department of Homeland Security, but the job's title seemed strategic. Jake flagged the classmate as an option and kept looking.

The next classmate was perfect.

Federal Bureau of Investigation.

Mike Jennings' demeanor could ratchet up a sailor's military bearing from two time zones away. Jake suspected that if he saw Jennings in sunglasses and a dark suit, he'd slap handcuffs on himself and confess to random crimes out of respect for the man's authority.

The FBI was probably too lax for Jennings, but it was the best the world could offer him. It was his perfect job.

Jake thought about contacting a classmate who, like the rest of the world, considered him a casualty of the Colorado Incident.

Such contact violated the rules of his witness protection, but the rule maker had taken his wife. "Screw you, Olivia."

Jake decided to reach out–smartly.

Could he launch a desperate appeal right there on LinkedIn? Could he try social media? No and no, he decided. Olivia would monitor that and shut it down, and if not, the chances of Jennings believing anything from someone claiming to be Jake Slate was zero.

"Shit."

He needed someone credible to connect him with Jennings, and the simple answer flooded his thoughts. Owing Jake his life, Andy Causey would help, if Jake could keep it safe for the American submarine commander's family.

"I need you, Andy."

But Jake refused to transfer his burdens to his classmate. There must be a middle ground, a safe way to communicate with Causey and have him contact Jennings.

Wondering if Causey could bring the affair to NCIS or push it up his naval chain of command, Jake doubted such attempts would work. The NCIS had no jurisdiction over Olivia or any other CIA wrongdoers in her camp, and the American Navy would have no interest helping the guy who threatened the *Lincoln* battle group.

Jake needed the FBI, but he feared the FBI might already know about the affair. He expected that some among their ranks would applaud the CIA for incarcerating the mercenary fleet's families.

But not Jennings.

If he knew, he'd oppose it.

Letting ideas cascade through his frontal cortex, Jake found nothing useful, and he let his subconscious mind work while he refocused on tactics. He called out to his French companion. "I'm done with my private work. You can come back whenever you want."

The response in French came through the breakroom's door. "I'll be there soon. Would you like some coffee, Mister Slate?"

"No, thanks. In fact, take your time with your cup. I'm enjoying my privacy." Jake glanced at his screen, seeking a status of his deployed units. The *Goliath-Specter* tandem remained together per Cahill's last report, and Volkov did what he did best—hunting submarines in secrecy.

None of the ships had risked radio transmissions during the last three hours, and Jake let them work in quiet. He grunted and turned his attention to his Aramaic lessons.

With his wife held captive, he needed to improve their semi-secret code. He could also picture Linda working out some scheme with Ariella. The ladies had common linguistic roots, with Arabic, Aramaic, and Hebrew sharing a Semitic heritage.

Anticipating one of the thrice-daily check-ins with his wife, Jake remembered to connect with his commanders' family members. Though he understood nothing the Volkovs said, he knew their son liked hearing their voices and seeing their faces. He double-checked the alarm on his display reminding himself to forward one broadcast of low bandwidth with the voices of Volkov's and Cahill's loved ones, and one with full videos when his commanders could expose antennas and download them.

After twenty minutes learning key words he'd need with Linda and studying Aramaic verb tenses, Jake heard his console chime and call his attention to a luxury hotel prison in Washington. He tapped an icon to accept the hail.

Wearing a labored smile, his wife appeared. "Hi, honey!"

"How are you, Linda?"

"Fine. What time's it there?"

Jake shifted to Aramaic. "About ten o'clock."

She responded in her native tongue. "You sound more confident with Aramaic."

"I study. I studied. I will more study."

Her smile widened. "You're trying hard. Doing good."

Jake realized that Aramaic was more than a code for her. It was her reminder of a better place and time. "You okay?"

"Yes." She continued, using small words and employing the codename for Ariella they'd created in their last conversation. "Strong flower okay, too. Strength of group."

"You're strength of me. You're strength of my navy."

A tear welled in her eye. "I'm scared."

"We're okay. Whole team my navy okay."

"Will this end okay?"

He couldn't know, but he feigned confidence. "Yes. I make it okay. Take you home." He was never going home, not to America while Olivia had power, and the first action he'd take after freeing his wife was flying her to Renard's bunker.

Renard's bunker.

With his mind swirling, Jake recognized stress chewing at his memory and causing him to forget details. So, he jotted down cryptic notes on a nearby pad, reminding him to connect with Renard's basecamp. The Frenchman might have left clues with trusted colleagues in his shelter outside of Avignon.

"Jake?"

"Sorry, honey. What more from strong flower?"

"She say we go nowhere. Cameras in rooms. We together not often in main room. Not much time together. Pierre family alone. Me with only strong flower and old people."

"What else? Men watch you?"

"Men watch me, yes."

"Stronger than strong flower?"

"I think so."

Jake accepted his wife's guardians as martial arts experts, special forces commandoes, or simply oversized bad asses who could crush skulls with a punch–even the female guard Jake had overheard talking during a check-in. There had to be female CIA guard, he reasoned, for moments when female detainees needed close monitoring. "You okay?"

"Yes. Okay enough."

"Understand." Jake sought his move. "You talk to strong flower now?"

Linda looked away from the monitor and then back to Jake. "Possible. She here waiting."

Finished with any pretense of secrecy, Jake relaxed and abandoned Aramaic for the rest of the conversation. "Can you let Ariella talk now?"

"I guess it's her turn. I miss you."

"Stay strong. I'll talk to you at the next check-in."

"I hate this."

"Try to enjoy the food, you foodie."

"The room service is great. I'm not going to lie. Okay, it's Ariella's turn. I miss you."

Linda walked away, and Jake heard a guard warning the women to cease whispering to each other in passing.

When the Israeli intelligence officer appeared, her expression oozed the survival, evasion, resistance, and escape protocols that pilots and other military personnel at risk of capture knew. But Jake sensed her reserved words complying with instructions from her captors in avoiding insinuations of imprisonment. "For Terry, do your job. I'm braced for all outcomes. For you, Jake, I find my stay here acceptable."

Wishing he had something insightful for her, Jake nodded. "Thanks. If I had anything useful to share, I'm sure it would be a burden for you to know it–not an asset."

The Israeli smirked. "Now, you're thinking like an intelligence officer."

"I'm doing my best."

A subtle but deadly look fell over Ariella's face. Then she made an abrupt shift to newlywed mode, her smile and glow a forced but believable mask. Her voice turned lighthearted as she played a role. "You know Terry's favorite insult, right?"

"Yeah. I'm glad you–"

Expecting Jake's blunder, she intercepted it. "Oh, don't say it or I'll start crying."

Wondering where she was taking the charade, he played along, grateful that she seemed to be conveying an actionable message. "I'd hate to make you cry."

"There are few things in a marriage upon which you can always count …" her pause let the weird grammar sink in. "But Terry's colorful swearing is something I hope to count on for a lifetime."

The words failed to land in Jake's logic, and he sought meaning in the use of 'count' twice. But as he replayed Cahill's favorite insult in his mind, he cringed at the thought of a naked man's buttocks.

Kiss me bare hairy arse.

"God willing, you'll have a long lifetime with him."

"It's funny what runs through my mind, now that we're married but far apart. I miss his freckles."

Jake couldn't remember a single freckle on the Australian's face, but he feigned agreement. "Understandable."

"I know I can count on you, Jake. Don't worry about me." Feigning levity, she continued. "Jake, do remember the date we met? You were so confident, but Terry was so smitten with me. I was expecting a pair of lions, but I found one lion and one little freckly kitten."

Jake attuned himself to her hints of repeated words, intentional inaccuracies, and strange grammar. He let her remarks linger for future mental processing. "Luckily, you pitied him, I guess."

"Did he ever tell you how close we came to not meeting each other?"

"Uh… no. That would've sucked."

"Yeah." Her throat tightened. "I'm sorry. I'm rambling."

If she were acting, he'd give her an Emmy. "No, it's fine. I know you must miss him."

"Thank you, Jake. You're a good friend." She perked up. "If my assignment with you guys had been delayed by only five days, I would've been leading some boring field assignment, and I never would've met Terry. But it ended up being the best month of my life, thanks to you guys."

"Really? Do tell."

Adding credibility, she embellished with feigned indignance. "Weren't you listening to the best man's speech at our wedding?"

He remembered Liam Walker, the best man, restricting his speech to a roasting of Cahill's helpless decline into amorous affection. "I thought I was paying attention. Maybe not." Knowing his escape from alcoholism with the medication naltrexone and the Sinclair Method was common fleet knowledge, Jake confirmed their tacit code. "I had a lot to drink."

She pounced on the opening. "Come on! Liam mentioned the craziness of why last November was my favorite month. I earned my first-degree karate blackbelt, I was the maid of honor for my best friend's wedding, and then the best day of my life was meeting Terry. Working with you guys nabbed me a husband and accelerated my promotion to lieutenant colonel."

Remembering Ariella had no single friends to support as a bridesmaid and the many times she'd told Jake how inferior karate was to Krav Maga, he committed her words to memory as a bank of clues. "Hey, we're a good group, and you earned your promotion."

"You guys spared me from a pain-in-the-ass assignment, and instead you gave me a hairy husband." Her face reasserted its cold, subtle death stare for a moment. Then she went neutral.

Jake had all he needed. The words 'ass' and 'hairy' flowed like gems, and her veiled message was taking shape. "No kidding. Only five days after the date we met, and only God knows where you'd be now."

Whether forced for show or issued as an honest release, a tear trickled from her eye. "Now you know my little secret. If you have nothing else..."

An odd idea entered Jake's awareness. "I might. Hold on."

"Okay?"

"I'm thinking... yeah. This might work. Can you get me in contact with a flag officer in the Israel Navy?"

"Not directly, but my boss can–"

The display froze and the audio ended. A man with a tenor voice addressed Jake. "State your intent."

Impressed to have kicked his listeners' first tripwire, Jake was candid. "Tactical, sir. I think I can play a trick to get rid of one Turkish submarine."

"Details."

"I take from Israel… this is going to get elaborate. I'll write it up so you can send it to your superiors and then pass it along to Lieutenant Colonel Dahan."

"Very well. You must have all tactical conversations approved or we'll shut off your access to the detainees."

"Understood. I'll keep it to small talk."

"You're back with the lieutenant colonel."

Ariella's face jumped in position and started moving again.

"Can you hear me, Ariella?"

"Yes. You were saying?"

"I'll send you written instructions. If you like the idea, send it along to your superiors in Aman."

"I await them. Anything else?"

"No. I'll forward our chat to Terry."

"Thank you, Jake. Take care of him."

"I will."

"I'll get Dmitry's parents." The unshakeable warrior departed, and the old couple appeared.

After quick salutations in misunderstood languages, Volkov's parents rattled a Russian message to their son.

When complete, Jake bid them farewell, shut off the connection, and sent multiple audio and video streams to a satellite queue for his commanders' download.

After sending the feeds, Jake sighed and reclined in his chair. Sensing his fatigue, he rubbed his eyes and considered his next move. Although tempted to check Aramaic words to verify what his wife had said, he saw a better use of his time.

He needed a secret door to the outside world. He needed a

channel opened to Renard's staff in the Frenchman's bunker, and he needed to extend that to his Naval Academy classmates.

Before risking the special console with its connection to Renard's bunker, he wanted to address a final unknown–the man who shared the command center with him.

After spending a day with a rotating trio of watch officers, Jake thought the command center's French staff lacked a vital trait.

None of them had gossiped about Renard.

Curiosity should have compelled them to interrogate the newly arrived American about his background, and there'd be no better way than chatting about their quirky mutual acquaintance.

Then Jake realized the faces Renard had shown him in the command center before his departure were different from the ones supporting him. After silently abusing himself for failing to notice earlier, he excused himself for the whirlwind day he'd endured.

As he stood and strode to the breakroom, he finalized his plan.

Commander Buisson looked up from the table where he was sipping coffee and reading his cell phone. "Would you like me to watch the consoles?"

"Sure. I'm going to step outside and talk to the guards."

Buisson frowned. "You can see them on the monitor."

"Exactly. I don't like their look. They're inattentive, and I'm going to remind them of their duty."

"Okay. Sure." Buisson tipped back his plastic cup, tossed it into a garbage can, and then marched out the breakroom behind the American.

When he saw the French officer sit, Jake stepped through the security door but propped it open with his foot. As the guards looked at him, he spoke softly. "You guys need anything? Water? Coffee?"

Shaking their heads, they thanked him and declined.

"Great. Just checking. But please listen to this very loud and strange conversation I'm going to have with Commander Buisson."

The guards frowned but nodded their agreement.

"Also note that I have no weapon. I'm going to act, and God willing, I'll be convincing."

"We work for you, as long as you honor the rules of this establishment. Remember, it's a civilian location, but we have military jurisdiction."

"Thanks. I know. Enjoy the show." Jake turned back into the room but kept a foot between the door and the latch.

Deepening his voice to sound like someone else, he laid the trap in English. "You there! Don't move."

Buisson bit on the charade. "Okay."

Recognizing the word 'okay' as adopted into French, Jake pushed harder. "When I tell you, move very slowly if you want to live. Nod three times if you understand."

Building Jake's case, the man obeyed the English command.

Jake pressed his advantage. "I have a gun to Mister Slate's head, but we only want him. If you obey, you can leave this place a free man. Nod three times if you understand."

The man nodded again.

"Very slowly, raise your hands."

Two hands rose above the Frenchman's head.

"Good. Now, keep facing forward, and stand."

Buisson obeyed.

"Now slowly turn and look at me."

The commander answered in perfect English. "If I see you, won't I become a liability to you?"

"I have a mask. I said look."

Buisson turned and revealed a horror that gave way to anger upon seeing the American standing alone.

Jake snorted. "My ass, you don't speak English."

In French, the man retorted. "I'm just shy about it. Why did you lie and scare me like that?"

"Because I just called your bluff, spy. Get out of here, tell Olivia to go to hell, and don't come back."

The Frenchman became indignant. "I am officially assigned

here in my duty as a naval officer in the French–"

"Really. You're a French naval officer?" Jake disallowed the man to answer and jumped to the real test. "Describe your date at the commencement party at the French Naval Academy?"

The man hesitated.

"Too bad, Buisson, or whoever you are. Every aspirant finds a date to that dance and remembers the night, even if he had to take his butt-ugly, one-legged sister."

"You caught me off guard. You lie and threaten me."

"Shut up!" Jake switched to French for the guards' understanding through the ajar door. "Here's your only warning. I can kill you with my bare hands, and that's actually the choice I hope you take, given my present mood. I would really find that therapeutic. But I suggest that you turn yourself over to these gentlemen for the crime of impersonating a French naval officer."

"You're making a big mistake."

Jake aimed his voice over his shoulder through the door. "You gentlemen are hearing this, right?"

"Yes, Mister Slate. But he has the proper security credentials."

Jake remembered the guards' faces from his original entrance with Renard into control center. His boss had been comfortable with them, and he knew his mentor would have warned him of unfamiliar people. He trusted them as much as any new acquaintance. "You'll still look into this, won't you?"

"Yes, sir. Of course." One guard entered the room. "Commander Buisson, will you turn yourself over willingly into my custody to allow an investigation into Mister Slate's accusations?"

"I will not. This is ludicrous."

The guard grunted. "Well, then. Shall I lock this door and leave you to resolve this in privacy with Mister Slate?"

Taking the hint, Jake embellished his position. "I have a lot of anger to work through, but I haven't found anyone's bones to break yet."

The spy's attitude corrected itself, and after his willing departure, Jake asked the guard to find the real officers who'd worked with Renard on prior missions.

Alone, he returned to a console and relaxed his mind with his ongoing study of Aramaic.

CHAPTER 10

Danielle Sutton second-guessed herself for joining the Frenchman's fleet.

Then she triple-guessed herself.

Then she forced herself to stop driving herself crazy.

The *Goliath's* domed bridge remained a cramped coffin under a black abyss, but the ship's executive officer–her executive officer–eased her unease. "These undersea loading and unloading procedures are a piece of cake. We're designed for it."

Refusing to show weakness, she eyed Walker. "I've heard. From Pierre, Terry, Jake, and you. I think Sergeui was even trying to tell me this morning in his broken English. But it's so damned unusual. I need to see it for myself."

"Fair point. We'll be through it soon enough."

Through a liquid crystal display, the *Goliath's* former commander added his opinion. "The ship's amazing at depth control and maneuvering for this very evolution. You'll forget that you're a commanding officer and feel like a spectator."

"I didn't sign up to watch movies. These sort of events are why I'm here. Plus, the action." She checked her ship's location on the chart and noticed it was seven miles outside of Israeli waters. "Speaking of which. What are we waiting for?"

Joining the conversation from the monitor, Cahill replied. "We're waiting for Jake's orders."

Trying to hide her thoughts, she narrowed her eyes, but the Australian commanding officer sensed her frustration.

"You joined us at the worst time or best time, depending on your point of view. This is as chaotic as it's ever been, and if you like order, you'll be miserable. But if you like excitement, you'll be happy as a pig in slop."

She pursed her lips. "Not sure I can consider myself a pig."

"Sorry. We bubbleheads aren't known for social grace."

Walker chortled. "I'm surprised he's even aware of social grace. By rights, he had to marry an Israeli. No other woman would tolerate him."

"Kiss me bare hairy arse, Liam. Danielle, please consider half rations for the wanker."

"I think he likes half rations. He barely eats."

"Watching me waistline." Walker aimed his nose at his former commanding officer. "And thankfully, you're sitting in the cargo bed out there while I'm in here enjoying Danielle's company much more than yours."

She challenged the pandering. "No sucking up."

"It's not sucking up. It's true. You're running this ship without any time to learn it. That's impressive enough, but we're surrounded by constant weirdness. Terry's commanding a submarine he's never set foot on, our patriarch is held hostage, and our American buddy's in charge of a fleet he never wanted to lead. Did I hit the major points?"

She snorted. "Not bad."

Cahill called out. "Are you seeing it? Message traffic."

Danielle faced a different monitor. "I am. Orders from Jake. He says to release you when it's tactically safe."

"Alright then. Let's do it."

She voiced her first concern. "You're still in charge of the *Goliath-Specter* tandem, Terry. I assume you concur with Jake's order to release you when it's tactically safe?"

"That's right."

"Aren't we about as tactically safe as we'll ever be?"

"That's right, too. You've reviewed the procedure?"

"I have. Offloading sounds easy compared to onboarding."

"That's also right. The *Specter's* positively buoyant by two thousand kilos, with a level trim. I see in our datalink that you've got the *Goliath* two thousand kilos heavy. When you release me, I'll float up, and you'll head down, but then the *Goliath* will recover itself right back to where you are. I'm ready to be detached."

"Understood."

"When I'm ten miles away, I'll launch a communications buoy telling Jake that we're separated. No need for you to risk exposing yourself, even with a buoy. You'll need that time to navigate to the rendezvous with the Israelis anyway, and Jake will give the final order once you're there, if not before."

"Right."

"We'll be in communications through the underwater phone, but I'll only use it if needed. Otherwise, silence."

Silence. That eerie sonic void under a black abyss. She struggled to welcome it. "If this process is automatic, at least from my end..."

"It is."

"Then I'm ready."

"Alright, then. Give Liam the order and watch him do it. You can learn while watching."

"Okay." She spoke to her executive officer. "Liam, release the *Specter*."

"Release the *Specter*, aye, ma'am." He tapped an icon and bounced his voice off panels, through a microphone above him, and to the entire ship. "Standby to release the *Specter*."

Like a supernova, floodlights illuminated the submarine cargo. With the depths' darkness penetrated, the *Specter* was blackness absorbing light within seeming reach of Danielle's fingertips.

The *Goliath's* wire-commanded rover hovered over the submarine's conning tower, offering a video of Jake's former ship under Cahill's command. As a dark screen rose to life with an external camera's view, she saw the *Specter*, the *Goliath*, and herself from a new perspective.

Unable to resist, she lifted her arm over her head and waved. From the rover's perspective, she saw herself from behind, standing next to Walker under a dome of bright light. "Wild."

Walker ignored her commentary and continued carrying out her order. "I am releasing the *Specter*." He tapped an icon, and clunking hydraulic valves echoed throughout the hull. Shadowy ram arms rotated away from the *Specter*, and a dark gap opened underneath the rising vessel and its bed.

Under her breath, she spoke. "Cool."

"If you like that, wait until we load one." Managing the water underneath the departing cargo, Walker shared his confidence, adding detail for his new commander's sake. "Terry's free, and we're descending at the predicted rate. Pumps are making us lighter, but we're still descending as expected. We'll reach sixty meters per protocol, to clear under Terry, and then we'll rise back to thirty meters."

"Very well."

Before Cahill's screen went dark with the loss of the short-range laser connection, he shouted his farewell. "Looking great! I'll scout ahead and clear the seas of–"

Walker announced the obvious. "He's gone."

"Shit. That was cool."

"Worth the price of admission?"

"Yeah. Next steps now. Chart us a course for our rendezvous with the Israelis."

"Already done, ma'am. Would you like to head there now?"

"I would. Recommended course and speed?"

"Six knots, on course zero-seven-four."

"Take us to our rendezvous."

As the *Goliath* glided forward, Danielle recalled a logical disconnect she'd learned during her interviews with Renard.

"I know we just had Terry's wedding in Israel, but weren't you... I mean 'we'. Weren't we fighting the Israelis only a year ago?"

Walker shrugged. "That's life in our line of business. We have enemies one day who are our clients the next. That's one reason we use humane torpedoes."

"What's another reason?"

"Jake's conscience. Well, that's how it started. But we all embrace the philosophy now."

"Normally only the submarines carry those, right?"

"Correct. Our present loadout is rare, but Jake wanted us to have a couple limpets and slow-kills on the *Goliath*. Not entirely sure why, but I guess it made logistical sense while we were swapping our heavyweights with the *Specter*."

Walker guided the conversation back to their pending custody of an old *Type-206*-class submarine. "I'm sure Pierre negotiated something with the Israelis to ease any remaining bad blood. Plus, we're doing them a service by literally taking out their trash."

"Pierre's latest predicament doesn't exactly overwhelm me with confidence in his negotiation skills."

Walker balked. "But he wasn't negotiating with the CIA or the United States Navy, for that matter. He started this mission by being extorted, and I trust him to negotiate that into negotiations, because he'd that good, if that make sense."

"It does. Sort of."

"And, if you'll excuse me disagreeing with you..."

"Pierre pays for your opinions, and he pays me to respect them."

"After the extortion, I give him credit. He found a way to join his family when they needed him. And his fleet is alive, well, and ready to fight the Turks or, God help us, the Americans."

"Didn't this very ship rescue a *Virginia*-class submarine from Iranian waters less than a year ago? Isn't there any sense of valor among the Americans for that?"

Walker smirked. "I'm sure there's valor among the fleet, but we deal with those in power, like flag rank officers, politicians, and CIA upper echelons. You know, a bunch of mongrels."

"Even mongrels should know better, but they seem to have short memories."

"Or selective memories." Walker segued into the present moment. "But sometimes selective memories can work to our advantage, like now. I'm hoping we don't run into anyone today we may have upset during our last trip into Israeli waters."

She sighed. "Fair point. I'll stop agonizing about it."

"We won't be with them long. In and out, and then we're back in business."

Ten minutes later, Danielle had a textual order from Jake to pick up the Israeli submarine, and she had the *Goliath* drifting with the current. The dome-shaped abyss around her remained a black canvas of secrets. "Do we have any idea where the *Rahab* is?"

"None, whatsoever, ma'am. We just sit and wait for them to welcome us."

An excited voice rang from the loudspeakers. "Bridge, control room. Active sonar bearing one-one-nine."

Before Danielle could ask for guidance in the unfamiliar situation, the clarification arrived as the report continued. "Sergeui believes it's a hail from an Israeli *Dolphin*-class submarine. He recommends following the receipt protocol."

Lacking an active, long-range combat sonar to signal back, Danielle tapped her memory of the protocol to acknowledge the Israeli vessel. "Very well, control room. Be advised that I will deploy all outboards."

"Understood, ma'am."

"Liam, deploy all outboards."

"Deploying all outboards."

Gentle clunks and hums echoed around her.

"All outboards are deployed, ma'am."

"Very well. And now, we wait." Her wait was short.

A semi-garbled Hebrew accent carried the code phrase for the *Goliath* that Jake had defined. "Container ship. Two knots. Course zero-two-five. Container ship. Two knots. Course zero-two-five."

Frustrated with her inability to answer, Danielle trusted the phantom Israeli submarine to hear her compliance. The stealth and data limitations that liquid water placed upon the undersea world filled her with both frustration and reverence. "On the outboards, make best speed. Course zero-two-five."

Walker obeyed, and the *Goliath* attained one-point-eight knots as its best speed on oversized speedboat motors.

Ahead, a point of light rose appeared, grew stronger, and then illuminated the silhouettes of two approaching divers. The duo swam to the dome and landed on it with suction cups.

"This doesn't seem batshit crazy to you?"

"Not at all. We just went through something like this with the *Indiana*."

Danielle snorted. "I seriously joined the right fleet."

"That's the spirit."

Groping for ideas to retain some control over her situation, herself, and her ship, she ransacked her mind for a way to contribute to the evolution. When she found a worthy idea, she shared it. "Shouldn't we get a whiteboard or tablet for them?"

Liam stooped and pulled a small whiteboard and marker from a cabinet. "We keep this here for such an occasion."

"Impressive." She had another idea. "How about a Hebrew translator?"

"No Hebrew translator, unfortunately. Jake's call to Israel was ad hoc. No preparation for talking to Israelis, but enough of them speak English, I'm sure."

The divers swiveled their backs to the dome while one of them lifted a waterproof phone.

"What are they doing?"

Walker chortled. "I think they're taking a selfie."

"Jesus Christ."

"Don't bring him into it. It's not his fault we're celebrities. This has got to be a diver's wet dream."

She gave him a cynical glare. "Can't help you there, Liam. I've never had one."

"Shit. Sorry."

"We're at war, there's at least one Israeli submarine within easy kill range, and they're treating us like a sheep in a petting zoo."

"It's not their war. Let them have their fun."

Before Danielle could decide how to respond to her new-found fame, a tablet appeared, and it spoke for the divers. "*Rahab* keel thirty meters. Six hundred yards. Course zero-three-one."

"Should we nod? Raise our thumbs? Give a round of applause?"

Walker scratched a note of simple compliance on his whiteboard confirming the *Goliath's* compliance. He aimed it at Danielle.

"How's this?"

She chuckled at the two capital letters he'd written, an 'O' and a 'K'. "Good enough."

Walker showed it to the divers, who offered a thumbs-up.

"Liam, right full rudder, steady course zero-three-one."

"My rudder is right full. Coming to course zero-three-one. I recommend letting me warn the divers first and then energizing the sidescan sonar."

"Sidescan sonar won't hurt them, will it?"

"Probably not, but combat sonars have fried divers before. Can't blame them for being sensitive."

"Very well. Tell them."

Walker scratched the note and showed the divers. After they acknowledged, one of them produced a black box and pressed its suction cups against the window.

"Now what are they doing? Have you seen this before?"

"Indeed, I have. It's right out of Jake's playbook. If this is what I think it is, we did the same thing with the *Indiana*. He knows we kept our magnetic induction unit after that mission."

Danielle looked at the tablet. "We're already communicating through the dome windows, but you're saying..."

"I'm saying standby for something really cool." Walker crouched, opened a cubby behind him, and stood with a similar black box. He pressed its suction cups on the window opposite the divers' box as a mirror image, and then he trailed his unit's USB cord to the nearest console. "There. We should have power and a connection. It's unsecure between the magnetic induction units. Any encryption will be handled elsewhere upstream in the network."

"What data are we expecting?"

The American commodore answered her. "*Goliath*, fleet headquarters. *Goliath*, fleet headquarters..."

"Sounds a bit formal for the infamous traitor-cowboy."

"That's just Jake. When he's in a mood, he can be a little ogre."

"Little? He's built like a house."

"With respect to his position, I mean."

"Got it. You should answer him."

"Right." Walker pressed keys. "Fleet headquarters, *Goliath*. We read you. Over."

Listening for cues about her accidental boss, Danielle noticed the immediate shift from junior admiral to everyone's buddy. She noted to watch that during this mission, and if she survived, future ones where the American might be in charge.

"Hey guys. I want to align to our fleet's daily encryption. Can you shift on my mark?

"One moment, Jake." Walker hurried through menus. "I'm ready to shift to daily encryption on your mark."

"Three, two, one. Mark."

Walker hit a final icon. "Can you hear me, Jake?"

"It worked. This may be our only secure two-way connection for a long time. But I don't trust it completely. Olivia and the CIA are probably listening. So, consider it tactically secure against Turkey but riddled with American eavesdroppers, and let's make our time count. How's the pickup going?"

Walker glanced at his commander.

Danielle slid to her executive officer's side, checked the display, and tapped the icon opening the microphone. "An unidentified Israeli submarine pinged us and then guided us in the right direction. Now we've got two divers on our bridge dome, which you probably assumed since we're talking to you."

"Good. That's what I wanted." Revealing fatigue, Jake's yawn was audible. "Excuse me. Anyway, I should've warned you about the induction communications box, but you guys seemed to have figured that out. Timing-wise, you should have the *Rahab* aboard you in an hour, two at most. Any concerns?"

"None. Other than being the wedge between two angry NATO nations, everything's fantastic."

Jake chuckled. "Welcome to Renard's Mercenary Fleet, Captain Sutton. I'm keeping this on audio to avoid overloading our bandwidth, but I'm sure your face is priceless right now."

Walker confirmed it. "Woman of steel."

She snorted. "I said 'no pandering'."

"I call it like I see it."

Jake's tone became businesslike. "If there's nothing serious on your end, I need Terry. Where is he?"

Walker took the bullet. "We detached him twenty minutes ago."

"Shit. Hail him on underwater comms."

Walker stepped to a different console. "I'm on it."

Learning the importance of keeping acoustic energy out of the water, Danielle challenged the American. "Can you explain the urgency?"

"Terry has information that could give everyone a secret number. We can use it for affirming who's on our side or not, or as a basis for encrypted messages."

"That's great, if it works."

"It will."

Walker snapped. "The *Specter* answers our hail. Shifting to secure underwater voice."

"Yeah, mate. What's wrong? Miss me already?"

Jake barked. "Can Terry hear me? I heard him."

Cahill's voice rang from one speaker, filled the bridge, and entered microphones piped to the American. "Jake! Good to talk to you. What's so urgent?"

"We're developing a secret code for our team, including our wives. Don't say it over this channel since it may be compromised. But after I'm muted, tell Danielle how many freckles Ariella counted on your bare hairy ass."

Cahill deadpanned his answer. "I'd love to."

"That's our secret number. Remember it for... whatever. Ariella obviously knows it, you know it, and soon Danielle will know it. Don't ask if I know it or not. Wrong question."

"I'll take care of it with Danielle. I need to hurry before I drive out of phone range, though."

"Fine. *Goliath*, mute me and have Terry tell Danielle the number."

Walker tapped icons. "Jake, can you hear me? Jake, can you hear me? Alright. He's muted. Go ahead, Terry."

"Twenty-three."

Smirking, Walker confirmed it. "Twenty-three is our secret number. What a bare hairy arse it must be."

"Laugh all you'd like at me bum. If there's nothing else, I'll be signing off."

Walker eyed Danielle.

"I'm good."

"We're good here, Terry. Happy hunting." Walker invoked a screen with the scanning sonar's view of the undersea world. "And we're alone again, except for a bunch of Israelis and Jake on mute."

While waiting for the *Rahab* to appear, Danielle spied a dark line shooting up from a diver. "Is that a communication line?"

"Good question. That would mean there's a diver support ship above us, which is probably the ship that's connecting us to Jake."

"Why didn't we hear it?"

"It's not a matter of hearing it. It's a matter of hearing something about it that makes it different from the thirty other ships making a racket in these waters. Except for collision hazards, we instruct the sonar team to ignore the merchant traffic and the fishing ships, which is what a dive ship behaves like."

An Israeli diver pressed the tablet against the window with an updated note. *Rahab* keel twenty-eight meters. Three hundred yards. Course zero-three-three.

"I assume that's not alarming, the change in depth."

"Nah. It's what you might expect with an unmanned drifting submarine."

"This fleet's practically turned you into a submariner."

"Guilty as charged. But you'll pick up on all these weird bubblehead nuances, too. You can't help it."

An image appeared on the scanning sonar, and Danielle pointed. "That's it? The *Rahab*?"

Walker gazed at the screen. Looks like the right depth. Right shape. Looks like an old, unwanted submarine waiting to be put out of its misery. May I slow to one knot, after I let the Israelis know?"

"Actually, no. Better idea. Tell them we've got it from here and that we recommend they let us maneuver freely."

"I'll do me best to summarize that."

Walker scratched his best brief and aimed it that the divers.

An Israeli raised his finger while his lips moved behind his facemask. Then he nodded and offered a thumbs-up.

"It's almost automatic from here. In fact, it should be, if you'll let me set the docking routine into motion."

Danielle liked the sound of that. "Set the docking routine into motion. Put the *Rahab* in our cargo bed."

Walker agreed, and the *Goliath* began its beautiful dance.

Floodlights bathed the cargo bay in an eerie glow as the waiting relic seemed to slide into the transport ship's arms. Danielle shot periodic glances at the display to double-check Walker's double-checking. Instead of seeing the errors she feared, she admired the *Goliath's* delicate computerized dance of shuffling water fore and aft while shedding water overboard to gain levity.

Much as the screens before her highlighted the transport vessel's automated grace, she ignored the technical spectacle in favor of the view through the windows.

Breathless, she absorbed the illusion of the *Rahab* falling through translucent molasses into the *Goliath's* waiting cradle.

"Per protocol, the system is stopping the ascent to allow us to assess for manual adjustments."

"Very well."

"We're askew in azimuth half a degree. I'm adjusting manually."

"Very well."

"Slowing to half a meter per minute."

She felt a gentle jolt.

"Contact! Engaging presses."

Mesmerized, Danielle watched the *Goliath's* retracted hydraulic arms rotate into the cargo's side like mechanical fingers.

"Done. Presses are engaged."

"That's it?"

"For our boarding procedure, it's a done deal. We've got a secure hold. We'll be in a weight battle with that thing since we can't push water into or out of it, but our presses are strong and we're the bigger ship. We'll muddle through and take this old beast to its grave."

"Tell the divers we've got their cargo and that we're leaving. I want to get out of here, away from that phantom Israeli submarine that's trailing us, and get into the action."

An hour later, Danielle led the *Goliath* to the northwest with its new cargo, making twelve and a half knots on the silent MESMA air-independent propulsion units. Ahead, the buffer zone between the approaching *Lincoln* battle group and the lurking Turks awaited.

Walker remained with her on the bridge, like a loyal dog.

Like a man who cared too much.

"Liam?"

"Yes."

"I'm going to ask a bitchy question, but I don't want to insult you with a tap dance around it. So, I'm just going to ask."

"I'm an open book. Go ahead."

"When do you mutiny?"

Refusing the bait for an argument, Walker impressed her with a terse answer. "I don't."

"But there are justified criteria for a mutiny, and mutiny isn't always bad, in theory."

"True. It's only bad ninety-nine-point-nine percent of the time."

"Be straight with me. I have no experience in this, and I was expecting six months to shakedown and learn the *Xerses*. I'd have to be a narcissist to think I could waltz in here and replace Terry."

"Your awareness of possible narcissism is why I won't need to lead a mutiny."

"I want to believe you, but there may come a point where you stop trusting me. I need to know where that is so I can deal with it, if we get there."

"Fair enough."

His calm listening skills impressed her, and she continued.

"What order do you fear me giving? I'm talking mortal terror."

"Mortal terror's part of the job, and the true answer is just about any order."

"I'm not buying it. Think of things that kill. Speed. Depth. Hostile weapons. Exposure of our masts. Making noise. What's the worst pitfall before me?"

"I honestly fear it all and am okay with it. It's healthy fear. You don't think I consider Terry immortal, do you?"

"No."

"Well, I'm giving you a chance. The whole crew is. So, why not give us a chance?"

She liked his logic and his tone. "Fair point. I'll make time to greet everyone and tour the ship. I haven't done that yet."

"We've all been busy. But if you think I'm the type to revolt without cause, ask yourself why the CIA never went after me family?"

"That's an odd argument to bring up, but I'll go with it. The quick and dirty answer is that they only went after the commanders."

"Right. I sent me wife on a vacation based upon Pierre's recommendation, but nobody's looking for her."

Wondering where Walker was taking the conversation, she listened in silence, trying to avoid leaping to conclusions.

Then he dropped the bomb. "But they had her."

She gasped, and the black dome above her became increasingly creepy. "You're an exec, not a commander. Why you?"

"You forgot the daisy chain."

She lowered her head, realized she'd forgotten the simple logic flow, and tried to forgive herself for her sensual overload.

Walker continued. "They knew Pierre would be under house arrest, which means they–or she, if it's Olivia on her own–knew that Jake would become commodore. Then Terry was the obvious choice to replace Jake."

"And you were the obvious choice to replace Terry."

"Right. But when you showed up, either by lucky timing or that knack Pierre has of doing the right thing at the right time, you caught the CIA off guard. And you hid your family before she, or they, could act."

"I'm still not seeing where you're going with this."

"They were jetting me wife to America but turned around and took her home about the time Olivia must have learned about your involvement. You may have saved her life just by showing up. I still sent her on vacation after that, in case Olivia changed her mind."

Emotions churned through Danielle. "I'm happy that I could help protect your wife. And I don't mean to be a cold bitch, but why would they let her go when she's the only leverage over this ship?"

"Because evil as she is, Olivia's a bloody brilliant analyst. She's devoured and rewritten my dossier umpteen times over the years, and she's drawn a very important conclusion."

"What's that?"

"Loyalty. I'm useless to her because I'm not the type to mutiny. Unlike Jake, who's been hurt, I don't expect horrible outcomes. Someone would actually have to harm me wife for real–not in me speculative imagination–before I'd retaliate."

Viewing her executive officer with newfound respect, Danielle completed his thought. "By then, our entire fleet would be against America already. So, there's no point in her pressuring you because you wouldn't snap until our entire fleet snaps."

"Right." Declaring the conversation over with his movement, he started towards the stairs. "Will you take the bridge and excuse me for a bit?"

"Sure." She felt like dirt for having prodded him, but she believed the relational damage would scar over with renewed strength. "Before you go, Liam…"

He stopped. "Ma'am."

"It's not mutiny to save me from myself. I consider that upward leadership. If my ignorance of submarine warfare or this ship's parameters sends me in the wrong direction, I'll be attentive to your voice."

"I'm no mutineer, but I'm happy as shit to speak me mind."

"Understood."

"Don't worry, I've got your back. But can you do me and the boys a favor?"

She braced for the jab. "Yes."

"Please don't accuse us of being that fragile. We're tough, and we'll take whatever you can dish out." He descended the stairs and clicked the door shut behind him.

CHAPTER 11

Stooped over the central charting table, Volkov recognized the *Wraith's* starting point within his self-defined hunting grounds. At the Levantine Basin's eastern end, between Cyprus and Lebanon, he considered himself prepared for the chase.

His first step was deploying the dolphins. "Helm, all stop."

"Coming to all stop."

"Very well." The *Wraith's* commander stood and addressed Anatoly. "I'm heading to the torpedo room to help launch the dolphins."

"Help? Vasily and the gang could do it in their sleep."

Volkov leaned into the sonar guru's ear. "Just take the damned deck and conn for me."

Anatoly nodded his agreement. "I'll get a replacement for my station. I have the deck and the conn."

During a stroll to the torpedo room, he tried shaking the distracting mental images of Danielle. But like a revolution, visions of her reserved smile, her glowing cheeks, and her radiant eyes assaulted him. Impossibly, her physique captivated him by fusing a feminine frame of taunting curves with the strong lines of a warrior's posture.

Consuming him deeper than her physique was her jaded demeanor. Although he could have perceived it as a weakness, he found it a bonding asset.

From what Renard had summarized, she'd suffered injustice and indignation in the Royal Navy, just like he'd suffered while commanding the *Krasnodar*.

Just like Cahill had suffered while commanding the *Rankin*.

Just like Jake had suffered while aboard the *Colorado*, before taking command of it through mutiny.

As an outcast scapegoat, Danielle fit perfectly within the team of cynical and overperforming outcasts who'd blossomed into mercenary commanders with points to prove.

But her gender was also unavoidable. Three of the commanders had penises and male DNA. Only the new arrival had a uterus. The others in the fleet seemed accepting of her womanhood, and Volkov accepted it, too.

But he hated its power over him.

And he enjoyed its power over him.

After knowing her for scant hours, he respected and feared her strength. Somehow, the world had forged her into a creature more commanding than he could have imagined.

Although she'd yet to prove herself in the mercenary fleet, Volkov knew she would. He sensed her courage, confidence, and competence. And he revered her for developing these qualities in a military world designed for males.

He caught himself admiring her under his breath. "So strong."

He tried to think about Turkish *Type-209* submarines, but Danielle Sutton retained control of his vital organs.

After all she'd accomplished, rising to command a frigate in the Royal Navy, she possessed a seemingly infinite set of natural attributes. She could grow a human inside her, give birth to a child, and nurture it. Then she could lead crews of hundreds to wipe out lives by the thousands.

Overpowering his senses, she'd turned the Russian submarine commander's innards to goo.

He eased his pace to slow his fluttering heart. "Get control of yourself, Dmitry."

In Volkov's reckoning, words had power. When he issued orders, people died. Better yet, they lived to escape in defeat. But in the battle against the insurgent chemicals within his flesh, his words failed.

His self-control was tenuous while he entered the torpedo room and watched technicians shut a breach door behind the loaded dolphins. He observed in silence while the men lowered a tarp to the deck, staging it to return the cetaceans from the tube to their tank upon their return.

More Serene than usual, the trainer leaned against a spare heavyweight torpedo–one addressed to the USS *Mason*–while monitoring the loading of his adopted children.

Volkov sought a conversation to keep thoughts of Danielle at bay. "They're ready, Vasily?"

"Yes! I'm ready to flood the tube."

"Very well." Volkov stepped to the nearest sound-powered phone, called Anatoly, and ordered the outer door opened to tube three. Once complete, he turned to the trainer. "Ready when you are."

Vasily told the technicians to flood the tube and begin a counter on his babies' holding of their breath. "They're ready."

"Very well." Volkov called the bridge again. "Anatoly, the dolphins are loaded in tube three. Verify that nobody has their hands anywhere near an active sonar control. I'll be ordering the muzzle door to tube three opened, soon."

Vasily smiled. "I love how you care about my babies."

"They've been good to us." Volkov made eye contact with the torpedo technician's supervisor. "Open the door to tube three."

As the man obeyed, the trainer seemed perky.

"You're strangely happy, Vasily."

"I am! I taught them to wait for me if we lose them. After Iran, I vowed to never lose them again, and I started to teach them."

"You abandoned them somewhere for training?"

"Well, yes. I thought it better to risk it intentionally outside of combat instead of accidentally again."

"Logical."

"First, I abandoned them in a bay for two hours in complete sonar silence. Mikhail was so agitated when I came back, but even he adjusted. Then I tried again, leaving them for four hours. Then eight. Then days. I used trackers to make sure I never lose them, but to them, it was the same as being alone. They thought themselves alone, but they learned to stay and wait."

"Great work."

"We reached up to three days. I hope to never test that in battle, though."

"Me neither. God willing, this mission's over before then." Volkov's thoughts aimed at personal concerns–this time, his parents instead of Danielle. "Can you handle your babies in the control room without me for about an hour?"

"Of course! Anatoly and I know what to do." The trainer took the hint and darted away.

Volkov turned and walked to his stateroom.

Arriving at his quarters, he closed the door and sat at his fold-out desk. After a few keystrokes and mouse clicks, he listened for a third time to his parents' voice from the latest check-in.

Speaking to them, he trusted they heard. "I think I'm in love, Mama. I think I found the one, if she'll have me." Thoughts of Danielle danced in his mind. "I thought I was married to the Navy, but the Navy rejected me. Then I thought I was married to this mercenary fleet, but now, I'm not sure."

Shutting his laptop, he sensed fatigue and succumbed to it. He lifted a sound-powered phone from its cradle and called his de facto executive officer.

"Control room, this is Anatoly."

"I need about an hour of down time. I'll take some rest and take a shower before settling in for our search."

"Understood, sir. I've got matters under control."

"You've confirmed communications with the dolphins?"

"Yes, sir. They're following the prescribed search pattern."

"Very well. I don't expect they'll find anything for a few hours. We couldn't get luckier than that."

"No, sir. I assume you want me to keep tube three empty for their return?"

"Right. Five loaded tubes are sufficient for this hunt."

"Understood. Uh… Dmitry?"

Volkov found the sonar guru's tone threatening but trusted their relationship enough to explore the man's sentiments. "Yes? Go ahead."

Anatoly lowered his voice. "Can I ask a personal question?"

"As long as nobody else hears you. You sound like you're preparing to make… an accusation?"

"Nobody can hear me. I'm crouched in a corner up here."

"Then go ahead."

"Dmitry, are you lovesick?"

In a fleeting moment, Volkov felt naked. In the next moment, he decided to accept his helplessness and commit to a full confession. "I don't know what lovesick means." He issued a long sigh. "But truth be told, I fear I'm in love with Miss Sutton." Volkov braced himself for the sonar ace's judgment.

Anatoly was kind. "Yeah, I thought so. I'm rooting for you, by the way. I think you'd be great together."

The *Wraith's* commander felt exposed but supported. "You knew? Is it that obvious?"

"You've been floating through the passageways."

Volkov pressed the phone closer to his cheek. "And?"

"And what?"

"Don't screw with me, Anatoly! Just because I was floating as you say, doesn't tell you about whom I've been thinking. You're leaving something out."

"There were rumors after Terry's wedding."

"And you always believe rumors?"

The sonar ace sighed. "Fine! Vasily told me."

Volkov chuckled. "I'll kill him."

"You know he can't keep a secret. Bearing your soul to him is the same as posting love poems on Instagram."

"I'll still kill him. That was in confidence."

"Would you rather keep it inside you?"

In Volkov's opinion, a grunt sufficed as a response.

"Come on, Dmitry. Don't blame him. You know he's socially inept, except maybe with his dolphins and, I suppose… uh, maybe some boyfriends?"

Volkov guffawed and enjoyed the shift to someone else's love life. "Oh, we do have much to talk about."

"I can't wait. Perhaps you shared a two-way confession."

"That discussion is for another time. This isn't a therapy ship, it's a combat submarine. Why don't you get back to it? I'm sure there are lonely dolphins that need coddling."

"Vasily's handling that. He already knocked two and a half of my guys out of their seats when he took over a console."

"Two and a half? That seems to violate a law of physics."

"I'll explain later. Or maybe not. I think you just had to see it to believe it."

"Get back to work, Anatoly. I'm getting some rest." Volkov hung up and then flopped into his rack. As visions of a beautiful British commanding officer teased him, he fell asleep.

Harsh knocking on his door woke him.

He tasted acrid copper in his mouth. "Come!"

A sonar technician jutted his head into the room. "The dolphins found a submerged contact!"

Volkov sprang from his bed and nearly mowed down the messenger while marching through the passageway. When he reached the control room, it buzzed with energy.

Anatoly began chattering a report, but Volkov silenced him with a finger and studied a display, announcing his assessment while he examined the data. "Medium-range submerged contact, bearing three o'clock from the dolphins, and you have high confidence in the dolphin's position?"

Anatoly replied. "Yes, sir."

"Let's do this smoothly, in one motion. Send them to mount their explosives, allow them their minimal turnaround time, and then wait for me to the order the detonations."

Having experienced every imaginable cetacean scenario, Anatoly seemed at ease with his commander's multi-faceted order. "Have the dolphins lay explosives, allow the minimal turnaround time, and then wait for you to order the detonations, aye, sir."

Volkov cast his voice throughout the control room. "I've ordered the dolphins to attack the submerged contact they've discovered. Until we learn more about the contact, designate it as Type-209 Bravo in the system."

"I'm designating the dolphins' new contact as Type-209 Bravo."

"Very well." Volkov announced his next steps. "I'll maneuver us onto a lag line of sight to escape the acquisition cone of a potential counterfire. Then I'll drive deeper towards Turkish territory and find another *Type-209*. We'll respect our distance to Type-209 Bravo while attempting to retrieve the dolphins to the northeast. God willing, we'll be done with this mess by tomorrow."

As he witnessed confident nods throughout the room, Volkov wondered if hubris had caught him, making him move hastily.

Time would tell.

Anatoly reminded him of his options. "Do you want a torpedo assigned to Type-209 Bravo?"

Appreciating the prodding, Volkov assessed his options. Limpets sufficed, whether the dolphins succeeded or not. This *Type-209* was Turkish, he decided. "Assign tubes one and two to Type-209 Bravo. Open the outer doors to tubes one and two."

Anatoly obeyed and then asked a follow-on question. "Do you have launch criteria?"

Sensing something slowing his mind, Volkov chewed on the concept and forced his brain to reach an answer. He thought aloud to entice his sonar ace's opinion. "If I shoot now, I could alert the target with launch sounds. That could ruin the dolphins' attack."

"True. But if you don't launch, we'll have nothing in motion as a backup plan. If the dolphins fail while you have nothing in the water, Type-209 Bravo will likely evade before you can get weapons on it."

"Let's see what Vasily says." Volkov stepped beside the seated dolphin trainer and bent forward. "What's your assessment of your babies' chances?"

"They'll mount the detonators by the conning tower like they always do. The problem will be the distance when you order the detonations. The range is always a crude guess at medium and long distances when we have nothing but Mikhail and Andrei's input."

"So, you want me to get closer?"

"I'm afraid so. That's the most aggressive thing you could do, and it matches with our need to complete this mission quickly. You could wait for an accurate range report while they're atop Type-209 Bravo, but that would take up valuable time."

"And I'd need torpedoes already in the water for that to matter. Otherwise, our adversary will hear our commands and run before our weapons arrive."

"I overheard you and Anatoly. You're right, and we need to admit the limitations of our communications with my babies. Nobody's ignorant enough anymore to mistake our chats with Mikhail and Andrei as innocent biological sounds. Our secret is out."

Volkov agreed that the ship-to-dolphin protocol had become vulnerable. "Of course. So, I either trust our dolphin attack, or I undermine it by launching now."

"I'm afraid so."

"And to support your babies, I need to drive closer to danger to assure that our detonation command reaches their explosives."

"At least we have dolphins. The best, Dmitry."

Volkov patted the trainer's back. "Yes, the best. Let's give them a chance to prove it again."

"Thank you, Dmitry. It will work."

"It will, if I don't get too close and entice a counterfire."

"Okay. Then don't get too close."

The *Wraith's* commander straightened his back. "Helm, right standard rudder, steady course zero-four-five."

"My rudder is right standard, coming to course zero-four-five."

"Very well." The deck rolled under Volkov's shoes, and he grabbed a railing for balance.

Minutes later, cetacean sounds chirped through speakers in the control room, and the trainer announced the significance. "My babies crossed a distance boundary from medium range to short. Reminder for everyone, that's reliably close to one nautical mile. I've been training them hard, and they've been practicing!"

Volkov was tempted to broadcast an acoustic message to the dolphins, but the sounds would undermine their effort. He used the best guess of their habitual swimming speeds to estimate their position as a basis for his target's location. After years with them, he considered their speeds and routines increasingly reliable and predictable. "Very well."

"We'll know more soon, Dmitry. They'll sprint now. Twenty knots! They'll be there in less than three minutes."

"Very well." Volkov shifted his attention to defense. "Anatoly, any sign of Type-209 Bravo, other than dolphin detection?"

"None."

"Very well. Also, keep one man listening for threats. This could be a trap."

"I already am, Dmitry."

"Very well."

Anatoly requested what every sonar technician wanted–a quiet ship without flow noise masking its hydrophones. "At our present speed, we face limits on what we can hear. I recommend slowing to six knots to acquire Type-209 Bravo on our sonar systems. You'd also create less chance of alerting Type-209 Bravo to our presence by slowing."

"True, but we're also racing a clock. Neither the Turks nor the Americans will wait for me. Best to resolve all encounters decisively. I need to take chances."

"Understood, sir."

As cetacean chirps filled the control room, the trainer half-stood from his chair. "Detonators are set! My babies are clear."

Volkov marveled at how small an explosive could cripple a submarine. With their blast power pointed downward, under their magnets and suction cups and aimed into the exposed steel, they posed mortal danger to submarines but trivial risk to the dolphins. "Transmit detonation sequence, one-quarter power."

A cascading series of whale-like whistles rang from the *Wraith's* bow-mounted sonar and into the sea, echoing through the hull. Anatoly announced the obvious. "Detonation sequence is transmitted, one-quarter power. Listening... no sign of detonation. Recommend half power."

"No time. Full power. Let's do this smartly and then move on to hunting our next target."

The booming sonic transmission reverberated, and as the sonar ace listened, he lifted his thumb. "Detonations! Two of them. Both explosives were successful."

"Excellent!" Volkov set his focus on his next victim.

CHAPTER 12

A sonar technician called out. "Active acoustic intercept, bearing two–"

Interrupting the report, two explosions ripped into the hull above Dogan, and the seas became two pitchers of deadly water pouring into his steel coffin.

From the corner of his eye, he saw a man reaching for the emergency blow switches in desperate hopes of voiding the main ballast tanks and rocketing to the surface.

Accustomed to thinking through frayed nerves, Dogan grasped a coherent thought.

Two holes above a control room, near a submarine's conning tower, marked the signature attack of dolphins serving the mercenary fleet. The attack was more than survivable. It was endurable, if the would-be victim declared himself something other than a victim.

Not a victim. Warrior.

His submarine could withstand two holes.

Surfacing meant defeat.

Staying submerged granted him hope of fighting back.

While the sailors around him wrestled with newfound sensations of mortal panic, Dogan found a strange comfort with the horrors. Though he was scared, his years of dealing with dreadful memories braced him better than those around him.

And the those around him needed him.

Courage enveloped him as saltwater peppered his face and drenched his cotton jumpsuit. He walked with defiance while locking eyes with the man whose white knuckles grasped the emergency air switches.

Dogan shouted over the inundation and spray. "Look at me!

Look at me! Look... at... me!"

The petrified man kept his gaze on his commander.

Dogan marched forward with his tennis shoes splashing in the sheets flowing across the deck plates.

"Sit down! Sit down! Depth control! Come to twenty-two meters! Do not broach! Twenty-two meters. Do not broach!"

Shaking, the terrified man remained a paralyzed statue.

Recalling the sailor's first name, Dogan tried again. "Yusuf, sit! Depth control! Twenty-two meters! Do not broach!"

Trembling hands released the switches. "Twenty... twenty-two meters. Do not broach, aye, sir."

The warrior Dogan turned, marched to his next sailor, and let his shoulder push through one of the unwelcomed water columns. Its power knocked him aside and unveiled the threat's power, but he'd braced for the sensation and regained his stability under his cold and soggy jumpsuit.

When he reached the trio of the helmsman, planesman, and their supervisor, he shouted his next command over the hissing salt shower. "All-ahead two-thirds, make turns for twelve knots! Right standard rudder, steady course zero-two-five!"

Frightened men agreed and obeyed, and the *Preveze's* commander trusted them to accelerate their drifting submarine.

Shielding his eyes from the spray, Dogan continued his unwanted shower while walking to the master chief. There, he found the veteran pushing fear from his own eyes. "Sir!"

"Lead damage control!"

"Already on it, sir. I sent two men to get the nearest kit. I will continue to lead damage control."

Again, Dogan barked his confidence towards everyone within earshot. "We can handle the flooding! We can keep depth control! We can evade and remain a fighting ship!"

A quick scan of wet faces gave Dogan immediate feedback. His crew revered him.

The tiny master chief reached for a microphone and spoke forcefully. "Flooding in the control room. We've been breached by two charges. Get damage control teams up here with shoring.

All spare hands bring blankets to cover electronics. We will remain shallow and fight the flooding."

Grateful the master chief had recognized the dangers of mixing electricity with saltwater, the commander of the *Preveze* nodded his approval. "Secure all electronic equipment!"

Throbbing adrenaline focused his thoughts, letting them flow in an ordered sequence.

Dangers outside the ship required action.

He grabbed the lead sonar technician, leaned into his ear, and shouted. "Snapshot, tube one. Five degrees lag from the bearing of the active acoustic intercept. And snapshot, tube two. Five degrees lead from the bearing of the intercept. Open the outer doors to tubes one and two. Launch both weapons when ready!"

As the sonar supervisor obeyed, Dogan picked up the nearest microphone and held it. He watched the master chief dodging downpours and braving the pelting spray while verifying that all sailors sent their consoles into sleep and suspend modes.

Two men appeared from behind an electronics cabinet carrying a canvas damage control bag and a chair.

A chair.

Something so simple had seemed an impossible asset against the danger until Dogan's men turned it into a footstool beside a water column. The extra height allowed the first man to reach the waterlogged lagging, rip it away, and expose the belching hole.

His sailors were fighting back.

Knowing they needed their captain's voice, Dogan keyed his microphone. "This is the captain. I confirm the master chief's summary of the damage. Engineering, disconnect the control room from the battery bus. Send technicians to disconnect backup power supplies, but keep power to the drain pump. Auxiliary division, get bilge pumps online. Line up and blow–do not await my further orders–blow sanitary tanks overboard to assist with buoyancy. Keep fighting like you've trained. Carry on."

He walked to his sonar supervisor. "Status of our weapons?"

"Both running normal, sir. We have wire control, but there's no sign of a target."

"I launched them to distract our enemies. I hope they drive them away."

"Understood, sir. Shall I keep them in active mode?"

"Yes. Distractions must be heard."

The supervisor's screen went dark, and the room's lighting shifted from white to red. "Damn it, sir!"

"I ordered everything deenergized. The electrical team's only doing what I asked."

"I can't work from here. I'll head to the torpedo room and use a fire-control console there."

"No. Send someone else. I want you here to bring up the sonar system again after we contain this flooding." Dogan glanced at the sonar consoles, which boasted some waterproofing against the saltwater spray.

"Aye, aye, sir." The man lifted a sound-powered phone to call for assistance.

Unwilling to remain idle, Dogan sought the next person to lead, but the water in his jumpsuit burdened him.

So, he stepped out of it, revealing dark underpants and a white tee-shirt that appeared sanguine under emergency lights. Then he moved beside the growing team of volunteers who labored under the ghostly red glow. He yelled. "Everyone, feel free to dress like me. Naked, if you need. This isn't a beauty contest."

As opportunities arose between propping vertical beams in the water columns and hammering rubber mats and wooden wedges between the beams and the hull, men liberated themselves from their soaking suits.

From nowhere, the executive officer appeared, his eyes puffy from sleeping after his midnight shift. "I can take over damage control, sir."

"Very well. The top priority is to verify at least one sonar console as being dry, and then reboot it. We need to listen."

"Understood, sir. Where will you be?"

"In the torpedo room, watching our weapons."

Before departing, Dogan crouched and peeked in the bilge.

Shimmering water crafted myriad optical illusions, and he grabbed a flashlight from his hip. Aiming the beam, he saw a better estimate of the danger.

Water had risen to half a meter.

The drain pump was losing the race against the columns.

Expecting the ship's speed and upward angle to offset the weight, he trusted the *Preveze* to hold its depth. He also expected the inflow to diminish as his sailors established their shoring.

He walked forward through watertight boundaries and entered the torpedo room. Appreciating the dryness of the ship's forwardmost compartment, he moved behind a technician seated by a console. Beside the technician, a young cook manned a sound-powered phone headset.

Trembling from his first brush with a watery grave, the youngster shook his head and called out. "What going on, sir? Nothing makes sense. We're being attacked, and my captain's wearing underwear and wet sneakers."

With the hissing and roaring removed from his ears, Dogan reminded himself to lower his volume. "And the day's not even over yet, lad."

"With all due respect, sir, have you gone crazy?"

"Crazy enough to get you home dry and alive. Are you in contact with the control room?"

The youngster responded to his commander's levity. "Yes, sir! I called them and was trying to find you."

"Well, you found me."

The seated man craned his neck. "We got lucky with one torpedo, sir, but I'm afraid it didn't last. Active return from the second weapon. Two pings only, spaced too far apart for targeting, and then it lost the target."

The *Preveze's* commander leaned over the seated man's shoulders and studied the data.

One of his counterfire torpedoes was useless, but the other offered the gift of information. The display showed two active returns from the leading weapon's seeker.

"Two returns are all I need to estimate course and speed."

"Are you going to shoot them, sir? I was going to recommend a steer to our second snapshot, but with the fuel remaining in the weapon, it would be a desperate tail chase."

Assessing the newfound advantage, Dogan made a rapid decision. "No. Let our weapons run out of fuel without steers. I want the mercenaries to think I have no idea where they are."

The technician smirked. "Yes, sir."

"Everyone else is keeping us afloat. The three of us right here, at this moment, are the entire tactical team of this ship. Are you ready to start tracking down our enemy?"

Both men beamed with anticipation. "Yes, sir!"

"Keep monitoring our torpedoes with one eye, but I want your best fire-control solution to that… that *Scorpène*. I'm absolutely certain that's what it is."

The sailor fiddled with dials and adjusted the solution. The *Scorpène* is nine miles away, making eight knots, course zero-four-five."

"Heading deeper into our chokepoint." Dogan let the data settle in his head. "It's quite possible they think they've beaten us, and now they're going after the *Sakarya*. I don't know if that's arrogant, efficient, or desperate."

"It could be all of that, sir."

"Right. And I…"

"Sir?"

"I have an idea. Don't be alarmed if you hear emergency air. I think I can fool them."

In the control room, the response team had halved the inflow from one column. With the master chief and the executive officer providing guidance, they'd left 'good enough' alone and shifted their attention to the second column.

Since his plans included sounding desperate, Dogan allowed himself continued liberal use of his loud announcing circuit. He stepped to a microphone and revealed his pending ruse. "Attention, this is the captain. We've survived the attack, and we're on an evasion course from any torpedoes our attacker may have launched. But we've also had a break. There were two active returns from one of our counterfire torpedoes."

The great news distracted the response team, who gave their commander quizzical stares.

With his microphone unkeyed, Dogan aimed a rigid arm at the downspout and yelled. "Listen while you work!"

As the sailors redirected their attention to the flooding, the *Preveze's* commander spoke again into his microphone. "I'm going to hunt down the bastard who attacked us, after I fool him–badly. I'll order our main ballast tank vents opened, and then I'll emergency blow. The air will signal our feigned defeat to our attacker, but in reality, it will mostly escape the tanks. I'll leave five seconds of air in the tanks to help our buoyancy. Carry on."

The executive officer offered a look of awe, which the *Preveze's* commander interpreted as concurrence with his plan.

Dogan walked to the man at the ship's control station and yelled. "Did you understand my announcement?"

Still shaking, the man seemed refocused on revenge. "Yes, sir. I like it! Let's do it."

"Open the main ballast tank vents."

As the man flipped switches, horizontal amber lines on the control panel disappeared, and then green circles rose below them.

"The main ballast tank vents are open."

"Very well. Emergency blow!"

Raging air hissed through huge pipes, and the world became a cacophony of flowing fluids.

Dogan counted twenty seconds. "Shut the main ballast tank vents!"

Green circles disappeared, replaced by a straight board of amber dashes. With the vents atop the tanks closed, they trapped the incoming air and allowed the submarine extra buoyancy.

The *Preveze's* commander counted another mental five seconds. "Secure the blow!"

In hopes of continued good news, Dogan checked the damage control team. The second column's flow now appeared halved, and he expected the drain pump to shoot water overboard as fast as the Mediterranean Sea could push it in.

Water management was reaching a stalemate with his team laboring towards an advantage.

In time, with continued effort, he knew they would have it.

They'd have it all.

An advantage over the water.

An advantage over the mercenary.

An advantage over their fear.

CHAPTER 13

Suspecting she'd overdone her valiant effort to embrace the unnerving dome, Danielle gave herself a break. The windows had proven their strength, and she needed to trust them, the bridge, and the *Goliath's* entire design.

That meant leaving behind the hemisphere of polycarbonate windows and seeing the ship's dark corners.

"Take the bridge, Liam. I'm going to tour the ship."

"Yes, ma'am. I can get you guide, if you'd like. Mister Johnson is always happy to show off the *Goliath* to new crewmembers."

She'd wanted to meet the crew. "Why not? Have him meet me in the control room?"

Walker scrunched his features. "Maybe I spoke too fast. He's happy to show off the port hull. But if I ask nicely, he'll probably meet you on this side of the catwalk."

"You can't order him, can you?"

"Not quite. When we left behind our proper navies, we shed much of our formality. We follow a hierarchy in battle, but when it's our personal time, I expect that wanker to tell me what he thinks when he thinks it."

"Thanks, Liam. I might enjoy meeting him. The catwalk is fine."

She darted down the stairs. As she reached for a watertight door, a peek in the bilge revealed the inverted triangular keel section, which provided stability and extra buoyancy, continuing underneath the ship. She then looked up, swung the door open, and stepped through its machined frame into the bizarre, circular-ribbed world of a submarine.

Lacking a torpedo room, the *Goliath* presented Danielle the tactical control room as its first cylindrical compartment. Four men staffed the space, with three seated in front of consoles, a supervisor hovering over them, and the extra bonus of the quirky Russian officer trailing a translator around the room.

The supervisor greeted her with a reserved smile. "Good afternoon, ma'am."

Anticipating someone announcing her arrival in the compartment, she digested another of many clues reminding her she'd left behind the Royal Navy. "Good afternoon. Anything interesting on sonar?"

"Not yet, ma'am. But it's just a matter of time. We always find something." Fostering teamwork among the eclectic group, the supervisor called to the *Wraith's* former executive officer and his Russian translator. "Isn't that right, Sergeui?"

The submarine officer heard the translation and then braved his answer in English. "Oh, I learn from Dmitry. I am best submarine warrior! Except, of course, for Dmitry. And maybe Jake. Yes, can't say I good as Jake. He really good." He frowned. "Maybe I not very good as Terry, either. But real good. Big competition. Glad I am on right team."

Danielle found the man likeable, and her polite smile rose easily. "Why don't you ever come up to the bridge?"

"I am happy inside big steel, not in sunlight. And no windows on real submarine."

"No arguments about that." Careful to inflict minimal distractions upon those doing their duties, she introduced herself to the others in the room and then continued her sternward walk.

She passed electronic cabinets that Renard had said were in abnormal locations compared to the *Scorpène*-class base design. Supposedly, the *Goliath* and *Xerses* provided luxurious space for submarine standards, but from her perspective, everything was tight, foreign, and cramped.

As she passed into the elongated berthing area, a sailor's snoring reminder her to be quiet. Placing her weight onto the balls of her tennis shoes, she squinted to avoid seeing unsavory male body parts on her way to the ghost-silent scullery.

She continued to the empty mess hall and kept walking until

she passed through the watertight door to the first MESMA section, where she tested her memory to recall the term 'MESMA' as an acronym for the French-designed Module-Energy, Sub-Marine, Autonomous ethanol-liquid-oxygen propulsion plant.

Oxygen starvation prevented the powerful machines she had cherished on surface combatants–the churning diesels and the explosive gas turbines–from operating under the water. Compared to those workhorses, and to her secondhand understanding of nuclear reactors, the MESMA system was a complex bomb of laughable output. With two men operating each plant under a pair of roving supervisors, the MESMA team comprised the largest unit of her new crew.

The temperamental little power plants consumed the most space and the most people. And with six plants providing the *Goliath* a mere thirteen submerged knots when unburdened by cargo, their presence riveted the horrors of undersea travel into her mind.

Oxygen starvation mattered, and she'd never considered it while it had been free in abundance on her frigate, the HMS *Westminster*. Now, the atmosphere she'd taken for granted since her first breath on Earth was precious.

For machines and people.

Finding new value in the life-sustaining gases within her confines, she inhaled through her nostrils. It was her first breath aboard the *Goliath* that included a respect for the stinky chemicals used to clean the air.

Motion caught her eye, and she welcomed the company.

With his jumpsuit unzipped and flopped over his waist, a technician exposed a sweat-marked tee-shirt. Noticing her movement, he looked up from his gauges. "Captain Sutton. To what do I owe the honor, ma'am?"

She appreciated his outward acceptance of his new and foreign commander. "I thought I'd see the ship and meet some of the crew."

"Great idea. Name's Torrence. Jason Torrence. I'd shake your hand, but…" he showed palms covered in lubrication oil.

"No offense taken. I'd rather see you doing your job than trying to be diplomatic."

A thin smile cracked his hard face. "We're off to a great start, ma'am. Can I help you find anything?"

"The intra-hull tunnel. Or the catwalk, whatever it's called."

"Either term's correct, and you're going the right way. Two compartments down, on your right, as you face aft."

She nodded, continued through the sultry air, and noticed sweat forming in uncomfortable places. Twenty-five meters and two MESMA plants later, she pulled an industrial-strength paper towel from a roll and ran it across her face. After verifying nobody was watching, she ran another towel over her sweatier areas.

A hidden voice startled her. "I can pretend I didn't see that if you'd like, ma'am. Or we can laugh it off."

She snapped her head in multiple directions.

"Over here." Perched halfway up the bulkhead with his lower body hidden, the sailor waved.

"You must be Johnson?"

On all fours, he craned his neck through the catwalk's door. "I am. Liam says you'd like a tour of the port hull."

"I've never been there, and I think it's about time."

"Well, if you'll ignore me ugly buttocks, I'll lead the way." He performed impressive gymnastics, pulling himself through the door, holding a rail above it, kicking his legs into the MESMA plant, and then somehow flipping himself back the way he came.

"That was impressive. You were a gymnast in a past life?"

"You get used to it. There's hardly room to turn around in there. There's basically only forward and reverse."

The claustrophobic fear developing within the *Goliath* gave her goosebumps. "Lead on."

He crawled ahead.

Following, she climbed to the door, ducked through it, and placed herself on all fours.

The confines scared her. Difficult to clean, the intra-hull tunnel smelled stale, and the precious air tasted thick. Unsure if she considered the lumbering buttocks blocking her view a welcomed presence, she risked a chat. "I imagine you do this all the time?"

Her tinny voice echoed, as did the sailor's response. "Less often than you might think. We like privacy on the port side. Other than moving food or swapping out supervisors every other shift or so, this tunnel's hardly used."

"I see. It's not the most comfortable of places."

Bowing her head to avoid the air-intake cross-connect, Danielle watched her multiple shadows stretch under the thin grating that served as a floor. Her labored breathing echoed off the bilge, where condensation reflected light from the twin rows of LED bulbs running beside the crossing air duct.

Johnson slithered around a hydraulic isolation valve which fed lever arms controlling the giant stern planes. "No need to play brave with me, ma'am. It's ugly, stinky, and downright creepy in here. I get the willies every time."

"I can't argue any of that." Her echoes carried her nervousness, and she wished to withdraw her statement. Instead, she let her eyes follow hydraulic lines to an oversized block of metal.

Keeping precise depth control, the block's arms glided with grace back and forth over a small fraction of their full range of motion.

Danielle craned her neck and watched the arms move outward through grease-coated holes into an invisible nook that shaped the hydrodynamic rear of the ship and housed the rocker that transferred the arms' piston-like movement into the arcing swing of the stern planes. "But even in this pace, there's something of beauty. That hydraulic controller just seems to belong. We had nothing like this on the *Westminster*."

"That was poetic, I think."

Opening herself, as a commanding officer should within limits, she shared a piece of her past. "I studied Economics at the academy. Didn't help much when I needed to learn all the technical systems. But no regrets in foregoing an engineering degree, and no regrets in making the effort to learn the technology on the job."

With a respectful tone, her escort replied. "Absolutely right, ma'am. No regrets." He reached the port door and exited with rehearsed ease.

Her exit proved more deliberate.

"Do you need any help, ma'am."

"Best that I learn by doing."

"Atta girl."

She grunted. "I once put a man in the brig for saying that."

"I meant no offense."

"I know. Unfortunately for the last sailor who said that, he did. He preceded that comment with something like…" She feigned a doofus' voice. "… so, you like being in tight spaces with a bunch of horny men."

Johnson chuckled. "There's one data point in favor of natural selection. I hope you castrated him, too."

As her head emerged in the port hull, Danielle twisted her torso and grabbed a bar attached above the door. "Nope. Scared the shit out of him first, then forgave him. When he got out of the brig, he was the *Westminster's* most fervent defender of gender equality."

"You made lemon-aid out of lemons."

She pulled her shoulders through the portal and then reached for a higher bar. With her waist freed, she walked her heels out and pushed her buttocks free. She drove her haunches backwards, making space for her legs to back into the compartment and transfer her weight to rungs mounted below the door.

She felt free as she stood and scanned the MESMA plant.

"Done like a pro, ma'am. I was afraid I was going to have to grab you. And after that little story of yours, I got to be honest. I might have hesitated if you started falling."

She tucked her shirt into her beige pants and patted down her wrinkles. "I don't think you'd let me fall, even if you had to go for the boobs or the vagina."

"Uh…"

"You seem like the first guy on the ship I can admit to having body parts."

"I guess so." His face flushed. "And if it came down to fondling you to keep your head from cracking open against a hydraulic valve, I assume you'd prefer that I do what I have to?"

"Just as quickly as you'd grab a dick. Spread the word. I'm not made of porcelain or girl cooties."

"Yes, ma'am. Well, now that we've got that settled, can I show you around?"

Finding him easy to trust, she sought his deeper confidence. "Not yet. Liam thinks highly of you, and you seem like the type of guy who keeps people working together."

"That's me. I love this job, if you can call it that."

"Mind if I ask a few hard questions."

"Go ahead. It's your ship."

"That's what my first question's about. It's my ship only by bad luck. I don't like commanding a vessel I've only studied on paper anymore than you should like me commanding it. So, be straight with me. What's the pulse of the crew about it?"

"Oh, bloody hell. First the boobs and then the…"

"Vagina."

"Right. Now you went for the jugular. Mine!"

Leaving her question's power unqualified, she shrugged.

"Okay. I'll share what I know. It's happening fast, but I'd say the guys are adjusting as well as can be expected."

"That's a fair attempt but only half an answer." Remembering she was probing a man's mind and emotions, she stuck with questions instead of orders. "Can you give me something about how you define 'as well as can be expected'?"

He glanced askance in thought. "Well, Terry's been the life-blood of this ship since it was built. He recruited every one of us, or he recruited someone who recruited someone. That's tough to overcome for any new commander, much less…" his voice trailed as he seemed caught in a trap.

"Relax. I'm not on a witch hunt. If I were, I'd be the top candidate as the only woman."

"Well, being the only woman is an issue, and then again it isn't. What I mean is, we're not used to women since most of us left the service while women were still rising through the ranks on submarines. And sure, women have been commanding Australian surface combatants for twenty-some years, but only the gunners, turbine techs, and Liam came from the surface fleet."

She eyed him. "So, most of the crew is unfamiliar with women, and as a surface warfare officer, I'm a double anomaly."

"That's right, ma'am. And to be honest, if I had to pick, the surface fleet thing's a bigger hurdle than being a lady."

"So, I've been promoted to 'lady' from 'girl' in one conversation."

His smile was sheepish. "I guess so."

"One more question before we tour the port hull."

Sounding relieved about his pending escape from the discussion, Johnson perked up. "Go ahead, ma'am."

"Another perfect segue. Is there a reason why I'm 'the captain', 'Captain Sutton', or 'ma'am'? Everyone else uses first names around here, and I get the feeling that was true for Terry, too."

"Not to be rude, but the rule around here is, until you see combat with the fleet, you don't get a first name. Applies to all new arrivals, including commanding officers, and you're the only new arrival on this deployment, except for the Russian riders."

"Fair enough. Looks like I'll have to earn it."

"With this upcoming exchange Jake's arranged for us, I'm pretty sure you'll get through that hurdle quickly, too."

She nodded.

"If you'd like, I'll spot you one, just this time."

"Sure."

"Come on, Danielle. I'll show you where we hide the best snacks from the starboard crew."

CHAPTER 14

Volkov stood over his sonar guru's shoulder. "You're sure there was no active return?"

With one muff behind his ear, Anatoly shook his head. "I can't be certain."

"I know that. I'm asking for your gut feel."

The guru shot his commander a sideways glance. "Your gut feel is better than mine."

"Perhaps not today." The *Wraith's* commander judged himself stronger than his infatuation with Danielle, and he considered his lovelorn loftiness a minor distraction. But the vulnerability of Renard's fleet, the imprisonment of families, and the CIA tyrant shifting from a partner to an enemy weighed upon him like the clock counting down Turkey's invasion of Syria and the subsequent American response. "I want your damned opinion."

Anatoly grunted. "Okay, then. Type-209 Bravo shot two weapons at us. One was behind us and was never a threat. The other wasn't a bad shot for a reactive fire."

"I gifted them a bearing when I ordered the detonations. We need to develop a better way to manage our dolphins. Our feigned biologic sounds aren't a secret anymore."

"Such is warfare. Most weapons eventually have a counter."

Volkov made a mental note to find better cetacean communication options. "Back to your opinion."

"Each ping's power level was low, but maybe eleven or twelve were significant." Anatoly paused in thought, or perhaps to entice his boss' reply, but then he continued. "Significant enough that I'd assign a dozen pings a ten percent chance of earning a detectable return from our hull."

"Statistically that's dangerous."

"Yes. If I run the odds, that weapon should have sniffed us on a ping or two."

"Apparently not enough for terminal homing." Volkov pondered a disconnect. "I can't help but think that at least one ping was successful. That would geo-locate us and allow for a weapon steer."

"Maybe the wire broke."

"I doubt it. Wires don't break easily anymore. They're too important and built for the task."

"Maybe one ping caught us, but it probably needed a confirmation ping before terminal homing or before an alerted operator would steer it."

Volkov appreciated his sonar ace's insights, which confirmed his suspicions. "Keep going. Keep speculating, assuming at least one ping earned a return."

"Okay. Three or more pings would have sent the weapon after us on its own algorithms, wire-commanded or not. But if I assume an attentive operator on Type-209 Bravo and a working wire, then I can't explain away even one ping. Like you said—we would've been geo-located by that. And with a second ping, they'd have our course and speed."

"I doubt they were attentive operators. I hope they were shitting their pants." Volkov qualified his confidence. "But they'll become attentive at some point, and they'll check the archived returns."

"That will tell them where we were, not where we are now. And your present course and speed is offset enough from what it was that we'll slip away even if they had our prior course and speed."

Gnawing at Volkov, a threat clung to his mind. While hunting the next *Type-209* more than finishing off the prior one, he desired another nugget of evidence that Type-209 Bravo was sidelined.

A junior sonar technician raised a finger and called out. "High-pressure air from Type-209 Bravo!"

Anatoly slid his headset over his ear and fell silent. "It's an emergency blow."

Volkov clenched his fist. "Yes!" Wary of overconfidence, he sought further data. "Hull popping? Any signs of surfacing?"

"They're too far away to hear that. But there's no question they're hitting an emergency blow."

"I'll count that as a victory."

The sonar guru grunted. "Agreed. Do want to add that to your report to Jake?"

"Yes. Do so, and then launch the communication buoy."

"I'll update the message and launch the buoy."

"We can breathe easier now." Volkov challenged his own statement. "But that was a damned good counterfire."

Anatoly slid a muff to his jawline. "They're in heightened state of alertness against American submarines. They may not have expected us specifically, but they were ready for action."

"Against a dolphin attack?"

Anatoly groaned. "I see your point. They shouldn't even know we're out here. You're right. The dolphin attack should've sent them into a panic, but they managed to shoot back based upon our detonation command. If they didn't know about us beforehand, they sure know that we're here now."

Volkov nodded "Pierre bribes the Egyptians for passage through the Suez, and I'm sure he pays them hush money, too, to remain quiet about the details they see. But everyone watches the Suez with human spies, and no amount of money can stop that."

"But we were heading from Pakistan to Toulon. We only stopped here to fight because of extortion by the Americans, and the Turks couldn't know that."

"They figured it out, or at least one submarine commander did. I need to understand the Turkish perspective and why one of their warships seemed ready for me."

"Maybe it's just a paranoid commander who refreshed his memory on our fleet's tactics after he and the whole world watched us transit through the Suez."

Volkov was unsure what to believe. "It could be that simple, I imagine."

Anatoly raised an eyebrow. "I can't say, Dmitry. These are the concerns of a commanding officer. That's your job to figure out, thankfully for me."

Volkov corrected his de facto executive officer. "It's your job, too, while Sergeui's gone. He's very quiet, not a natural leader, but he's very smart. I look to him for confirming my most important decisions. Nods, winks, confidence in his face. But now that you're my accidental executive officer, you must be my verification of sanity."

"I can do that."

To lessen the tension of battle, Volkov chided him. "I also need you ready to lead the crew if I die."

"You said you were in great health!"

The *Wraith's* commander clutched his chest. "Since you know about my personal business, you know that I could collapse at any second with a broken heart."

Anatoly grunted. "Can I get back to finding you another Type-209?"

"Yes, and do it fast." Volkov strolled behind the row of seated sailors, glancing at their Subtics monitors, until he reached the dolphin trainer. He stooped beside his friend. "Any contact?"

"Too much contact. My babies are calling me, but I can't answer. I hate this."

"I know. They're my sailors, but they're your children."

The trainer issued a soft groan.

"Maybe before our next mission, you can teach them to call less frequently when we can't respond. It might lessen Mikhail's anxiety."

"I was going to adjust their communication protocols, but there was no time. I invested every minute into making sure they'll wait for me if we lose them again."

Volkov grunted. "But isn't that comforting? We can always come back for them if we need to, can't we?"

Vasily turned his head and showed his friend determined eyes. "Promise me that you'll never abandon them."

"If we lose them, I'll charter fishing boats, dinghies, jet skis, garbage scowls, or whatever it takes to find them again. They're far too important."

In silent appreciation, Vasily nodded and returned his attention to the monitor showing unrequited calls from the dolphins.

At the far console, Anatoly twisted his torso towards his boss. "I'm launching the communications buoy."

"Go ahead."

The sonar ace tapped an icon. "Communications buoy is away."

"Very well."

A quiet sonar technician clasped his headset and curled forward in the posture Volkov recognized as a warning.

The *Wraith's* commander hissed across the room. "Anatoly!" As his intended audience made eye contact, Volkov gestured towards the quiet technician.

Trailing his tethered headset, Anatoly stood, walked to his colleague, and then bent forward to examine his screen. He looked up. "He's got something bearing zero-six-eight."

Assertive, Volkov declared the new discovery a target. "Designate the contact as Type-209 Charlie. Assign tubes one and two to Type-209 Charlie."

Energized, Anatoly returned to his console. "I'm designating the new contact as Type-209 Charlie and assigning tubes one and two to Type-209 Charlie."

The quiet sonar technician validated his commander's decision. "Submerged contact, bearing zero-six-nine, bearing rate, one-point-three degrees per minute to the right. I have blade rate on a seven-bladed screw correlating to eleven knots for a Turkish *Type-209* submarine, fourteen-hundred-ton displacement variant."

Volkov announced his intentions. "Attention in the control room, we have a Turkish submarine designated Type-209 Charlie. I intend to engage Type-209 Charlie with a single limpet weapon from tube one. Tube two is the backup limpet weapon.

I intend to fire as soon as the system is ready. Our ship is already on a lag line of site to evade counterfire cones."

Pausing his speech, he scanned his sailors for their understanding and possible dissent. All eyes showed confidence.

The *Wraith's* commander continued. "I believe that Type-209 Charlie heard the distress of Type-209 Bravo and is racing to assist. I expect it will slow to listen for us. Therefore, I will act quickly. If anyone sees a flaw, speak!"

A seated technician broke the silence. "Tube one is ready."

Seeking a final verification, Volkov inquired. "Parameters?"

"Three-mile run to seeker enable, pre-enable run speed forty knots, passive search, submerged target only–ceiling twenty meters."

"Check fire! Check fire! Give me the system's range estimate. You've got blade rate and bearing rate. Use them!"

Facing his monitor, the technician double-checked. "System range estimate to Type-209 Charlie is five nautical miles."

"Tighten this! Make it go active right in their laps. Increase the enable run to four miles."

The young man's fingers danced against a capacitive touchscreen. "Tube one now has a four-mile run to seeker enable."

"Very well, shoot tube one."

Volkov's ears popped with the impulse ejection.

The young sonar technician confirmed it. "Tube one, away. Normal launch. I have wire control.

"Very well." Volkov reconsidered his tag-and-run tactic. "I'm going to shoot the backup as well. I need as many limpets on Type-209 Charlie as possible, since I won't linger to attack again. Get tube two ready with a five-mile run to enable."

"Five miles?"

"Yes. Type-209 Charlie will be evading after our first weapon enables."

Tethered to his headset, Anatoly skulked behind the junior technicians and intercepted the order for his apprentices. "Tube two, five-mile run to enable. I'm balancing the team's workload… and tube two is ready, sir!"

"Shoot tube two."

With two weapons racing towards his target, Volkov dared to wish for a rapid victory.

A sonar technician called out. "I've lost broadband flow noise on Type-209 Charlie. Blade rate's falling off... now making turns for six knots. I'm also hearing up-Doppler on their fifty-hertz electric bus. I think they're slowing, but they've turned towards us..."

Anatoly hunched over the junior technician's shoulders, helping him analyze the dynamics. He then angled his face towards the *Wraith's* commander. "He's right, Dmitry. Type-209 Charlie has slowed to six knots, but the speed has increased in the line of sight. They've turned towards us."

Volkov summarized the scenario. "They've slowed to hunt us, with a respectable idea of our location, probably from a radio broadcast from Type-209 Bravo. Lucky for us, we caught them before they arrived on station."

Vasily corrected his boss. "Not lucky, Dmitry. Cause and effect–thanks to my babies attracting them here giftwrapped!"

Volkov smirked. "Very well. Thanks to Vasily's babies and some good fortune, we retain the advantage. Steer the weapons accordingly and finish this."

Anatoly handled the adjustments and then updated his commander. "We've injected steers into both weapons."

"Very well."

"Do you want to reload your torpedoes, Dmitry? We have no more limpets in the tubes."

"Not until Type-209 Charlie is running the other way."

"Understood, sir."

Unable to resist a bragging opportunity, Vasily boasted. "Aren't you glad you trusted my babies? Thanks to them, you had tubes one and two loaded for Type-209 Charlie."

Volkov aided his friend's stage performance. "Your dolphins shaped this battle and gifted us two submarines."

"That's what you pay them for, Dmitry–in mackerel and exciting excursions in exotic waters around the *Wraith*!"

"Let's wait until the limpets hit before we celebrate."

"Okay." Vasily's pink cheeks suggested that his full celebration was unstoppable.

Anatoly gave Volkov his next gem of data. "We're out of the expected counterfire seeker cone."

"Very well. Helm, all-ahead one-third. Make turns for five knots."

As the ship slowed, Anatoly shared an update. "Torpedo one has entered passive search mode, slowed to twenty-eight knots, and it's already detected the target's propeller blades."

"Excellent!"

As Volkov waited for his first weapon and the target to converge, Anatoly conveyed more good news. "Torpedo two has shifted to passive search mode, twenty-eight knots, and it's also detected the target's blades."

"Very well."

Anatoly became animated. "Type-209 Charlie's accelerating! We've got rapid blade rate. Cavitation. Extensive engineering sounds. Noisemakers! Recommend active searches, both weapons!"

"Send both weapons into active searches."

Time ticked away as Volkov enjoyed dominance over his adversary.

Within minutes, both weapons reached their targets and released fifty limpets towards its hull. The seas became a chorus of electronic wailing, and the Turkish submarine was louder than a rock concert.

"How many limpets landed?"

Wide-eyed, Anatoly chortled. "We're having trouble counting, there's so many. At least thirty. Maybe forty. Both weapons arrived on optimum trajectories."

Volkov pursed his lips and replied. "They'll need two days on the surface to pry them all off."

A brief shadow passed over Anatoly's face. "This may not be over in two days."

The sonar ace's thought irked the *Wraith's* commander. "If the

Americans can't make up their mind on Turkey by then, we'll turn against them and force their damned decision."

His entire control room fell into a silent shock.

Hubris.

Defeating two submarines, each built when most of his sailors were in diapers, was expected. Turning against the world's greatest naval arsenal was a graver matter.

Worried he'd gone overboard with his confidence, Volkov retreated to Vasily's side and begat a new conversation. "Are you sure you'll get your babies back, even without communicating?"

Scrunching his features, Vasily appeared perplexed. "Yes, but I don't want to test them. You've hit both your targets. You could transmit the return-to-ship signal to guide them home."

Volkov resisted the temptation. "Each submarine we defeated can still listen and launch torpedoes. And God knows if there's a silent American *Virginia*-class seeking us at this very moment."

The trainer's shoulders slumped. "I know. That's why I'm not asking. It's for situations like this that I trained them to wait."

"I'm sure they'll wait for you."

"What's next for us? What do we do now?"

Volkov sought the right words and then leaned into his friend's ear for the illusion of privacy, knowing the *Wraith's* walking version of a Twitter tweet would share the poorly kept secret. "Jake's instructions to the commanders were clear. After handling the Turkish submarines, we will turn and prepare to strike their surface fleet. It's only if Jake decides otherwise that we would turn against the *Lincoln* battle group."

Vasily nodded. "You weren't joking about driving an American decision, were you?"

"No. I wasn't. But I shared it the wrong way and at the wrong time. I've worried everyone."

"Those orders would be terrifying. You can't share them without making everyone worry."

"Terrifying, indeed. But we're getting ahead of ourselves."

Volkov reasserted control over his staff. "Anatoly, prepare a communications buoy for Jake with the status of Typ-209 Charlie."

"I'm preparing a communications buoy with the status of Type-209 Charlie, sir."

Volkov stepped to the central table to plot a course southwest with the intent of standing, as best a solitary *Scorpène* submarine could, against the Turkish surface fleet–and any submarines protecting it."

CHAPTER 15

In his monitor, Jake studied the face of the naval officer standing between the guards outside the control center's door.

Recognizing the man from the group Renard had introduced before his departure, he thought he'd found an ally. The officer's face also seemed familiar from a distant memory from past missions aboard the *Specter*.

Suspicious of the newcomer's identity, Jake pressed an intercom button and launched his examination in French. "What year did you graduate from *l'Ecole Navale*?"

Ready for the test, the man volunteered a quick answer into the microphone outside the command center's door. "Two thousand and four."

"Describe your date at the commencement celebration."

The man smirked. "She's the one that got away. Then I married a harpy, and I'm still paying for it. Come to think of it, I should see if Celeste is available, I–"

"Good enough. Describe the most beautiful date of the evening–yours excluded."

The officer hesitated in apparent thought before replying. "There was a sleek blonde in a strapless evening dress. She moved with the grace of queen across a chessboard, and more eyes watched her than the fireworks. Two drunk Dutch Marines drew their dress swords to fight for her hand in a dance, but then a sly aspirant from the British Naval Academy swept her away while they bickered."

The silliness aligned with Jake's recollection of his summer exchange. "What about the guy who brought her?"

"Fifteen kilos overweight and a spineless jellyfish. That's why the woman stood out. We learned later that she was his second

144

cousin, trying to help boost his reputation."

"Good answers, but possibly rehearsed. So, let's try something new. Which professor did you hate the most?"

The man grunted. "Doctor Legrand. We called him 'Le Grand Penis' for his sadistic enjoyment in screwing over young men. He issued more failing grades than high marks in Physics, and the entire class signed a petition for his removal."

"And?"

"And the superintendent explained to us the concept of tenure and then reminded us of the concept of military insubordination. Afraid to lose our commissions, we returned to our lessons, including those who had to repeat Physics classes with a non-demonic professor."

"Did you have to repeat?"

"I was hoping you wouldn't ask. But damn it, yes."

The frustration seemed genuine, and Jake tapped a button unlocking the door to his new companion.

When the man entered the room, his voice echoed across its emptiness. "You look like you could use some help."

Jake had been awake for thirty hours. "Yeah. I'm going to need a break soon."

The French commander strolled down a side aisle towards Jake. "I must be blunt. You appear in need of a break now."

"It's a rough mission."

"Rougher than you may realize. The group of us who've been supporting Pierre for the last two years were blocked from entrance by a Naval Group executive order. I can only assume one of Pierre's enemies bribed or threatened someone in the company."

"Shit. Olivia."

"Olivia McDonald? His CIA contact?"

Jake kicked back his chair and faced the man. "She's turned from an ally to a hostage-taker. She has Pierre, his family, Volkov's parents, Cahill's wife, and my wife."

Revealing concern, the commander was upset. "I only overheard half of Pierre's conversations with her, but I never trusted her."

"Well, she's shown her true colors, and it's exhausting. Let me update you on the fleet, and I'll get some rest." Jake scanned the center. "Where does Pierre normally sleep?"

"Oh? You haven't seen the vault yet, have you?"

"The what?"

"Shit! The imposter officers wouldn't have mentioned it, would they? May I give you a key?"

"Slowly. I'm still learning to trust you."

The man lifted a chain over his neck and extended it. "The key on this chain opens your private vault. It's a Faraday cage and has one hundred and thirty decibels or better of sonic isolation across all frequencies of human speech. It's downright eerie in there."

"Where?"

The commander pointed. "That door."

"Shit. I thought that was a broom closet. I'm not trusting you until I open the door and see for myself, though." Jake tossed the chain back to the commander. "In fact, you open it."

A chime alarmed at a console, and maintaining his focus on his new colleague, Jake resisted the urge to look.

Wide-eyed, the commander glared. "Aren't you going to look?"

"It can wait."

"That's your fleet calling you. I recognize the sound."

"I'm glad you do. Open the damned door."

Hurrying, the French officer reached the room, inserted the key, and turned the latch.

Behind him, Jake glanced through the doorframe and saw two consoles in the center of a quiet room. Trusting the man's identity, he granted him the dignity of using his name. "Keep the key, Commander Laurent. If Pierre didn't mention this room, he might not think I need it."

"What about your private communications?"

Jake stretched his palm towards the door. "You'll be in here instead of me."

"Understood."

"In fact, go in there now while I see who's calling me."

"I thought I was earning your trust."

"You are. My limited trust, thus far. Like I said. It's been a rough mission."

"It's your command center." Commander Laurent entered the vault and shut the door.

Alone, Jake rushed to the chiming console and read Volkov's report. For the first time since learning of his wife's capture, he felt hope and expressed it in a whisper to himself. "Holy Shit, Dmitry. You make it look too easy."

Jake typed a response for his entire fleet, announcing the *Wraith's* success to his commanders, and he copied Olivia on the message. He sent word of Volkov's victory against two Turkish *Type-209's* into the network feeding his ships, and then he sent an obligatory textual copy to the American intelligence machine.

He thought about freeing Commander Laurent from his cage, but he awaited Olivia's reply.

She hailed him thirty seconds later.

As he accepted her call, tired lines stretched across her face, and dark circles underscored her eyes. "Two out of three is what I expected by now, but you're just getting started."

"Your gratitude is overwhelming."

"Take out the third, and then move the *Goliath* into position for action against Turkish ground troops."

"Before we go down that road, can you get me some reconnaissance on the surfaced Turkish boats?"

"You think I wasn't going to verify it?"

"I know you are, but I want the information as a double-check, and I want to see the footage for myself to assess my team's performance. Maybe there's something there I can use to make sure Terry takes down number three."

"I'll see what I can do. Don't get cocky. This is far from over." She extended her arm towards the camera, and then she disappeared.

Hours from his next check-in with his wife, Jake walked to the vault and knocked.

The commander opened the door. "Any news?"

"Volkov took out two *Type-209s*. I mean three, really, since he got an Egyptian one by accident yesterday."

"Impressive, even for Dmitry. That leaves only one more before you can finish the first phase of your obligation."

"I see that you're up to speed on the situation."

"It's ugly, and I don't envy you. All this pressure, and Pierre is taken from you. Arrogant as he is, he's still a reassuring presence."

The comment spurred a memory. "I need about another thirty minutes of privacy."

Laurent went back into the room. "I'm at your service." He closed the door behind himself.

Jake walked to the leftmost console with Renard's secret server and connection to his bunker.

First, he sought a friendly face, although he couldn't know to whom it would belong until he called.

He typed Marie Renard's birthday and clicked the icon that seemed logical as a request to place a video call.

And someone answered, revealing a familiar face from a decade-old memory.

"Holy shit."

Former French naval aviator, Alain LeClerc, seemed youthful for his sixty years. Time had stopped for him after he'd flown Jake and Olivia to Algeria to flee French authorities, earning him a king's ransom from Renard. "Jake! I was hoping Pierre left you a way to call me!"

"LeClerc? Andrew LeClerc?"

"It's 'Alain LeClerc', but that's a very good memory for how long it's been."

"Shit. So, you're the guy Pierre leaves in charge when Henri's not around."

"Indeed! I wish our circumstances were better. Your friends and families are already caught. I am saddened."

"Me, too. So, do you know what's going on?"

"Pierre gave me some insight."

"I didn't even know that you and he were still close."

LeClerc became solemn, recalling the deceased sister and nephew Renard had lost to a drunk driver long ago. "He's still my brother-in-law, as far as I'm concerned. And I'm a wealthy man, thanks to him. It's a privilege to serve him."

"I thought delivering me from France and ditching your aircraft over the Med was service enough."

A broad smile covered LeClerc's face. "This is hardly a sacrifice. I see that Pierre's house staff keeps the Suttons comfortable, I tell them what I can about their daughter's affairs, which is thankfully little, and I otherwise enjoy Pierre's champagne and caviar with my wife. Pierre instructed me to bring her here, and this is essentially a nice family vacation."

"Great." Jake's demeanor downshifted. "I need you to take a break from that vacation and do me an important favor."

"Of course."

"Alain, do you have a Facebook account?"

"I don't like your tone, but yes."

"I need you to reach out to someone. Or better yet, have a cousin's brother-in-law's best friend reach out–someone as far from Olivia's view that will agree to help you."

"Depends where you're going with this. I don't want to endanger uninvolved people, and you know that Pierre supports that."

"I need one of my Naval Academy classmates to contact you. Then you'll update him on my needs and have him connect to another classmate."

"That seems like an extra step."

"Agreed. But the first guy knows I'm alive, which puts in him in a super-minority. And since I just saved his life, he kind of owes me, which puts him in a mega-minority."

"Now I get it."

"The first guy's name is Andrew Causey. The problem is, he's still on active duty. Well, that's maybe not even the biggest problem. The biggest problem is that Olivia knows he owes me. She might predict that I'd start with him if I tried to contact anyone."

"I can likely do better than distant roommates and social media. I could send a man to find him where he is, depending where that might be."

Jake recalled Renard's global network of operatives. "That would be wonderful. I think he's still stationed in Bahrain, though. On some desk job finishing up for retirement. He wasn't too keen on sticking around in the Navy after what he endured."

LeClerc reached forward to manipulate his computer. "I believe Pierre has a man in Bahrain. Let me see... he left a list of operatives by code names and contact information."

"No kidding? On the American base?"

"You don't need to know. Just know that I can get to your classmate. I can have a pizza delivered to his home with a courier who will share whatever information you have for him. You'll need something secret to tell him that nobody else would know, to gain his confidence. Do you know what you want to tell him?"

Impressed with Renard's network, Jake ran through memories of the *Indiana's* escape from Iranian waters. "I do. I have a ton of data to prove to Andy that you're working on my behalf. I'll jot down some details before you set your man in action. But we ultimately need to get to the second guy, Michael Jennings, with the FBI."

LeClerc's face glowed with enthusiasm. "The FBI? You have quite a group of classmates."

"Yeah, and now you're a vital part of it. But how can Causey contact Jennings without danger?"

"Pierre's taught me a few things. Causey could leave a fingerprint. Jennings would have access to verify that. He could offer his hair for DNA, too. Of course, we'll get a photo of Causey complying with all this."

Jake hoped it would work. "And I write a note for Jennings to be delivered with Causey's stamp of legitimacy?"

"That's essentially it. Jennings will doubt the complete communications chain, but I assume that piquing his interest to have him contact you is sufficient. He should be willing to do that. If you can write up a note for Causey, and one for him to send to Jennings, I'll put this in motion."

"I have that all covered." Jake had already typed the words he wanted to share with each classmate and had saved them to a USB drive. He reached for the stick and inserted it into Renard's private server. I'm ready to send it."

"Go ahead. Ah, one other thing. I promised the Suttons that you'd update them on their daughter.

Jake wondered how Renard stayed sane moving mountains one moment and then nurturing scared people the next. "Put them on."

"They're waiting outside my room. Hold on."

While waiting, Jake felt momentum shifting in his favor, and he remembered to check the encrypted hard drive.

The *Goliath's* file revealed several upgrades, but one caught his eye. To his surprise, Renard had deployed lighter rounds to the transport ship, along with the replacement railgun cannibalized from the *Xerses*. "You slippery bastard."

According to the tests, the lighter rounds could reach one hundred and fifty nautical miles–great for interfering with Turkish ground forces.

Great for sending rounds into the *Lincoln* battle group.

Then he saw a note he'd stenciled on paper reminding him to verify the secret number. Digging into the *Goliath's* deck log archives, he found the day of the month Ariella had first set foot aboard the ship in dry dock.

November eighteenth. Adding five days to it, queued by the false boring assignment she'd claimed to have escaped, he arrived at twenty-three freckles on Cahill's bare hairy ass.

A minute later, a worried elderly couple sat in front of the monitor, flanked by lady resembling a younger version of Danielle.

The father spoke. "Hello? Is Mister Renard there?"

"Sorry, no. He's been detained, Mister and Misses Sutton. I work for him, and my name is Jake. Danielle is safe and doing the exciting work she loves. What can I tell you about your daughter to ease your concerns?"

CHAPTER 16

Waking from a nap, Danielle smelled the metal surrounding her. The tinny sink and shower reminded her of a warship, but the walls curving into a roof and floor emphasized the confinement of her underwater quarters.

She'd just slept in a casket within a steel burial ground, and as she let rapid-fire thoughts careen through her mind, she reduced herself to an idiot.

She was commanding a ship beyond her knowledge, carrying an abandoned relic as her cargo, jamming her warship between two hostile NATO allies, and obeying the insane orders of an international terrorist named Jake Slate.

But she'd yielded to slumber and had endured the disorientation of waking in a strange prison. Having survived her first sleep cycle aboard a submerged vessel, she silently congratulated herself as she hurried through her toiletries and put on fresh clothes.

Her next disorientation came as she sought breakfast and remembered the *Goliath* lacked a wardroom. With the commanding officer and executive officer as the only sailors with lofty titles, the ship forced her to dine with the commoners.

Having enjoyed private quarters with her own staff on the *Westminster*, she ordered a side dish of humility with her eggs and sausage.

"There you go, ma'am." The cook offered a friendly smile. "Coffee, tea, and juices are at the end of the line. Just yell if you need something."

"Thanks."

A quartet of sailors occupied a table in an otherwise empty mess hall. She sat alone with her thoughts while eating food she found surprisingly tasty.

Two men in their late twenties approached with trays. "Mind if we join you, ma'am?"

"If you don't mind me leaving in about five minutes."

"We'll keep you company until you go."

She nodded, and they sat opposite her.

One introduced himself. "Williams, gunner."

"Evans, better gunner."

She extended her hand over the table, and the men accepted her handshake. "Are you guys the oncoming watch?"

"Yes, ma'am. And not to brag, when it comes time to light someone up, we're your battle stations gunners."

"Tell me about that. What makes you the best? Well, first best and next best."

While Evans wrestled a piece of bacon into his mouth, Williams answered. "You can probably guess that it's not about long-range hits. That's all controlled by electronic guidance and the rounds' fins. The real talent comes into play with short-range shots."

After washing down his mouthful with coffee, Evans bragged in an Australian accent. "We once put rounds into a bloody North Korean submarine that was caught right in our cargo bay. Try doing that without cutting holes in your own ship!"

"Yeah. Our rounds come out of the muzzle at Mach Seven. They just keep going and going."

While swallowing a mouthful of her hurried breakfast, she recalled Renard's summary of a drowned North Korean crew's gruesome fate. "Pierre told me about that."

"It was the first time someone unexpected landed in our cargo bay, but it wasn't the last."

She grunted. "Huh. That's how you met Dmitry, sort of?"

Evans answered. "The North Korean sub was a surprise. We thought we were rescuing a South Korean submarine–we found it eventually–but the first attempt nabbed us the enemy. Nasty surprise. But when we nabbed Dmitry in his *Kilo* submarine, we'd already beaten him into submission. It was hardly dramatic. It was just the icing on the cake."

"I'm glad you guys didn't shoot him."

Williams smirked. "Word's out that he's fond of you, ma'am."

"Seriously?"

"It's a small fleet, and everyone's talking about how he couldn't keep his eyes off you at Terry's wedding."

"Yeah, I caught that."

Probing for gossip, Williams continued. "I guess he's a better submarine commander than a romantic."

She humanized herself for the duo, and for the crew to whom they'd surely blab. "He wasn't a complete moron."

"Woah, I guess you know him better than we do."

She washed down her final bite with orange juice. "Maybe. Excuse me, guys. I need to get to the bridge." She stood, took a step, and stopped. "Wait. I thought the port crew stuck to themselves. One of you shouldn't be here."

Evans turned red. "Guilty, ma'am! When Williams told me you were getting in line for chow, I made a special trip to meet you."

She offered her polite smile and departed.

Passing through the tactical control room, she found the skeletal midnight staff wearing foggy faces of caffeine-laced fatigue. She took comfort in Sergeui's absence, trusting that her submarine officer had rested during the night.

On the bridge, Walker was a thin ghost under sanguine lighting, but his smile was a genuine welcome. "Did you get some rest, ma'am?"

"Enough."

He stood in silence.

"You seem uneasy. What's wrong?"

"If I may, we're still getting used to you replacing Terry." He rephrased his sentiment. "I'm still getting used to it. Until you showed up, all our commanders were pilfered from some sort of crisis. That's how Renard works—finding people in distress, and there aren't any secrets about the jacked up scenarios that screwed them over."

"Except for me."

He shrugged. "Yeah. I'm wondering when you'll tell your story and keep us all from speculating."

The invitation pushed beyond a boundary. Though he'd been an ally, Walker remained a stranger. She deflected. "Didn't Pierre tell you?"

"No. That's his way. He likes to be mysterious."

Easing her defenses, she revealed a filtered version. "The summary is, my squadron commodore wanted me more than I wanted him, and when I had to turn him down, he called in favors to ruin my career."

Walker grunted. "Sounds like a tool."

Finding the Australian increasingly approachable, she shared more. "He seemed like a good man at first. We actually went on a few dates, but I had to back off."

"Was he too aggressive?"

"No. Too married."

"Oh shit."

"I'm not going to play dumb. I knew better than to date within my chain of command, but…" Owning her mistake, she rephrased. "Well, shit. No 'buts'. I screwed up. I also knew about his wife, but he said they were waiting to sign the divorce papers. The truth ended up being quite different, and when it blew up, he claimed I started everything and made advances at him."

"Typical mongrel."

"He claimed that I ruined his marriage with my advances, and he had the legal corps push me out of the Royal Navy."

"That's crap."

Silent, she wanted to avoid reliving the pain.

Walker continued. "That's the sort of bullshit that created the first three commanders before you. Kind of shared misery."

As she let the comment linger, she accepted a newfound sense of belonging. And she noted that the 'Wounded Kitten Club' of Renard's Mercenary Fleet somehow turned damaged housecats into roaring lions. She reaffirmed her decision of signing up with the Frenchman.

Then Walker's body stench interrupted her serenity. Eyeing him, she forgot her verbal filters. "You look like shit."

He grunted. "I'm sure I do."

"When's the last time you slept?"

"Somewhere in the Suez, I think."

"Well, as your commanding officer..."

He raised his palms. "Okay, okay. I'll go down after chow." He perked up. "I almost forgot. Jake's been sending some news. We get most of the major international papers, with images filtered out for bandwidth. But we've got all the verbiage you could want on the Turkish advancement."

"So, it's happening?"

"As of last night. They're in Syria, and President Trump isn't stopping them."

"At least we no longer have to speculate about it."

"And it gets better. While you were sleeping, Dmitry took out two Turkish submarines."

The Russian's stock doubled in her reckoning. "Just like that?"

"Just like that."

"Am I wrong to expect Terry to handle just one?"

"Maybe he will, but remember that he doesn't have weaponized dolphins, at least not yet. Supposedly we're training the females we stole from Iran. So, Terry has to hunt the good old-fashioned way, with sonar only."

Before checking the chart, she looked out the windows to relax her eyes, but dark water shielded her view of the Israeli relic.

Then, turning her nose towards a display, she verified the *Goliath's* location as it left the Levantine Basin and pushed deeper between Cyprus and mainland Turkey. She also examined the mercenary fleet submarines' locations.

Cahill had the *Specter* four miles ahead of the *Goliath*, and Volkov had the *Wraith* off the northeast tip of Cyprus, poised for softening the Turkish surface fleet. But a doubt nagged her. "How accurate are these positions?"

"Shitty, compared to what you're used to. We don't get radar returns or real-time data. We get what we get when they can launch buoys, or when they think they're isolated enough to raise an antenna and broadcast."

"Terry's position is crucial. That's the one I need to know."

Walker recited the plan Danielle knew, but she let him engrain it in their minds. "His zigzagging is fast enough to be heard, but not too fast to look like he's trying to attract attention. He'll launch a buoy each time he reaches the far left of his pattern, about every seventy-five minutes. That'll keep us honest on his location, after Jake receives it and rebroadcasts it."

"Except for the seventy-four minutes when we're guessing."

"Right."

"And we can't hear him directly on our sonar?"

"Off and on, depending on his aspect, the water temperature, the sea bottom–when his sound arrives after bouncing off it."

"I clearly have more studying to do about submarine combat."

"I've learned on the job, as will you."

She grabbed the segue. "And I'll be fine up here alone. It's time to let me lead the ship without you."

"I can take a hint. Sergeui should be on watch in thirty minutes, after chow. He'll have your back while I'm sleeping."

"See you." As she heard his steps echo down the stairs, she thought Walker might have her back even during his sleep.

Half an hour later, a request arrived over the open microphone. "Sergeui here. Can me and translator to bridge come?"

Welcoming the company under the eerie red dome, she pressed an icon unlocking the door.

Two pairs of footsteps echoed, and then two Russian men accompanied her.

Sergeui seemed mesmerized by the hemispherical abyss around him. "Maybe submarine should have windows."

His translator, a portly man, was a pale statue.

"Is he okay?"

Sergeui examined his companion. "He fine." The submariner gave a second look. "Maybe not." He shook the translator, who mumbled something in Russian.

"He looks terrified."

"Maybe. Who knows? Maybe I be his translator while he wake up."

"To what do I owe the pleasure of your company?"

The submarine officer deadpanned his response. "Huh?"

She remembered the language barrier. "Why are you here?"

"We hear Terry on sonar. Good fix. You good stay slow and quiet behind him."

She studied the petrified translator and aimed her palm at a foldout seat against the aft bulkhead. "He should sit."

"*Da*. Come, Leonid. Over here." Sergeui helped him down.

"Him." She pointed. "Feel better soon?"

Sergeui nodded and waved off her concern. "He translator midnight *Wraith* watch with me. Tough. Be fine."

Danielle checked the *Goliath's* speed. Five knots kept it quiet while matching Cahill's forward zigzagging advance.

As time tested her patience, she fell into a cascade of random thoughts that swept her from the dangers of the deep. But her respite in her imagination was fleeting.

The sonar supervisor's voice shot from the loudspeaker. "Torpedo in the water!"

Recalling the plan, Danielle found the right icon, tapped it, and then issued the confirmation. A message revealed her success in launching a buoy containing the *Goliath's* Subtics tactical system's bearing and bearing rate to the torpedo.

"Good! You no wait! Jake send to Terry. We triangle!"

She shot the submariner a sideways glance. "We what?"

Surprising her, the recovered translator stood and removed the language barrier. "He means we'll triangulate the torpedo's position, course, and speed with Terry's data. Jake will relay our data to Terry, and he should be able to backtrack its course to the submarine that launched it."

"Welcome back from the dead."

"Sorry. It's just … I don't like it up here."

Sergeui stepped to console and lifted a headset over his ears. "Real torpedo. I hear. Team make good system info."

"Is this a threat to our ship?"

The translator checked with the submarine officer, who shook his head and answered in English. "We safe. Problem for Terry, though."

"Which way will he evade, and at what speed?"

After the Russians exchanged words, the portly man answered. "We need something from Terry on the torpedo. Ideally, he'll send his evasion course, too. Or we can estimate his course now that he's speeding up. Or we can call him on the underwater phone and risk revealing our presence. It's a complex matter."

Her adrenaline pushed her heart rate. "No shit."

Over the loudspeaker, a welcomed voice soothed her. "This is Liam in the control room. Private line, ma'am?"

She lifted a boom microphone headset and slipped it over her pulled-back hair. "Can you hear me, Liam?"

"Yes, ma'am. It's just you and me on this line. I recommend that I stay down here in the control room and handle the ship based upon your orders. Sergeui should stay up there as your advisor."

"Agreed. Keep talking."

"Right. The key here is to trust the ship. We've got info from Jake from Terry's latest buoy, and Terry's easy to track while he's running loud from the torpedo. We even have a good enough solution on the Turk that I'm confident Terry will hit it."

"What about Terry's' evasion?"

"Just like we planned. We didn't get lucky enough for him to evade without help, but we'll follow our plan and help. Let the ship handle it."

She remembered respecting the *Westminster's* automation when watching it demonstrated, but she preferred inserting human brains into her command loops. "How's your confidence?"

"Good. We have some time. I'll show you a simulation of the next seven minutes, compressed into twenty seconds. Can you see it?"

She found the right screen "Yes."

"Here we go."

An icon of the *Specter* raced to the south ahead of the pursuing torpedo. The *Goliath* moved on a perpendicular course, slowed, and then released its relic cargo into the weapon's path. Then the transport ship turned back, slowed, and evaded.

"I know we planned this, but Jake set this trap into motion after only two hours of thought."

"It'll work."

"If it doesn't?"

"Then you surface and see how fast we can fly."

A pang of terror paralyzed her and then receded. After it ebbed, she acknowledged it as a sane person's valid response. "I'll trust the system. What orders do you need from me?"

"Use the open mike over the ship-wide circuit so that everyone hears you. It'll make sure nobody misses a beat and is ready to back you up. I'll confirm your orders over the control room's open mike to the bridge, and my fingers will be the only ones that touch the system to carry them out."

"Agreed. Keep going. Recommendations?"

"Let's start with accelerating to our maximum submerged speed of turns for thirteen knots, which gives us twelve and a half with the cargo. And let's come... I'm checking the system... come right with standard rudder to course one-seven-zero."

She tapped an icon to open the microphone circuit, and then she cast her voice upward. "Helm, all-ahead standard, make maximum submerged turns."

Walker's tone was reverent. "Answering all-ahead standard, accelerating to maximum submerged turns of thirteen knots, ma'am."

"Very well." She lowered her voice into the boom microphone jutting from her jaw. "You're sure the system can release the *Rahab* at the right time, steer us clear, and send us on the right evasion course?"

"The ship's built for it. When you're ready, tell me to set the ship on automated maneuvers to release the cargo and clear datum."

The peculiar jargon frustrated her. "Clear what?"

"Sorry. In 'bubblehead', that means 'get the hell out of here'."

"Clear datum?"

"Right. But no hurry on that. We're still... four minutes away from tossing the *Rahab*. So, now's a good time to review the scenario."

She looked at a tactical overview. Still adjusting to the wicked uncertainty of anything's location under the water, she tried to make sense of the shifting fuzziness.

The *Specter* sprinted south from a torpedo that chased it with a credible chance of intercepting the fleeing submarine. Two counterfire weapons fanned outward from Cahill's launch point, boxing in the ensnared the Turk, and the *Goliath* was racing to insert itself between the hostile weapon and her colleague's submarine.

Not racing. Lumbering.

In her understanding of a proper navy, frigates warp-jumped to speeds approaching thirty knots faster than the *Goliath's* submerged mass gained an inch, and the ultimate goal of twelve and a half knots with their cargo's flow friction left her wanting for bigger battery cells or for a full-blown nuclear reactor.

For lack of options, she accepted what the hybrid beast could offer. "Looks like everything's going as planned."

Walker remained her rock. "Sometimes our plans work. This one will. It already is."

"Any reason I shouldn't shift to automated maneuvering now?"

"No, ma'am. You can always take it back when you want. If you issue any rudder, engine order, or depth command, I'll shift us back to manual."

"Alright." She raised her voice. "Control room, shift the ship to automated maneuvers to release the cargo and clear datum."

Walker answered over the open circuit. "Shifting to automated maneuvers to release the cargo and clear datum. The ship is shifted to automated maneuvers, ma'am."

"Very well."

In her ear, Walker nudged her. "Want to watch it happen?"

"You mean turning on the outside lights?"

"Why not? It should be a show, and we should be watching."

"Roger that. I'll handle it from... on second thought, hold on." Gaining comfort with the routine, she angled her jaw up. "Control room, turn on the cargo bay lights."

"Turning on the cargo bay lights, ma'am."

Over her left shoulder, a small sun rose and illuminated the Israeli metallic mass. She reverted to her hushed tones. "So, now we just watch and wait?"

"I'll keep one eye on the system and the sonar team down here. You should get a sanity check from Sergeui."

"Right." She looked to the submarine officer. "You're okay with all this?"

Two thumbs up and a goofy smile confirmed the Russian man's confidence.

During tense minutes, icons shifted forward, side-to-side, and back again as the imperfections of sonic data jostled the chess pieces. Danielle began to respect the informational uncertainty for the artwork it commanded from those who fought beneath the waves.

"The release is coming up, ma'am."

Accepting Walker's hint, she checked the timing. "Agreed. What's our jargon for a 'brace for erratic maneuvers' warning?"

"Not entirely necessary. The system's going to make this gentle on us. A polite warning–"

"Oh, for God's sake, Liam. I'm not a child." She confirmed the timing on a screen and then aimed her voice upward. "Prepare to release the cargo per automated system maneuvers in twelve seconds. Everyone, hold on to something."

She heard Walker's exhausted chuckling. "Perfect. I was rambling a bit."

"Keep it up. I'll squash it if you get annoying. But like you said, let's sit back and watch. Can you see the *Rahab* on a monitor?"

"Everyone on the ship's watching through a monitor. We've never done it quite like this before."

"Now you tell–"

Lights flashed on a display, and then hydraulic valves clunked throughout her ship.

While she gasped and beheld the *Goliath's* beautiful brilliance, the gentle beast released its cargo.

But the *Rahab* went nowhere.

"Liam?"

"Hold on a bit."

As she grabbed the nearest railing, the *Goliath* jutted its bows downward into the dark depths. A gentle angle teetered her into a console while she craned her neck to watch the silent, impossible ten-ton dance outside the dome.

While flow friction slowed the *Rahab*, the *Goliath* gave itself a backing bell to slow faster. Like a palm releasing a pebble, the transport ship's open fingers bid farewell to the Israeli relic. As the dying submarine's stern slipped from the last tendrils of artificial light and into the black abyss, the *Goliath* righted itself and banked away.

"Holy shit."

"Agreed, ma'am. But we're not done yet. The torpedo's getting close."

She checked a screen. "It looks like we're in the right geometry for it to pick up the *Rahab*."

Tension gripped Walker's voice. "The torpedo's seeker just went active. We'll know soon if we've got the geometry right, or if we got something wrong."

"Are you holding out doubts on me?"

"No, ma'am. I always get the willies when a no-shit angry heavyweight passes two miles from us."

She probed his resolve. "We could surface and run to be sure."

"You know the cost of that as well as I do."

"What do you recommend?"

"I say we stay submerged, but I could argue it either way based upon too many factors to discuss right now. I hate to bugger out on you, but this is a command decision."

She aimed her voice to the open microphone. "We're passing within dangerous range of the hostile torpedo, but we will stay the course and trust the *Goliath* to escape. If the weapon acquires us instead of the *Rahab*, we'll surface and run. We may not have the speed to outrun a torpedo, but we'll keep fighting as long as we're in the fight. Until then, we trust the system. Carry on."

Walker exhaled into her ear. "I hope you're right. At least if we die, we know we followed a captain with balls."

"So I've been told before." Breathless, she watched the icon of the weapon glide behind that of the *Goliath*. Over the loudspeaker, the torpedo's shrill pings haunted her.

The cyclic acoustic threats grew louder, spiking her adrenaline, but then they became softer.

Walker announced his findings over the loudspeaker. "We're clear of the torpedo, and it's acquired the *Rahab*. It's going to absorb the warhead."

She sighed. "Very well."

"And I have more good news. Terry's first weapon reached the Turk and is deploying limpets. A bunch. Terry got them."

CHAPTER 17

Dogan reached his limits with the *Preveze*.

Shoring had restricted the dolphins' damage to flowing faucets, and his crew had removed metal doors from lockers and propped them as funnels guiding the streams into the bilge.

Though humid, the control room was functional down to thirty meters, and his standing orders had precluded testing it deeper.

The shallowness strained his crew's capacity to monitor and avoid merchant ships, which were collision threats against his conning tower. Worse, the surface swells begat constant rocking, downing a third of his crew with seasickness.

He envied his adversary in the *Scorpène*-class warship he trailed, the submarine he believed was the *Wraith*.

An adversary with a MESMA system who could stay submerged for days without excursions to snorkel depth.

An adversary with a newer ship of quieter design.

An adversary without downspouts in his control room.

An adversary with weaponized dolphins.

Unless the rogue mercenaries had altered their tactics, he knew his adversary by name.

Having tracked his opponent around Cyprus' northeastern tip, Dogan sensed combat fatigue balancing the thrilling buzz of the tactical advantage he'd earned over a rising star.

Dmitry Volkov, the former commanding officer of the improved Russian *Kilo*-class submarine, *Krasnodar*, and present captain of the *Wraith*, enjoyed a mystique among the international submarine community.

Images of the Russian legend's past battles danced in Dogan's mind as he recalled the briefs he'd received about the mercenary fleet.

In the Black Sea, the Russian commander had forced a stalemate against his future employers, despite breaches in the *Krasnodar's* hull and a shorted battery. After switching teams to the Frenchman's fleet, he'd become the first person to shoot down helicopters with submarine-launched anti-air missiles.

Then videos from curious fishermen supported rumors of Volkov upending several skillful and well-equipped commanders of Israel's submarine fleet. Finally, he'd surprised Dogan with his dolphin attack on the *Preveze* before moving to his next victim, turning the *Sakarya* into helpless limpet farm.

But despite the Russian mercenary's prowess, Dogan had claimed the advantage.

Not a victim. Warrior.

He verified his firing solution on a display and then sent death towards the Russian. "Shoot tube three."

Air pressure dipped, popping Dogan's ears, and a sailor announced the status over the flowing faucets. "Tube three away. Normal launch. I have wire control."

Mixed emotions swirled within Dogan as he lamented his attack, which might send a ship of submarine brethren to their deaths.

Although furious about the dolphin attack, he credited the legend with sparing his crew. A simple two-weapon follow-up salvo of heavyweights would have boxed in and doomed the *Preveze*, but Volkov had spared them.

To his detriment.

Wanting for humane weapons to return the favor of a survivable shot, Dogan had no choice but to send heavyweight reapers towards the *Wraith's* stern.

Without the sound-quieting and undersea propulsion advantages to overtake the *Wraith*, Dogan had run out of options. He'd wanted to continue following Volkov in the nonviolent cat-and-mouse game, the type made famous in the Cold War, especially since he was winning. But duty dictated otherwise.

Volkov's course and speed suggested his targeting of Turkish naval assets.

Had the Russian turned away from his homeland, Dogan would have let him go, out of respect for a legend and as a reciprocal gesture of mercy. But the mercenary aimed the *Wraith* towards the Turkish surface fleet that stood ready to challenge the encroaching American battle group.

Duty demanded action, and as the *Preveze's* battery drained faster than the *Wraith's*, time precluded a better option than heavyweight destruction.

But Dogan's disadvantages in maneuvering against Volkov had made for a mediocre shot–a tail chase challenging his weapon's seeker to acquire the jogging *Wraith* and taxing the torpedo's fuel capacity. If the Russian were truly superhuman, he'd find a way to evade.

Dogan left the verdict to fate.

"Very well. I'm turning to avoid possible counterfire. Helm, left ten-degrees rudder, steady on course three-one-five."

During the turn, the rocking deck rolled, and sheets of incoming water sloshed over the bolstered locker doors. Splattering fluid landed against metal cabinets that had proven their watertight integrity during prior maneuvers.

"Steady on course three-one-five, sir."

"Very well."

A sonar technician barked an unexpected report.

"Loud explosion, heard on the towed array sonar, bearing zero-two-nine or two-four-one. I need another turn to resolve the ambiguity."

Fearing his torpedo had detonated on accident, Dogan denied the request. "No turn. Not yet. Do you still control our weapon?"

"Yes, sir. It's running normally."

"Then what blew up?"

"I'm not sure, sir. We're listening for wreckage, but the explosion might be too far away."

"Damn it, then. You can have your turn. Helm, left ten-degrees rudder, steady course two-one-five."

After the deck tilted through the turn, the sonar technician called out. "The towed array is steady. I've resolved the ambiguity and hear wreckage on bearing two-four-one." As he continued his report, the man's throat tightened. "An air-tight compartment is collapsing at crush depth. It's the *Burakreis*, sir."

Dogan silently agreed with the assessment but voiced his hopes. "We don't know that. Don't jump to conclusions." After a quick look, he noted his battery reserves above the minimum to sprint from one hostile torpedo, an imperfect but sufficient margin to investigate the explosion. "I'll stay on this course for two minutes to get a bearing rate. From that and data from my prior course, I want a range estimate to the wreckage."

"Aye, sir!"

Wearing a windbreaker to keep errant splashes off his cotton jumpsuit, another technician shared his findings. "Limpets, sir! I have to assume it's the *Burakreis*. It's covered in limpets, as badly as the *Sakarya*."

Dogan agreed that the *Wraith's* counterpart, the mythical nuisance *Specter*, had tagged his countrymen on the *Burakreis*. "Very well. Until we learn otherwise, designate the contact with limpets as the *Burakreis*. Give me a bearing."

"Bearing to the *Burakreis* is three-two-seven."

Dogan stood. "You're sure? No ambiguity?"

"Not with limpets, sir. We have them on our bow and hull arrays, too. Everyone in our operating areas will hear them for days."

"That bearing means they've retreated from the battle, and we're deeper into their assigned battlespace than they are."

"Correct, sir. I'm sure they ran from the limpet weapon."

Dogan slowed his breathing and gathered his thoughts. "That gives us insight into the *Specter's* location. The mercenaries put a submarine on either side of Cyprus, like we did. That means our countrymen survived, and..."

Appearing before him, his executive officer voiced hope. "Sir, that sinking hull could be the *Specter*. Maybe the *Burakreis* won the exchange."

169

Dogan refused to accept it. "The evidence suggests it, but I can't... we need to find out."

A sonar operator yelled. "Hull popping. The *Burakreis* is surfacing."

"Very well. We'll know more when they broadcast." Reconsidering his tactics, the *Preveze's* commander allowed his submarine a respite from the hunt. "I'm not waiting for a one-way broadcast from Squadron. Let's hear what our brothers have to say and snorkel for a bit. Line up to charge the battery and bring the ship to snorkel depth!"

The deck remained level during the trivial short rise.

"Executive officer, man the periscope."

"Aye, sir." The executive officer stepped beside his captain, invoked the cylinder's rise, and scanned for interfering ships. "Upon initial sweep, I see no close contacts."

"Very well. Raise the snorkel mast. Raise the radio mast."

As the sailor at the ship's control panel obeyed, clicks and clunks signaled the desired movements.

"Commence snorkeling. Radio operator, line me up for encrypted high-frequency voice, low power aimed at the *Burakreis*."

"You're lined up on the radio, sir. Low power."

"Hail the *Burakreis*."

"Hailing... connection acknowledged. You're a 'go', sir."

Dogan grabbed a microphone from the radio box above his head and keyed it. "*Burakreis, Preveze*. Radio check. Over. *Burakreis, Preveze*. Radio check. Over. *Burakreis, Preveze*–"

A nervous voice rang from the overhead speakers. "*Preveze, Burakreis*. Radio check confirmed. What are you doing here? Over."

"*Burakreis, Preveze*. Shall we dispense with formalities?"

"Hell, yes. Shit, Ozan, I don't know if I sunk a *Scorpène* or not. But they got me with two limpet torpedoes. These mercenaries use tactics we've never trained against."

To calm the man he'd known for years in the small Turkish submarine fleet, Dogan agreed to first names. "You sound like you've survived quite an exchange, Mirac."

Hearing from a fellow victim of the mercenary fleet, the *Burakreis'* commander sounded less flustered. "I heard from Squadron that you and Eyman both had encounters, too."

"Eyman's taking the *Sakarya* back home to remove the limpets, and I've got two badly plugged holes in my control room from the damned dolphins."

"I should count my blessings. I'll take limpets over holes any day, annoying as they are."

"Tell me what happened."

"The *Scorpène*, the *Specter*, I guess, since it was the *Wraith* carrying the dolphins..."

"Good guess. Let's assume it."

"The *Specter* was in a hurry, making eleven knots. Didn't seem to care about being quiet as much as hurrying. I didn't question it, and I took the shot. And it was good, but the explosion happened much sooner than my range estimate. I definitely hit something submerged, though."

"The *Goliath*?"

"Possibly. That makes the best sense. But what if an American was spying on us and got in the way? That could spell disaster and retribution. I'm speculating at this point, but damn it, Ozan. I don't know whom I killed!"

"Get your tail home. You're no good out here, and you'd face a full day trying to pry off limpets with divers."

"I'm already fleeing. I've done what I can. What about the *Wraith*, though? What news should I share with Squadron?"

"I'll take credit for a little ruse. After the dolphin attack, I stayed submerged and hit an emergency blow, but with my vents open. I'm pretty sure I convinced Captain Volkov I was defeated. He must've accepted the ruse since he moved on immediately to attacking Eyman's boat."

"Genius, Ozan. Spectacular."

"I trailed him as far as I could, but he's got longer legs with the MESMA system, and I couldn't overtake him without becoming loud enough for him to hear me."

"But you took a shot?"

"Yes. It's still out there, with wire control." Ozan looked to a console. "It's mediocre, but I'm letting it run."

After a pause, the captain of the *Burakreis* spoke. "I've got more news. It's not on the broadcast yet, but the commodore told me before you and I started this conversation. Our air assets finished laying a sonobuoy field as a buffer against submerged hostility, and the American battle group didn't challenge it. They let us drop it."

Dogan approved his fleet's boldness. "Excellent."

"Volkov won't get through, and the *Goliath* won't reach gunfire range of our troops without being heard."

"Hold on, Mirac. Maybe I can scare Volkov into that sonobuoy field." Releasing the microphone key, Dogan yelled to his team. "Set our weapon to an active search."

"I'm setting our weapon to active."

"Inform me of any returns."

"Aye, sir."

Dogan returned to his ship-to-ship conversation. "Mirac, can you send me any acoustic data you gained on the *Specter*?"

"Not over this channel, but I'll send it to Squadron for them to broadcast to you."

"Thanks. What else have you got for me?"

"Nothing. Just pick up where I left off. We need to know who I hit. Damn it, Ozan. I need to know."

"We all do. I'll take it from here. *Preveze*, out!" Dogan put away his microphone. "Secure snorkeling. Lower all masts and antennas. Make your depth twenty-five meters."

The downspouts strengthened with the increased depth, but the submarine leveled per Dogan's orders.

"Everyone begin searching for–"

"New contact, bearing zero-five-four!"

Unsure how many more surprises he could withstand, Dogan felt his heart race. "Slow to all-ahead one-third!"

"Slowing to all-ahead one-third, sir."

"Get me information on that new contact."

"I've got blade rate. Cleanly machined blades. It's a warship."

"All stop! Rig for ultra-quiet! Snapshot, tube one, five degrees lag from the new contact. Snapshot, tube two, five degrees lead. Open the outer doors to tubes one and two. Correction! Open all outer doors!"

As a frenzy of activity unfurled around the control room's twin fountains, one sonar operator shouted above the din. "Reduction gears, *Scorpène*-class submarine!"

"Give me the new contact's speed! Correlate blade rate to a *Scorpène*-class submarine."

"Five-point-two knots, sir."

Dogan eyed a screen. The high bearing rate and slow speed suggested a close encounter. The system indicated the range below two miles and closing.

At that distance, the first submarine to launch was the second submarine to die. Mutually assured destruction.

No escape.

"Blade rate on two five-bladed screws. It's the *Goliath*."

Adrenaline sent Dogan's mind into hyperdrive. "Designate the new contact as the *Goliath*. God willing, we'll get lucky and they don't hear us."

"The *Goliath's* opening its outer doors. I recommend firing!"

"Check your fire! Check your fire! I'm not committing us to suicide. Not yet."

The executive officer scowled. "Sacrificing ourselves in a one-for-one exchange with the *Goliath* accomplishes the mission, sir."

"I know that. Watch yourself. And check our speeds."

A sonar operator yelled. "The *Goliath* is coming to all-stop."

The executive officer continued. "What will you do, sir?"

Dogan allowed himself tranquil seconds of rational thought. "Nobody's doing anything rash yet. Not us. Not the *Goliath*. Everyone's calm."

"What of it, sir?"

"It may be time to show off my English."

The executive officer scowled harder. "I disagree with your

intent."

"Your one disagreement from being relieved of duty. Line me up on the underwater phone. I'm hailing the *Goliath*."

CHAPTER 18

Danielle had heard rumors of close-aboard undersea encounters, and as she entered one, every muscle in her body tightened. Her breathing became labored.

Wide-eyed, Sergeui repeated himself. "Too close! You shoot, we die! You shoot, we die!"

She snapped. "I got it!"

"Remember you no shoot!"

"Shut up!"

Her rock, Walker, hissed in her ear. "This is really bad."

"Recommendations!"

"Play it cool for now. I have no idea beyond that, other than trying to drift away unnoticed."

"They came to all stop and opened their outer doors, Liam."

"I was trying to be optimistic."

"I need a realist."

"Right, then. This is bad, but we have some advantages."

"Like what? Don't candy-coat this."

"If we surface, we're much faster than they are, and I'm sure they know it. And we've survived torpedoes before. So, if either of us has a chance of surviving an exchange, it's us."

She recalled Renard's boasting about the *Goliath* sacrificing its port bow to torpedoes multiple times to save the ship. But those actions involved lightweight torpedoes, while the weapons ensconced within the nearby Turkish *Type-209* could vaporize complete compartments of her ship.

She kept her thoughts about that silent. "Let's keep it from coming to that."

Recognizing her predicament as a test of wills, she cast aside concerns about the unfamiliar underwater world and embraced her raw leadership challenge. Courage, conviction, and competence were her best assets, but she needed one technical answer before asserting herself. "Are there any limits, like range or aspect, on my ability to shoot this submarine?"

"Five hundred yards is the minimum enable distance, but let me check with the team about aspect limitations."

"Hurry."

Sergeui and the translator were ghouls under the red light, and the system's solution by Danielle's fingers showed the Turkish *Type-209*–the *Preveze* by process of elimination–gliding within a nautical mile of her starboard quarter.

Walker responded. "Each torpedo nest is canted six degrees outward. With respect to that offset, you can't shoot over the shoulder more than one-hundred-sixty degrees in either direction for targets within half a nautical mile. Anti-circular-run safeguards would prevent the weapons from arming. Your complete blind spot is therefore twenty-eight degrees, centered in your baffles."

She envisioned the geometric limitation and remembered to avoid letting the *Goliath's* tail point at the Turk. "Understood. Get every torpedo we've got aimed at that submarine, including the humane ones."

"I'm assigning every weapon to the close-aboard submarine, ma'am."

"Very well." She lowered her vocal volume. "And I want a channel opened to the *Preveze*."

"The underwater phone? Acoustic communications?"

"Yes, unencrypted, low power. And get me a Turkish translator up here ASAP!"

"I'm not sure..."

"I wasn't asking."

"Yes, ma'am. One moment... You're lined up. And I'm having both our translators sent to you."

"Very well." She grabbed the appropriate microphone and let her arm dangle.

Sergeui queried her. "You to talk to them?"

Knowing Walker listened while she answered the Russian, she thought out loud. "I'm deciding what to say, if anything. Even something in English that's gibberish to them could avert hostilities." During quiet moments of intense thought, the loudest sound in Danielle's ears was her pulse.

A male voice with a Turkish accent, garbled as encoding algorithms corrected the water's interference, cracked the tension. "Undersea transport ship, this is the naval unit off your starboard quarter, request dialogue. Over."

Unhesitating, Danielle capitalized upon the chance to deflate a two-ship conflagration. "Naval unit off my starboard quarter, this is undersea transport ship. Dialogue is open. Over."

"Undersea transport ship, this is naval unit off your starboard quarter, state your intention. Over."

Danielle grunted. "Naval unit off my starboard quarter, before I state my intention, I suggest that we address each other by simpler names. We don't have time for formalities. Over."

The ensuing pause concerned her, but then the man answered. "Call me 'Captain'. Over."

"Captain, call me 'Captain' as well. My intentions are my own, but I can accomplish them without a fatal one-for-one exchange. Over."

"Understood, Captain. I can accomplish my goals without a weapons exchange as well, but I can't let you depart without an agreement about your intentions. Over."

Part of her wanted to launch her weapons and send the man into the abyss, but her rational mind prevailed. "That may be a problem, Captain." Unsure of her next move, she deflected. "Is my English clear to you? Over."

"I was schooled at the University of Chicago, Captain. Am I coming across clearly? Over."

"Clearly, yes." She muted the phone. "Liam, have the Turkish translators listen from the control room. This guy wants to speak English, maybe as a show of strength, maybe as a gesture of peace. Not sure. But I'll let him continue.

"Understood, ma'am."

She checked icons showing each ship drifting towards a final separation outside half a nautical mile. Digesting the inevitability of her confinement, she ransacked her mind for ideas until one took root. She clicked the phone's key. "We should set rules of engagement, Captain. No need to destroy each other unless we mean to. Over."

The Turkish submarine's commander became stern. "Let me be perfectly clear, Captain. This may be a pleasant conversation over hair and nails to you, but this is deadly. I will not negotiate anything leading to my mission's failure, and I will not hesitate to commit to mutual destruction. Over."

She released her microphone and addressed Walker. "Hair and nails... I think he's torqued about dealing with a woman."

"A Turkish commander would be, but it may have been a jab to throw you off. Don't let it."

"Right." She keyed her microphone. "I won't hesitate either, Captain. If you take hostile action, I shoot back, and we all die. Over."

"Very well, Captain. I believe we understand one another. What do you propose? Over."

"As a first step, I suggest that we keep talking. Silence would create suspicion. Over."

"Agreed. We run communications checks every thirty seconds between conversations. Over."

"Agreed. I intend to take thirty seconds now to discuss options with my crew. Over."

"Understood, Captain. Over."

Danielle snapped into the headset boom by her jaw. "Liam, set up a twenty-five-second timer. Start it every time the Turkish captain and I finish speaking, and get my attention if it alarms. Dedicate two men to monitoring the alarm."

"Understood, ma'am. I'm setting up and staffing a timer for twenty-five seconds."

Focusing on the immediate crisis, Danielle ignored Jake's low-bandwidth teletype updates. She looked to Sergeui for an update and as a test of his alertness. "Where's Terry?"

The submarine officer passed the test, proving he'd remained alert to his duties. "We can't hear Terry. Too far. Jake broadcast say he seven miles. Terry turn and come for us, but slow."

The translator clarified. "Jake said Terry's battery was at six percent after his sprint. He's coming back towards us on his MESMA system, limited to five knots. They don't know of our predicament, though."

"I'm sure they don't."

"There's more. Maybe relevant. Dmitry is only twelve miles away, but he had to evade a torpedo and his battery is down to seven percent. Sergeui guesses that the submarine you're talking to is the one that shot at Dmitry."

Her adversary's will to kill was proven. "Shit. The man's not afraid to shoot."

"Be careful what you say, please. I didn't learn English to die under this accursed dome."

"And I didn't join the Royal Navy to die in a mercenary fleet, either." She keyed her microphone. "Captain, I propose that we avoid outside communications. If either of us inform our chains of command, we would be inviting unwanted interference. No floating of wires. No launching of buoys. Nothing but you and me talking. Over."

"Agreed. Over."

She remarked under her breath. "He's terse."

Sergeui shrugged.

"Never mind." She keyed her microphone. "I also propose that we keep our propellers at all-stop. I would consider your acceleration an attempted evasion and a prelude to an attack. Over."

A pause ensued as the Turk considered her offer. "Agreed. Over."

Danielle sought ideas. "Am I leaving anything out, guys? I only get one chance at this."

The Russians shrugged as Walker lamented in her headset. "I can't think of anything."

She keyed her microphone. "Do you have any demands, Captain? Over."

"Yes. I'm quite aware of your dolphins. I will blast active sonar at any dolphin I hear. I will deafen and attempt to bake them. Am I clear? Over."

Knowing the cetaceans were distant, she yielded the easy concession. "Clear. Agreed. Over." After lowering the underwater phone's handset, she sought additional input from her team. "Who's under the most time pressure here, me or him? I want opinions."

Surprising her, Sergeui answered first. "We have six MESMA. Energy forever. Him battery only. Him toxic air in days. Maybe hours depending. Oh, him flooding from dolphins. Need pump. Pump drain battery."

"Got it. What about mission deadlines? We're the ones trying to attack his countrymen, but he's only playing defense. That's our disadvantage."

From the control room, Walker answered. "He doesn't know our deadline. President Trump's slow reaction is thankfully buying us time. We really don't have a deadline yet, to be honest. Alarm! Twenty-five seconds."

She keyed her microphone. "Communications check. Over."

"Communications check acknowledged. Do you have more demands, Captain? Over."

"I'm in no hurry to issue orders, Captain. I can wait all day. Over."

"As can I, Captain. I'm sure you understand my mission parameters. Over."

She spoke to Walker. "Do you see an opening to talk about his mission? This is an information battle as much as tactical."

Walker perked up. "Yeah. Explore that!"

Keying her underwater phone, she took the opening. "Captain, you mentioned mission parameters. Do you have any demands of me? Over."

"Yes. I cannot let you transit farther to the north or to the east. Over."

"Understood. Over."

"Understood and what, Captain? Your understanding doesn't

mean compliance. Over."

"I've agreed to remain at all-stop. As have you, and I trust that agreement is still in place. Over."

He sounded irritated. "No semantic games, Captain. I meant about your ultimate intention. Over."

"I can accomplish my mission without farther transit to the north or to the east. Over."

Walker hissed. "Ah... okay. You're the captain."

She double-checked her muted microphone to avoid revealing her secrets. "It wasn't a complete lie. I can reach all the Turkish ships and some of their ground troops from here."

"He may doubt that. He's not aware of our lightweight rounds, but well played."

As if overhearing her executive officer's concerns, the Turk protested. "I find that hard to believe, Captain. Over."

She lowered her microphone and fell silent.

Walker prodded her. "Aren't you going to answer?"

Wondering where she drew her newfound strength, she felt like a badass within her own skin. "Let him feel the tension. Warn me at twenty-five seconds."

"Bloody hell, you have ice-water in your veins."

"Twenty-five seconds, Liam."

"Aye, ma'am... and now. Twenty-five seconds."

She lifted her microphone. "Communications check. Over."

"So, you're not answering me. Over."

"You didn't ask a question. Over."

As the Turk replied, the underwater connection broke. "I... holding... geometry in..."

"Liam, can you boost the sensitivity of this channel?"

"Increasing gain. It may get staticky."

"I'll deal with staticky." She shifted her voice to the underwater phone. "Say again all. Over."

The Turk's voice was stern but slower, and the promised static created an annoying hiss. "I will hold you to that. But I am concerned about holding our relative geometry. As a submarine officer, you know that changes in depth, aspects, and angles can give one of us an advantage. Over."

Walker balked. "He recognized your accent and knows the Brits didn't commission female submarine officers until five years ago. It's another jab to throw you off."

"Understood, Liam." She ignored the jab and responded. "Captain, I can deploy my outboard motors to hold us in a locked geometry. That would remove the variable of random relative motions."

Fifteen seconds of hesitation suggested the Turk's doubt, but he broke the silence. "Explain the procedure. Over."

"I will deploy four outboard motors to hold our relative positions. You'll drift with the current and rotate freely without steerageway, but my motors will hold me in a geosynchronous orbit around you, always seeing the same side of my ship, like the moon to the earth. Over."

"How long to do this? Over."

"Less than one minute. Over."

"Agreed. Deploy your outboards. Over."

Unsure if she should interpret the statement as an order or an agreement, she accepted it without challenge. "I will deploy my outboards. I'm sure you'll hear them. Over."

"Understood. Over."

She called to Walker. "I trust you're already on this, Liam?"

"Ready and waiting. One icon away from it."

Under the red light, she raised her voice to the open microphone to remind her crew of her presence. "Lower all outboards."

Walker answered over the bridge's circuit. "I'm lowering all outboards. All outboards are lowered."

"Very well." She addressed the submarine. "My outboards are lowered, Captain. Over."

"Understood. Over."

Her executive officer qualified the ship's abilities. "I'm staffing a console with our best cargo loading operator. This'll be manual work since our outboards are automated only with respect to objects we can detect in our cargo bay."

Walker's comment about the limitation sparked a bold idea, and she made note to develop it between verbal volleys with the Turkish commander. "Very well. I didn't overstate our abilities, did I?"

"To hear our outboard operator speak, he can handle it in his sleep. He's playing with a couple outboards now."

Like whispering a confession, she lowered her voice. "Can we sneak out an advantage here by opening range or changing our aspect a small amount that the Turk wouldn't notice?"

"No, ma'am. I recommend you double-check with Sergeui about placing the *Preveze* at a disadvantage, but there's nothing we can gain as an advantage for ourselves. And... alarm. Twenty-five seconds."

"Understood." She called out to the Turk. "Communications check. Over."

"Communications check acknowledged. I recommend relaxing these checks to two minutes. Over."

"I propose five minutes. There's no need to force unnecessary conversations, and we can police each through our sonar systems. Over."

"Agreed. Five minutes. Over."

She released the underwater phone's key. "Liam, reset the timer to four minutes, fifty-five seconds."

"I've reset the timer to... shit."

"What's wrong?"

"Check your incoming data stream from Jake."

Wanting to continue ignoring the American's repeated request for her status, she yielded to Walker's prodding and found interesting news. "I assume you're referring to Jake's order to cease movement towards Turkey's national water or its ground forces."

"Exactly, ma'am."

"Well, lucky us. We're already obeying him by being stuck in this forsaken Turkish dance. But I thought we conceded that the CIA is listening to his broadcasts? His order is essentially Jake's open defiance. I can't see him doing that while his wife's in custody."

"Good point, ma'am. He knows Olivia's sniffing his orders. I've got a few theories brewing in me head, but I don't like any of them."

Danielle drew a dangerous conclusion. "Me neither. I think I know what's happening."

"I'm all ears."

"He's using us as a bargaining chip, and his timing couldn't be any worse."

CHAPTER 19

As he studied Olivia's list of targets, Jake disbelieved her audacity. Some targets were military, but most were components of the Turkish economy.

Since she knew about his fleet's recent attacks on Greek natural gas assets, he recognized her tactic of incremental commitment. Olivia's list covered similar types of Turkish targets–pipelines, pumping stations, and processing plants–but more of them than the mercenaries had attacked in Greece. Jake suspected she'd pile on civilian targets of the *Goliath's* railguns, if the transport ship survived to do her bidding.

By raising the stakes in Turkey, she pulled him into a slow escalation of his personal limits, and he wondered how far she'd go.

After ordering his fleet to cease motion towards Turkey, he glared at her in his console and lied. "I just forwarded your targets' coordinates to my fleet."

"I didn't order an attack yet. That was a preparatory list."

Fearing the *Goliath's* demise and Olivia's endgame, Jake played poker against the CIA's best. He tapped a nervous toe against the tiled floor, trying to deflect, stall, or do whatever rainmakers did when yammering. "I know that, but they need to envision the attacks and start analyzing them. They need to start plotting courses to move Danielle into position and then figure out where Terry and Dmitry should be to protect her."

"That's your job."

"In case you forgot, I'm new at this and landed here against my will." A silent clock ticked in Jake's mind, counting down until his sneaky cease-motion order reached Olivia, assuming she'd truly tapped into the network between his command center and his fleet.

"Shouldn't you find the *Goliath* before giving it orders?"

He compounded his lying by feigning unwarranted confidence. "The *Goliath* isn't sunk. I'm just having trouble communicating. You know that submarines can't always broadcast due to tactical restraints."

"You need to do better."

"Why don't you help me find it? Why not tell me what the American submarine that's spying on us heard during Terry's torpedo exchange."

"That was a rookie's demand. Pierre really left a chump in charge."

He'd grown callous to her repeated stabs. "How about some aerial reconnaissance, then? Do you see the *Goliath* floating on fire somewhere? Or maybe, just maybe, you can tell me where the damned *Preveze* is. Dmitry damaged it, but I don't know if it's sunk, skulking home, or still fighting."

"Find the *Goliath* and put it where it belongs." She reached towards the display, and it went blank.

In silence, Jake's tired mind wrestled for understanding. The slow escalation from military targets to economic infrastructure was logical in countering the Turkish advance, but it bothered him. He questioned how quickly Olivia would order him to rain down shells over the one-million-plus inhabitants of Mersin.

He feared how quickly she'd turn Turkish sentiment, even international sentiment, against his fleet.

Then, he realized her endgame.

She wasn't just using Renard's fleet. She was destroying it.

"Bitch."

The final outcome would establish her as the CIA's queen, the one who resolved an international catastrophe by setting up a mutual win for Turkey and the United States.

That meant establishing a common enemy and defeating it.

Renard's Mercenary Fleet.

She'd lose her quasi-personal navy, but her power would grow beyond needing Renard anymore. Done with her decade-long power struggle with the Frenchman, she was discarding him, his crews, and selected family members.

She's poised the fleet as a sacrifice to the *Lincoln* battle group, the Turkish fleet, or both. When the clashing nations could focus on Renard's armada as a common enemy, tensions between the NATO allies would ebb, politicians would take credit, of which Olivia would grab a royal ransom's worth.

She'd gone mad with power.

Quick bursts of text arrived from his submarines, jostling Jake from his revelations of his former lover. He prayed for good news while examining the incoming messages.

Volkov reported a half-charged battery and his slow, snorkeling trek as he brought the *Wraith* towards the datum of the *Specter's* attack on the *Burakreis*. Then, after ordering Cahill to report, Jake learned the *Specter's* battery was at forty percent while snorkeling back towards the hostile exchange's datum.

Jake spoke under his breath. "At least I have two submarines." He inhaled while drawing courage for his next order. Instead of typing it, he recorded his voice to convey his conviction.

"Olivia's ordering us to attack civilian targets. When we did this in Greece, we defined our own limits. But she's got a big list, and I'm sure it's designed to inflict too many civilian casualties and make us look like villains. She wants to make us into a common enemy for America and Turkey, and that means we're already dead unless we fight back. So, we're going to disengage from the Turks and unite our forces to make the Americans think twice before taking us down."

He paused his monologue, gathered his next thoughts, and continued. "I don't know if the *Goliath* is still alive, but I will issue orders assuming so. If it's not, the orders still stand for Dmitry and Terry. Since I suspect this communication channel is compromised, I'll give coordinates with our agreed-upon secret number, which everyone but Dmitry knows. Don't worry Dmitry, I've got a number for you."

He stopped again, called up a chart, and guessed the location of the American armada. Stationing his ships at the *Lincoln* battle group's assumed southeastern flank, he wanted his small fleet halfway between Cyprus and Port Said.

Then he set himself to solving math problems. After a minute of crunching numbers and checking his calculations, he dictated the cryptic coordinates into an audio file.

"I'm giving coordinates where I want the *Goliath* stationed. That's our ground zero. Terry, I'll want you four miles line-of-site range from ground zero bearing two-seven-zero. Dmitry, four miles line-of-site range from ground zero bearing three-one-five. Here come the encoded coordinates."

He started with the Anglophones. "For Terry and Danielle, multiply the following base numbers by our secret number. Round up to the sixth decimal place for the ground zero's coordinates. Your base numbers are one-point-four-four-three-two-three-two-five-one-seven north and one-point-zero-six-five-two-four-two-six-zero east."

Next was Volkov, but Jake wanted a layer of confusion to slow his eavesdroppers. He walked to the leftmost monitor and hailed Renard's bunker.

Devouring a piece of salmon on toast, Alain LeClerc answered. "Jake! I was going to hail you. Andrew Causey complied with your request! I've sent his response to your FBI man through one of Pierre's men in Washington. Mister Jennings should meet a new friend outside his entrance to work this morning."

Appreciating Renard's network, the one that had found him fifteen years earlier, Jake shook his head in silence awe.

LeClerc continued. "Commander Causey also suggested three other service academy graduates who've taken jobs in federal law enforcement. I'm reaching out them. Causey was eager to help!"

Knowing that one classmate stood by him comforted Jake. "Great work, Alain. I need another favor, though. Can you get me a Russian translator quickly?"

"In Pierre's world, translators grow on trees. There's one in the house, not far, I think."

Write this down. I'll type it after I dictate it so that you can triple-check it later."

The Frenchman set aside his food and lifted a pencil and pad. "Okay. Go ahead."

Jake dictated. "I want the translator to record an audio file of this in Russian that I can send to Dmitry. Here goes. Ready?"

"Yes! Go!"

"Dmitry, multiply the following base numbers by the number of holes I put into the *Krasnodar* with my slow-kill weapon the day I met you with the *Specter*. Round up to the sixth decimal place for ground-zero's coordinates. Your base numbers are two-point-five-five-three-four-one-one-three-eight-five north and two-point-four-eight-eight-four-six-zero-zero-zero east."

Wide-eyed, LeClerc scribbled notes and showed them to Jake.

"Perfect. Your handwriting is impeccable. No need for a follow-up note. Just make sure the numbers are correct after the translation and then email me the audio file."

"Consider it done. Twenty minutes maybe?"

"Make it ten." Jake shut off the connection and then returned to his working console.

When the leftmost console chimed minutes later, Jake stepped to it and answered.

LeClerc appeared. "I've emailed you the audio file. The Russian translator double-checked it, but I'm having it sent to another of translator to verify. I assume if it's wrong you can simply rebroadcast it?"

"Not simply, but yeah. That's a good verification. Thanks, Alain."

"My pleasure. I'll keep reaching out to your service academy network with Commander Causey's stamp of approval. I should have something soon for you."

Jake dismissed LeClerc and returned to his console. Before broadcasting, he added another audio order. "Terry, race ahead to ground zero and sweep for enemies. If you run into anything that smells like an American surface combatant, put a slow-kill in it. Let them piss their pants and then get some damage control training. That'll be our first and last warning. If you run into an American submarine, use a limpet. No heavyweights unless we're forced."

His heart sank with the next order. "Dmitry, check on Danielle on the way. Give yourself two hours to search for the *Goliath* and then continue to the rendezvous. God willing, they're still alive."

Jake broadcast the audio files and waited for the consequences. While doing so, he decided to nap, having been awake for a day and a half. He marched to the vault and knocked.

The control center's other inhabitant opened the door.

"Commander Laurent, I need some privacy."

"Of course. I'll monitor events for you."

Strolling into the room after Laurent stepped out, Jake left the door open to overhear sounds in the control center. He also dialed up the volume of the two consoles within the vault to roust him if his commanders hailed him.

He flopped onto the foldout bed and lay atop its blanket. Sleep overcame him, but then he awoke a seeming instant later. Checking the clock, he noticed he'd slept forty minutes.

As he cleared his head, he heard Laurent calling to him. "You have a call from Pierre's bunker."

Jake darted to the console and accepted LeClerc's call. "What's going on?"

"Great news! I have Mister Colvert here from the FBI's office in Lyon. Your classmate sent him here via helicopter with a phone that's encrypted with the FBI's security."

The suited man standing beside LeClerc looked young. "I'm just the messenger, sir. I don't know the details about your situation and don't need to know. But I must hold the phone and observe the conversation between you and Agent Jennings. Are you ready for Agent Jennings?"

Jake's heart burst with hope, and his throat tightened. "Yes."

Colvert extended the phone towards the screen, revealing the hard lines of Jennings face. "So, it's true. You really are part of that mercenary fleet."

"It's me. I can't say how much I appreciate this, Mike."

"Four years by the bay, my friend. I won't waste your time. I can't believe your claims until I see for myself, and I'm light-years from getting a warrant to break into your wife's hotel room. But I have eyes and ears on the ground investigating. So far, the hotel room is impenetrable by audio, visual, or thermal. That tells me that professionals are holed up in there, and it has a CIA smell to it."

"Can't you just break in and rescue her?"

"No, sorry. I need more evidence to act."

"So, it's just another standoff."

"Until we get evidence and can start acting. I see this as a possible kidnapping and hostage scenario. And since it's supposedly the CIA, my boss is working backchannels for info. That could take a while, since we hate sharing secrets across agencies. My bosses are also reaching out to Aman in Israel to verify the captivity of Lieutenant Commander Ariella Dahan."

"This is asinine."

"I know, but I've got to be honest. Accusing the CIA of foul play against you and Renard is a tough sell. But since your wife's an American citizen, I'm using my jurisdiction to investigate her disappearance and abduction across state lines. We'll also learn how much Aman cares about Dahan if they pressure the CIA."

"You believe me, don't you, Mike? When I say my wife's held hostage, I can't see a scenario where I'd make that up."

"You've done some nasty shit in your life, Jake. You've also done good work, too, per the rumors. But I can only extend my trust to an investigation, and I must consider Olivia McDonald and the CIA innocent until the evidence says otherwise. But you have my commitment to a balls-out investigation."

Jake appreciated the sentiment but rejected its sufficiency. "When I say I'll kill Americans, you believe me, don't you?"

"The sailors and marines on those ships have no idea what's going on. Don't kill them for doing their jobs."

Jake reaffirmed his conviction. "If I allow myself one moment of weakness on this commitment, Olivia will see through it."

"I can't negotiate a hostage situation if you're shooting shells and torpedoes at the *Lincoln* battle group."

"Why not? I can always threaten to kill more of them if we need a bargaining chip."

"Careful with that."

"Do you want to believe my conviction or not?"

Jennings looked away, processing the question. "I believe you, but don't do anything irreversible until we talk again."

"You mean like taking out three Turkish submarines? I've got my back against the wall, and I'm being manipulated into irreversible decisions."

"I've made this a top priority, but it's dicey when one agency points a finger at another."

Having recorded his check-ins, Jake had an idea. "Would a video of my wife being held against her will help?"

"It would, if she makes the right claims. Your note from Andy Causey didn't mention that you had access to video."

"I wasn't sure it would help. I've got a lot on my mind. By the way, you'll need translators for Aramaic."

"Understood. Send it to my operative in Renard's bunker, and I'll have it analyzed. If your wife claims kidnapping and captivity on video, it would be enough for a warrant, but don't get your hopes up. The CIA knows this game, and I'm sure they told her what not to say."

Jake recalled the conversations and agreed. Then he had an idea. "If Linda could say she was captive in a live video feed, and you had access to it, could you act?"

"Definitely. You got something in mind?"

"Not yet. I was hoping you've been through this enough times to have an idea."

"If she claimed her captivity in your video, that would be enough for the warrant, but that might trigger a backlash from her captors."

"I don't want to put her in worse danger." Jake thought further and added his next idea. "What if her message was masked enough that you could unravel it immediately, but her captors would need a few minutes?"

"I think it's a stretch. I can't put a secret code in front of a judge. Even if I did, I don't see how a judge would unravel it faster than CIA experts."

"Not a code, but how about a mix of Arabic and Aramaic? You could have one Chaldean Iraqi translator turn it into English in seconds. The CIA would be caught off guard because we haven't used Arabic yet."

Jennings' eyes narrowed. "Maybe. We'd have to coordinate the timing and have a judge, translator, and an infiltration team standing by, which I can handle on my end. But I'd need a solid plan to set it up, and don't see how you'd tell her what to say without them cutting her off before she could make her claim."

Jake snorted. "I've got an idea."

"I'm listening."

"My mother-in-law. If I played a recording of Linda's mother instructing her while switching languages in mid-sentence like she always does, in her thick accent and particular dialects, Linda would get it instantly. But CIA translators would need to rewind a few times."

Jennings's eyes angled away in thought before he answered. "That's actually worth a shot. But we'd only get one chance at it. I can use FBI Aramaic and Arabic speakers to handle this instead of burdening your mother-in-law."

"I'd prefer the personal touch. I want Linda to know the words are from her mother. They have that way of communicating, little slang words and inflections, that will throw off listeners. And I think the CIA would allow the video."

"Really?"

"Olivia McDonald. She'd do anything to avoid looking weak, and she's allowed all foreign languages during check-ins so far. She might permit a quick recorded note to Linda from her mother."

"Roger that. If she does, we roll with it. If not, we'll work a

Plan B. Where can I find Linda's mother?"

"She's got a dress shop in Ferndale, Michigan. Can you send someone there to shop for wedding dress?"

"Consider it done. I'll make sure your mother-in-law knows the right words to say. And I'll have her instruct Linda to say them as a mix of Aramaic and Arabic to slow down the CIA when she claims her captivity. I'll have my translators, or a damned good trilingual Chaldean translator, with the judge for immediate translation and issuing of the warrant."

"I can't thank you enough, Mike."

"It's my duty and my pleasure, Jake."

"Anything else for me?"

"No. I'll put things in motion. Again, I urge you, nothing irreversible."

"It's just saber-rattling for now, but my ships will defend themselves. I'm not just a victim here. I'm the commodore of the mercenary fleet. Please hurry before I'm forced to prove it."

CHAPTER 20

Like déjà vu, the master chief confessed an agitated crew. "Sir, the men are restless."

Tired from an exhausting hour drifting in lockstep with the *Goliath*, Dogan grunted. "That means they're paying attention."

The tiny man leaned into his commander's ear. "There's talk of cowardice, taking orders from a woman who's not even representing an accursed legitimate navy."

Dogan glared at the veteran. "What's your opinion?"

"I don't speak enough English to know what's being said, but I don't like her treating you like your equal."

Inhaling to calm his rising ire, Dogan planned his next careful steps. "You're right. I'll put an end to this." The timer on the nearest screen showed two and half minutes until his next phone check with the *Goliath*, but he asserted himself and grabbed the underwater phone's handset. "Captain, do you have a Turkish translator?"

The female commanding officer, a surprise replacement for Terrance Cahill, held her ground. "I'm concerned about you asking that, Captain. That question suggests a change in our communication protocols. Over."

Certain he could squeeze a few ounces from his bladder, he fibbed. "I need use to the toilet. I want my executive officer to handle communications while I tend to that. Over."

She impressed him with a rapid counter. "We've both honored the ground rules. I propose a thirty-minute break from communications. Over."

"Agreed. Thirty minutes starting now. Over."

Dogan faced his master chief. "I made her back off. Start a thirty-minute timer. Have the corpsman meet me in my quarters, and have all off-watch personnel meet in the crew's dining area."

"I'll see to it, sir."

The *Preveze's* commander marched to his stateroom and shut the door. Clearing his mind while voiding his bladder, he felt dark doubts clawing at him.

Victim. Victim. Victim.

Quelling his inner demons, he whispered. "Never again a helpless victim. I am a warrior."

When finished, he skipped the steps of flushing and washing his hands, following his own orders of water preservation while stranded in the standoff.

He sat at his foldout table and reached towards his safe. While he twisted dials and clicked open the latch, the corpsman knocked.

"Come."

Senior Chief Asker moved with an uncomfortable caution. "You wanted me, sir."

Dogan kicked his guest chair towards the corpsman. "Sit."

Asker sat and remained quiet.

"What's wrong with you?"

"Nothing, sir. Other than a deadly standoff that has everyone rightly terrified, I'm doing quite well. I'm not regretting for a second forgoing a peaceful retirement for this."

Dogan snorted. "Fair enough. Maybe I'm being too cavalier. I can't tell. There's no protocol for this. No knowing what's right or wrong. I don't know if I should negotiate peace with that woman or send us all to the afterlife."

The opening encouraged Dogan's confidant. "That's the problem. She's a woman, and she's operating well beyond any bounds I understand. I know we have women in our own Navy, but call me old-fashioned."

"It's not 'old-fashioned' I'm worried about. It's zealotry."

"Understood, sir. I do hear... well, I'm sure you can imagine what's being said, especially by the younger sailors."

Gripping the handle of his Ruger Nine Millimeter pistol,

Dogan retrieved it from the safe and strapped its belt around his waist.

"What are you doing?"

"Commanding my ship. And you're going to help me, unless you want to side with the potential mutiny."

"I'm always with you. Even in this disaster."

"Then act. I need you."

"How?"

Dogan lifted the lanyard holding his key to the *Preveze's* gun locker over his head and extended it.

Asker raised his palms. "I can't."

"I'm not asking you to arm yourself, only the right men."

Trembling, the corpsman accepted the lanyard.

"Find twelve men with the courage and sense to follow me. In fact, I bet you already know who they are. List some names now."

Asker hesitated. "Sir, I–"

"You want to stay alive or die a martyr's death, whichever is appropriate, correct?"

"To be honest, I prefer the former."

"As do I. But we must face reality. The names."

Asker announced four sailors Dogan recognized as men who valued loyalty over other sentiments.

"Stop there. On my authority, place each of the first four in charge of a group of three. They know you have my confidence, and my gun locker key will serve as a marker if they doubt you. Wait. Let's bolster that. Take a photograph of me giving you the lanyard."

Asker withdrew his phone and took a shaking selfie.

"Now, who are your next eight men?"

The next four names invoked images of loyal men, but they were newer arrivals to the *Preveze* and worthy of modest doubt. The last four were young men too scared to choose a side, but Dogan expected them to join the loyalists when promised firearms.

"I want four groups of three stationed with pistols in the engine room, auxiliary machinery room, torpedo room, and control room. They'll shoot anyone who revolts, aiming first to injure–legs and abdomens. If anyone still resists, the loyalists will shoot to kill."

"Sir, this is too much."

Dogan uttered the words naval commanders feared saying outside of training scenarios. "Deadly force is authorized."

"Uh…"

"Are you hearing me?"

Asker's throat was tight. "Deadly force is authorized, aye, sir."

"After you distribute twelve pistols with spare magazines to the first four loyalists, you'll prepare syringes with tranquilizers, strong enough to put down an elephant, and distribute one to each loyalist."

"I like that better than shooting people."

"Have the first four and the control trio ignore my order of meeting in the crew's dining area. Have them instead take their guard posts in the compartments I mentioned with weapons for the other eight. Tell the rest to head to their guard posts after they attend my crew's meeting. Got it?"

"I'll take care of it, sir." Asker departed.

Alone, Dogan contemplated his personal hell and questioned how he'd landed on a razor's edge. Giving time for his orders to unfold and reverse the rising revolt, he distracted himself with tactical considerations.

Time was his ally while he pinned down the *Goliath*. With the transport ship's railguns submerged, they were fangless vipers. Every minute locked in the stalemate was a minute his nation's military machine marched into forsaken lands in Syria.

But with the *Preveze* submerged, every resource for his survival died a slow death.

Time was also his enemy.

Lifting water from the bilges, his drain pump devoured the ship's main battery's reserves faster than the atmosphere-cleaning machines. If nothing changed, carbon dioxide poisoning would kill him and his crew, unless the incoming downspouts dragged them first to their watery graves.

Victim. Victim. Victim.

Not a victim. Submarine commander.

He wondered what allowed the *Goliath's* commanding officer's patience. Per his reckoning, she had orders to send railgun rounds into the Turkish military machine—surface ships, aircraft on runways, or ground forces driving through Syria. Her tolerance of remaining locked in a spiraling death dance stymied him.

He abandoned hope of unraveling that mystery while seated in his quarters, and his thoughts returned to the innards of his submarine.

He pondered a ploy and removed the bullets from a spare magazine and then exchanged it with the loaded one. He tucked the unloaded Ruger's barrel into the web belt under his lower back.

As multiple footsteps shuffled outside his locked door, Dogan reached into his safe and withdrew the binder with his orders and then tucked them under his arm.

When the *Preveze* seemed quiet, he strode to the dining area with his unloaded pistol and his mission orders.

The banter fell as he appeared before his crew.

Inviting honest answers, Dogan leaned against a bulkhead to hide the Ruger. "Stand up if you wish to declare me a coward."

In a sea of uncomfortable gestures, a young sailor with angry eyes stood. "You cow to a woman! How can you?"

As others drew inspiration from the young dissident, they rose from their seats.

With a sideways glance, Dogan looked to his master chief for interference.

Courageous, the tiny man met the challenge. "You've just committed an act of insubordination, sailor, and you're one step from mutiny."

With that single comment, the rising men hesitated. Some remained half-standing while others returned to their seats. But the defiant youngster remained standing.

The master chief then faced his commander and pushed himself to the edge of disrespect. "But others aboard this ship agree with this sailor's accusation, and I recommend that the captain answers."

Silence enveloped the dining area.

"Very well." Dogan met the young sailor's stare. "How do you understand the present mission I'm leading on the *Preveze*?"

Caught off guard, the youngster floundered. "We kill infidels." Showing himself a cut above a mindless martyr, the sailor qualified his statement. "Although I don't know all the details, I do know that courage and valor are necessities to carry out our duties. But I see only stalling and talking."

Dogan let the man finish but immediately pounced. "I respect your opinion. Will you allow my defense?"

The youngster remained standing in defiance, but his posture betrayed his stayed aggression. "Yes."

Teetering on mutiny's edge, the master chief intervened. "That's 'yes, sir', sailor. Leave yourself an opening to back down, lad."

"Yes, sir."

Casting his eyes over the twenty men before him, the master chief continued. "That goes for everyone. The captain stands accused, but he is our captain unless legal fault is found against him. You will hear him out."

Several supporters and undecided sailors gave the *Preveze's* commander hope. "Yes, master chief."

Dogan addressed the standing sailor. "We kill infidels, yes. Ultimately, diplomacy fails, and we must go to war." He withdrew his pistol from his back and held its barrel. "Here. Catch." He lobbed it to the sailor, who gasped and caught it. "And here are my orders." The *Preveze's* commander slid the binder from under his arm and handed it to the nearest man. "Pass that to him."

In astonished silence, the standing sailor held the Ruger and the orders.

Dogan continued. "On page three you'll see a summary of my

orders. Read it."

The youngster's eyes flitted across the page.

"What did you glean from them, sailor?"

"We are to prevent any enemy's maritime forces from reaching attack range of our surface fleet and our ground forces in Syria."

"Was there a priority?"

"Yes, sir. Protect the ground forces first. All naval assets are expendable to protect ground forces."

"There were also lists of possible threats, such as the American *Lincoln* battle group, but the Israelis, Egyptians, Greeks, and even that mercenary fleet were listed too, right?"

"Yes, sir. But this proves my point. We're expendable. We need to behave as such."

"Believe me, lad, I would very much enjoy being the captain who sacrificed himself to protect his people and rid the planet of the *Goliath*. But should I sacrifice this ship and its crew when I can accomplish my mission otherwise?"

"I don't know how you can, sir. We're unable to maneuver. We can't move."

"Nor can the *Goliath*. Last I checked, its railguns don't work under water."

"You can't keep us here forever, sir. We're slowly dying."

"No, I can't, but we have the upper hand. Our troops are gaining ground as we speak. And since the Americans tasked the *Goliath* to fight in their stead, the Americans have shown an unwillingness to intervene for themselves. Therefore, the longer we delay the *Goliath*, the longer we protect our troops, and the more successful we become in our mission."

"But it's not complete until it's complete, sir. There's a simple way to complete it, and that's with a torpedo."

The master chief intervened. "Careful to whom you attempt to give orders, sailor."

Dogan raised his palm. "It's okay, master chief. For his sake, I'll take the sailor's opinion as a recommendation–not an order." He turned back to the dissident. "I don't deny that a torpedo would work. But instead of breaking their ships and bodies, I prefer to wrestle with them, right here in this deplorable scenario, and break their wills."

The youngster's eyes betrayed a glimmer of respect.

Dogan continued. "We are unbreakable because we are defending our people and our way of life. They are greedy mercenaries working for profit. Shame on us if we can't outlast them."

Digesting his new perspective, the young sailor handed the weapon and the mission brief to a junior officer. "I hadn't considered that."

"You need to, son." Dogan eyed his crew. "All of you do."

The former dissident met his captain's stare. "It's possible that I was out of line, sir."

As the junior officer brought the weapon and mission brief to his commander, Dogan accepted them. "Yes, it is. And you were. Now sit with your fellow crewman, sailor."

The youngster obeyed.

Dogan raised his voice. "All of you will continue your duties until this battle is over. All of you will demonstrate unbreakable wills." He stared down the disarmed dissident. "If we survive, you'll see me for an administrative hearing. I suggest you brace yourself for reduced pay, a reduction in rank, and scullery duty."

Newfound respect filled the eyes of the *Preveze's* crew, and then Dogan noticed his corpsman in the passageway. "Approach."

Senior Chief Asker approached. "Sir?"

Dogan leaned into the corpsman's ear. "Status on the guards?"

"They're stationed, sir. Three in the control room. One each elsewhere awaiting the others."

Dogan faced his men. "I have armed guards stationed throughout the ship. I've authorized deadly force against any potential mutineer. Do your duties, show strong wills, and then I'll relax that order. Until then, your fates are in your hands. Everyone back to your stations."

After clearing his head during his walk to his quarters, Dogan put the bullets back into his weapon and donned the Ruger's belt. Armed, he went to the control room and spied three loyal guards in the humid steel jungle.

His executive officer accosted him. "What's going on with the guards?"

"Didn't you just forget a word?"

The executive officer frowned. "Sir?"

"Yes, that was the word you forgot. Rephrase your question with military bearing if you want an answer."

"What's going on with the guards, sir?"

"They're here on my orders, which I suggest you obey along with everyone else on this ship."

"Of course, sir."

"How much time is left on my thirty-minute count?"

"Six minutes, sir."

Unwilling to wait, Dogan sought decisive action to maintain the momentum of regaining his crew's confidence.

Annoyed with the incessant downpour, he stepped around a guard to the conning platform and grabbed the underwater phone. "Captain, I intend to perform welding operations. It will be loud, but I believe now is the appropriate time. Over."

The *Goliath's* commanding officer's compliance shocked him. "Agreed. I concur with your welding operations. Over."

Unsure why she'd allowed the risk of attracting unwanted listeners to their stalemate, Dogan accepted the gift. "Executive officer, reset the communications clock to five minutes and get a welding team up here. We're going to make a lot of noise."

"I'm resetting the communications clock to five minutes and will assemble a welding team, sir."

"Very well."

Letting himself internalize the rapid developments within his flesh and within his ship, Dogan moved to his foldout captain's chair and sat.

Before relaxation could free his muscles from tension, the *Goliath's* commander stupefied him. Her tone was inviting. "Captain, I have a proposition. Over."

Dogan stood and reached for the handset. "Very well. I'm listening, Captain. Over."

"I no longer represent my prior employers. I identify myself as Danielle Sutton, commanding officer of the mercenary vessel, *Goliath*, and I offer my services to the Turkish Navy in standing against its American enemies. Over."

CHAPTER 21

Danielle's heart raced.

When the Turkish commander answered, his tone was level. "I understand, Captain. I can't answer yet, but I will consider your proposal. You're demanding a lot of trust. Over."

She keyed her microphone. "Understood. Over."

Walker's voice entered her ear. "He'll probably want to raise an antenna and bring your offer to his fleet."

She responded in the boom receiver at her jaw. "Liam, get up here. I'm tired of talking into three different microphones."

"On my way, ma'am."

Tapping an icon, she unlocked the door for Walker's entry to the bridge. Then she slid off her headset and dangled it on a hook.

Quiet footsteps brought her Australian rock to her side. "Quite a day we're having, huh?"

"It's fantastic, except for buddying up with my former enemy to attack history's fiercest battle group."

"I didn't say it was necessarily a good day."

"And my former enemy is far from saying 'yes'. Unless he's a simpleton, his mind's a beehive right now."

"Not to overstep any bounds, but did you come up with that offer by yourself? I didn't see it in Jake's feed. He doesn't know about our predicament, unless the *Wraith* or *Specter* has found us and figured it out."

She smirked. "It came to me, and I bounced the idea off Sergeui."

The Russian shrugged. "Sound good to me. What we lose?"

"Just asking… you guys didn't think to ask me?"

Danielle was honest. "If I asked you, I knew you'd talk me out of it."

Walker folded his arms. "I might have. So, now what?"

"We wait."

"You don't want to invite the Turk to periscope depth with us so that we can both phone home?"

"Not yet. Let's see if he's as sly as I hope."

"Sly?" Walker scowled. "You're working well over my head on this, ma'am."

"Call it woman's intuition."

"If whatever you're concocting works, I'll call it a miracle."

The Turkish captain's voice was somewhat garbled. "Captain, I'm beginning welding operations. Over."

She protested. "Captain, before you announce our presence to the entire Mediterranean Sea, may I share an idea with you? Over."

Walker eyed her. "You asked him for permission. That was intentional?"

She wanted to quell Walker's ongoing commentary, but she welcomed his challenges to warn her of missteps. "That's still woman's intuition."

"Right. I'm not equipped for that."

Over the underwater phone, the Turk answered. "If your idea is about joining forces, Captain, I'm hesitant. Explain yourself. Over."

"I won't ask you to attack Americans. I only ask to appear united against them. I want to make a show, release you, and then let you go about your business. Over."

"Explain what you mean by a show and releasing me? Over."

"We'll put you in my cargo bed, surface, and show a united front to the Americans. It would help both our causes. Over."

"Why in your cargo bed? Over."

"To hunt the Americans three times faster than you can on your own power. The Americans would know that. But we can't make noise to reveal ourselves under water, or else an American anti-submarine asset will ruin everything. Over."

"Understood. I will delay welding while I consider this. But I make no promise to yielding control of my ship. Over."

"To be blunt, Captain. This is a win for you. Over."

"You presume much. How so? Over."

"You can claim this stalemate as a victory. Nobody in your chain of command needs to know my mission changed. You can say you found me and then scared me into turning back. Over."

"Only a coward would turn back from our stalemate. Over."

"Then declare me a coward. I'm a woman who took over this ship by accident after a disgraceful exit from the Royal Navy. Over."

"You have a point. Over."

"I will say the opposite to the Americans. I will claim that I convinced you to join us. If you're in my cargo bed, the threat is real enough for them to honor. Over."

She expected a hesitation that never materialized as the Turk flowed with her dialogue. "Three diesel submarines and your *Goliath* may sound powerful, but these are the sort of nuisances a carrier battle group trains to destroy. Over."

"Agreed, but four submerged torpedo launchers are enough to make the Americans hesitate. We would test their wills. Over."

The flowing conversation yielded to a stagnant pause.

Walker broke the silence. "I don't think you offended him. Not sure why he's silent all of a sudden."

"I didn't offend him. Something I said struck a chord."

When he recommenced the dialogue, the Turk spoke with reverence. "You wish to break the Americans' will? Over."

Enthusiasm overpowered her attempts at stoicism. "Got him! Damn it, Liam. I've got him! He wants to team up. Did you hear it in his voice?"

"Uh... not really."

Crediting herself with recognizing the verbal subtlety that Walker's male DNA denied him hearing, she keyed the phone's handset. "Exactly, Captain. I know we can do it. Over."

"I find your request logical, but you're asking for great trust. Your fleet's tactics are known. You've captured unwilling submarines before, such as the *Krasnodar*. That creates an unacceptable risk of me appearing as a victim. Over."

She muted her microphone. "Shit!"

Walker tried to encourage her. "Don't give up, Danielle. You've still got him. We can propose some mitigation. Something."

Hearing her first name signaled her unofficial acceptance into the fleet. "I'm open to ideas. I'll stall, but we need to hurry." She keyed the phone. "Understood, Captain. I am assessing ways to mitigate that for you. Over."

"Understood. Over."

Fearing her advantage slipping away, she found a clueless expression in her executive officer's face.

But the bantering Russians caught her interest.

"Gentlemen?"

They continued, louder.

She barked. "Gentlemen!"

Sergeui's face revealed consternation, and she feared the Russian would shit himself during his internal battle of ideas. Before his bowels released, his face lit up. "Sergeui hero!"

She glared at him. "Quickly, Sergeui."

"Might work. We... *suka blyat*." He grabbed the translator's shoulders and rattled off his idea.

Struggling to keep up, the interpreter uttered broken phrases. "Let the *Preveze* launch a torpedo..." He added his own opinion. "I already don't like that."

"Translate without the commentary."

"Sorry... short range... one hundred yards. Close enough to kill the *Preveze* if detonated. Far enough to load into our bed. But not in our bed exactly. Cradled against two hydraulic arms. But not the arms. Their structural connection to the hull. Starboard hull. By our ears. Oh, I'm afraid he's rambling."

She had hung on every word. "I understand. Keep translating!"

"He says the torpedo will be connected to a wire on the *Preveze*. Same danger as a torpedo in the *Preveze's* tubes, but a visible sign to Turkey that he negotiated with us. We tell the Americans it's a sign of trust between us our new ally."

"Damn it, that's brilliant, Sergeui."

The Russian officer beamed. "I told you. Hero!"

"Can it be done, Liam?"

"I am trying my hardest to convince myself otherwise, but I can't. If the *Preveze* floats it past a wire-clearance maneuver and then lets it drift, we can see it on scanning sonar and scoop it up. It's nontrivial, but it's the sort of operation we're built for."

"Not to be a bitch, but you've claimed this ship was built for every operation. A jack of all trades is a master of none. What's the real risk?"

"They could arm the torpedo's magnetic influence field, and we'd never know it until it detected our hull and went boom."

"At one hundred yards, could they survive?"

"Maybe. I don't know. We need Sergeui to answer."

The translator relayed the submariner's input. "A submarine can withstand shockwaves that kills its crew. If the *Preveze* is bow-on, the crew could hide in the engine room and have a chance of surviving. But if broadside, even if the ship stays intact, the shockwave will kill everyone inside."

"Can the Turk launch a weapon and place it close aboard to his broadside? Remember, he can't maneuver."

Russian banter preceded the interpreter's response. "He can't drive the weapon that close to himself due to anti-circular safeguards. But a *Type-209* has an outboard. Let him deploy it and use it to orient himself broadside to his weapon."

While making her decision, Danielle slowed her breathing. Overloaded by second opinions and advice, she committed to the exchange and reached for the microphone. "Captain, I think I have a solution. Over."

"I'm listening. Over."

After dumping a load of information on her former adversary, she'd won over her Turkish ally.

Thirty minutes later, Danielle had every scanning sonar on the *Goliath* energized, every light illuminated, and hope stirring in every heart of two ship's crews.

Scanning sonar showed the compliant *Preveze* drifting broadside to a torpedo her team had heard launched, and her four outboard motors shuffled her closer to the submarine.

As a gesture of trust, she announced her progress. "I'm three hundred yards off your starboard beam, Captain. Over."

"Understood. Do you see my torpedo yet? Over."

"Not yet. Likely in another hundred yards. Over."

As she hoped, the oblong instrument of destruction appeared on her display, pixilated in bright green by scanning sonar. Then she recognized her limits. "I don't know this ship well enough to handle this, and I assume there's no automated routine?"

Walker was gentle. "I couldn't handle it either. This isn't ship handling. It's cargo loading. Fortunately, our expert's been nudging us towards the *Preveze* and is confident he can do this. I'd like to help him by deploying the rover to give him better visibility."

"Very well. Deploy the rover."

Watching through external cameras offering multiple views over the *Goliath's* topside superstructures and its cargo bed, Danielle watched a hatch flip open atop the starboard hull.

From the opening, the self-propelled roving camera emerged on its tether and darted above her view.

"Who's controlling that?"

"Another expert. We've got an expert and a backup for all our cool toys."

"Understood."

"If I may." Walker reached in front of her and tapped icons, giving her an improved perspective of the *Goliath* from selected cameras and the new perspective of the rover.

"I can't argue the view. I can see how it gives our team a vantage point to get the job done."

"The guy working the outboards can work us left, right, back and forth all day. The poor bastard I worry about is the guy handling depth control. That's going to be the arse-ache, since the weapon's so small and landing off our centerline axis."

"Now you tell me?"

"He'll move slow. Really slow. And I trust me boys."

She eyed him.

"Sorry. Your boys."

"Terry's boys. I'm just borrowing them."

She glued her eyes to the monitor as the pixelated cylindrical image grew larger. A camera on the ship's port hull glimpsed the torpedo's underside over the *Goliath*. It was misaligned, but then outboard activity twisted the transport ship onto the same axis.

Facing her fear, she looked out the window and saw the illusion of the weapon gliding towards her, like a celestial body. "Is anyone else freaked out about this?"

"Maybe Sergeui no hero. Maybe I am idiot for this idea."

Walker's report cut the tension. "I see a long oval forming off the port side. Yes, ma'am, that's a sidescan sonar detection of the *Preveze*. If we die, they die."

Having kept tabs on the submarine through passive sonar–a triviality with the *Preveze's* hissing downpour–she knew it was there. But she was learning the sketchiness of passive range estimates, and seeing the vessel on scanning sonar was a relief.

She keyed her microphone. "We're underneath your weapon, Captain, and we see you on sidescan sonar. Over."

"Understood, Captain. Over."

Landing the weapon against welded joints consumed long minutes that passed in slow anxiety. After allowing her team the time to move with caution, she held her breath and watched the *Goliath* rise into the weapon.

With a clunk, it landed against her starboard hull and two hydraulic arm joints.

Sergeui turned white. "No. No. Me Idiot!"

"What? Don't tell me you forgot something."

"Sorry. I forgot something."

She wanted to rip off his Russian head.

"But have idea. Need translator."

After the rapid Russian exchange, the interpreter explained Sergeui's intent. "The torpedo is neutrally buoyant. The only way we can hold it is by going to the surface and lifting it from the water. But if we do that, we can't load the *Preveze*."

Butterflies flittered in Danielle's stomach. "I'm waiting for a very important 'however'."

"However, if you take a slight down angle with forward motion, flow friction will keep it pressed against the hull and the rocker arms."

Her tension eased. "Liam?"

"That's doable. The *Preveze* would need to take the same angle and speed, or close to it. We can make minor corrections, but–"

"But the ship's designed for it."

He sighed. "Right."

"Make it happen while I have a chat with our future Turkish guests."

Half an hour later, the *Preveze* and its diplomatic torpedo were aboard the *Goliath*, moving with a three-degree down angle at one-point-eight knots.

"Captain, are you ready to surface? Over."

"After what you just did, I'm quite ready. Take us up. Over."

CHAPTER 22

While awaiting news from his FBI classmate and from his commanders, Jake napped.

He awoke to knocking on the vault's open door. "What?"

Commander Laurent had refused to allow an unproven French naval officer to replace him. His enthusiasm in rousting the American suggested that his round-the-clock loyalty had paid off in excitement. "Wake up! Wake up! You won't believe this."

"What is it?"

"The *Goliath* is surfaced and hailing you."

In disbelief, the mercenary fleet's acting commodore released his fears of deceased shipmates while darting past Laurent. "Surfaced? Shit. Are they okay?"

"Yes. Maybe. They're at risk of detection by the Americans, but I think that's her point. You have to see this for yourself."

Jake rubbed sleep from his eyes and then refocused them on Danielle Sutton's face. "What's going on?"

Her businesslike focus impressed him. "Quick summary. The maneuver with the *Rahab* was flawless. It absorbed the torpedo from the *Burakreis*. But when I transited towards a possible launch position, I ran into the *Preveze*, which you can see is now in my cargo bed." She paused to allow her boss to speak.

Jake flipped through screens showing varied views of the Turkish submarine from the *Goliath's* cameras. He was surprised, but given his fleet's rampant audacity, he really wasn't. "I see that. Pretty damned impressive, but I'll withhold my questions for the sake of time. Keep talking."

She continued her report. "I was within mutually-assured-destruction range and locked in a stalemate with the *Preveze* until you issued your order to rendezvous and face the Americans. Under those orders, I was able to negotiate an agreement with the *Preveze's* captain, Commander Ozan Dogan, to unite in a show of force against the Americans. That's how he willingly ended up aboard the *Goliath*."

"I see." As his mind kicked into awareness, Jake saw an anomaly in a camera view. "He's there willingly. That's great, and it answers one question. But I don't like what I think I see dangling on your starboard hull."

"It's an armed torpedo, under wire control. I don't like it either, but I considered it no more dangerous than the torpedoes inside the *Preveze*. If Commander Dogan wants to destroy me, he can command-detonate any one of them."

Finding a slight inaccuracy with her statement, Jake recalled that detonating a dry torpedo required breaking into its circuitry and overriding safeguards. A weapon of that power needed to be convinced it was immersed in water a safe distance from its host vessel before invoking its detonation algorithms.

Per his estimate, the Turks could have armed an interior torpedo within hours and had probably been working on it since the beginning of the stalemate.

He considered Danielle's gambit wise and gave the *Goliath's* temporary commander credit for winning her high-stakes gamble. "Agreed. Keep talking."

"Either way, he'd die with us in any attack. The torpedo on my hull is a trophy for him and a bargaining chip for you. It lets him defend his position with his fleet, claiming he forced us to surface and turn back. And it's evidence of negotiations between us and the Turks you can use against the Americans."

Rapid-fire thoughts raced through Jake's head, and his rising bile reminded him he was a poor substitute for the sly diplomatic fox, Pierre Renard. Quelling his doubts, he promised himself to think clearly and free his captive loved ones. "I'm following you so far. Keep going."

"You can see that he survived Dmitry's dolphin attack and

kept fighting. Two holes in his control room. He's snorkeling now and making welding repairs. I'm pretty sure he's also having an interesting discussion with his fleet right now."

"Did you make any offers or concessions to the Turks?"

"Other than what you see, I offered our services to stand against the Americans. I didn't mention any price or qualifications, but I doubt they'll want to turn against the Americans. They're playing defense. We're the only ones who need to show signs of aggression."

Jake agreed. "Good thinking. Any signs of other warships?"

"None. If we're being watched, it's by someone quiet. It may be wishful thinking, but the Americans could be circling the wagons around the battle group, including their submarines, and waiting to see what's left over after we and the Turks beat each other up."

"It's possible, but I don't like you being surfaced, whether it's a message to the Americans or not."

To his horror and excitement, Olivia hailed him. "Hold on Danielle. Olivia's calling. I think you earned her attention."

"If I did, it's time for me to submerge again."

Appreciating Danielle's broad vision, he agreed. "If you don't hear from me in two minutes, do exactly that."

"Understood."

Jake switched to Olivia. "To what do I owe the pleasure?"

Her natural flow with unnatural news made the CIA renegade unreadable. "The *Goliath* isn't where I told you to put it."

Unsure if Olivia had eyes, ears, or both on his flagship, he stalled. "If you'll cut me some slack, I just found it myself."

"Where the hell's it going?"

Jolted by her refusal to acknowledge the *Preveze's* teamwork, Jake bought more time. "Look, you know how ugly it can get during a torpedo exchange. Danielle was under fire and needed to maneuver. We're getting things back in order."

Lifting a drone's reconnaissance photo of the *Goliath-Preveze* tandem, the CIA beast played her card. "Then what the fuck's this?"

Jake shifted gears from ignoramus to ogre, embellishing his position. "Oh, that? That's my new friend, Commander Ozan Dogan from the Turkish Navy. In fact, I'm making a lot of new friends with my new NATO ally. Ozan's talking to his friends in his fleet headquarters. Did you know that my fleet plus their fleet is enough to hurt your fleet really, really bad?"

"This isn't the deal, Jake."

"Deal? How about fuck you, you have my wife. Give her back. Give all the captives back, and I'll send my ships to Toulon."

Her eyes became black rage. "You really fucked this up, Jake. You're responsible for what happens next." She cut him off.

His heart raced, and he invoked the screen to the *Goliath*. "Submerge, Danielle. Warn the *Preveze* and head under. Shit could get ugly fast. I'll send you more information as I get it."

"I'm submerging."

Jake slid to the leftmost console and hailed the bunker.

An unfamiliar face appeared. After a quick exchange, Jake told the underling to find LeClerc and the FBI man.

Minutes later, the former aviator and the youthful but bleary-eyed FBI agent from Lyon appeared.

"Guys, I need Mike Jennings. Now."

The young FBI man scowled and answered in French. "I think I understand, but you just spoke English."

Jake shifted to his second language. "Shit. Rough times. I need Jennings!"

The FBI agent fiddled with his phone and then aimed it at the display.

The Naval Academy classmate appeared. "I'm here, Jake. What's the status?"

"The *Goliath* just surfaced with the Turkish submarine, *Preveze* in its cargo bed. There's a loose alliance between my fleet and the *Preveze* to appear united against the *Lincoln* battle group."

Jennings face turned black. "Do not attack any American assets."

"Would that deny my wife's rights as an American citizen?"

The FBI officer sounded exasperated. "You need to use common sense."

"Common sense didn't place my wife in captivity. I'm fighting tyranny with tyranny."

"Stick with the plan. Everything's ready. If you can just wait until your next scheduled check-in with your wife."

"Shit."

"Shit, what?"

"I just pissed off Olivia. There may not be another check-in."

Jennings slumped his shoulders. "That was bad. Can you repair it?"

"Maybe if I kiss her ass real hard."

"Do it."

Jake returned to his working console and hailed the CIA rogue.

After twenty seconds, she answered. "I hope you've got a plan to fix this."

"Of course, I do. I've made my show of power, and I think you believe my conviction."

Her features were unmoving.

"Now that I've made my point, and I believe that you believe I'm willing to sacrifice everything. Now that you see that, perhaps we can work together."

"I'm listening."

"I know I can't fight a carrier battle group. So, I'll have the *Goliath* take the *Preveze* north to Turkish waters. Then they'll part ways, pretend to be friends, and then I'll send the *Goliath* the long way around Cyprus. The *Specter* and *Wraith* will already be there in secret, clearing a launch area, and then the *Goliath* will start raining down hell fury on your targets."

"What guarantee can you give me?"

"If the *Preveze's* commander wanted the *Goliath* dead, he would've pulled the trigger already. But he's just a guy doing his job, and he just wants to go home and brag about stalling the infamous mercenary fleet."

"Get it done." She reached towards her screen to end the conversation.

Jake yelled. "Olivia!"

"What?"

"Can I talk to my wife? I'm in full compliance now, and I'd like to assure her of her safety through my compliance."

"Why should I?"

"Who can argue with compliant detainees? They're less likely to fight back, more likely to give you any information you want, and more likely to encourage me and the commanders to keep obeying you."

"I'll give you a check-in in five minutes." She hung up before Jake could respond.

Still expecting that the CIA monitored his communications, Jake upheld his part of the ruse and issued Danielle a textual order to surface again and follow a course straight to the nearest Turkish coastline with the intent of dropping off the *Preveze* in its home waters.

He then slid to the leftmost console with the bunker connection. "Olivia says I can have a chat in five minutes."

Jennings eyed the mercenary fleet's commodore. "Are you ready?"

After checking his phone's video of his mother-in-law's greeting, Jake's racing heart said 'no', but he was trapped. "Yes."

"I'm ready here, then. Tentative entry is in five minutes. We'll update that as you talk to Linda. I see that the feed you set up between your check-ins and Renard's bunker is working. I'll verify that the judge and translators are ready, and I'll get my team ready for ingress."

"This is happening fast."

"It always does, but this is what I do. I've got it covered on my end. You just talk to your wife, run the video, and keep this line open for my cues."

Four minutes later, the chime for a check-in request made Jake gasp. He tapped the icon to bring up his wife's face. "Linda."

"Jake! This isn't our normal check-in time, but they let me

call you."

He stuck with English. "I know. I've been 'good', for lack of better word. I'm just going with the flow, and I was allowed to talk to you thanks to my improved attitude."

"Awesome. Any chance we can go home?"

"Not until the job's done. I need more time."

She frowned. "Oh."

"But I got a hold of your mom. I told her you're okay. Of course, she didn't believe me. But she sends her love."

"That's sweet, Jake."

"She was concerned and even recorded a message for you."

A tear welled in Linda's eye. "Okay."

"She's a bit hard to hear. So, watch and listen very closely." He lifted his phone and played his mother-in-law's throaty mix of the dual-language Arabic-Aramaic code that approached Navajo levels of murkiness. He understood a fraction of it, but he knew its contents.

The FBI was next door ready to break into Linda's room as soon as they had a warrant. To get that warrant, Linda needed to say in a clear and slow mix of Arabic and Aramaic that she'd been kidnapped and held against her will. The FBI is watching your husband talk to you right now. Say it right now."

"Jake?"

"Obey your mother! Now!"

She uttered her dual-language code. "I have been kidnapped and am being held against my will."

Jake aimed his gaze to the Jennings' image.

The FBI officer nodded and raised a finger. He scribbled on a pad and then revealed the lettering. "Translation with judge in process. Keep stalling."

Unsure what to say, Jake switched to English. "I know, honey. I'm sorry that you're sad."

Another glance at Jennings showed progress. 'She gave us what we needed. Warrant is signed! Entry in thirty seconds.'

Jake checked the time on his console and then faced his wife. "Do you have any news for your kids? They're staying with your mom, but they're justifiably worried."

Confused, Linda spoke in a wavering voice. "Tell them I love them."

Twenty seconds. "I know."

"Linda? Do you trust me completely?"

"Of course, I trust you, Jake."

Fifteen seconds. He switched to Aramaic. "You fall to floor soon."

"I go to floor? Hide?" Before answering, he looked to the monitor with the FBI officer.

Hidden in the hotel room beside that of the captives, Jennings pushed his latest notes into Jake's view. 'Twelve seconds. Timing is precise.' The Naval Academy graduate lowered the pad, raised his palms, and then curled a finger closed with each passing second.

Watching the fingered countdown with his peripheral vision, Jake looked back to his wife. "When I say. Ready?"

"Yes."

Five seconds. "Soon. Very soon." He howled in English. "Hit the floor!"

Linda dived off screen.

The banging thud of a door being knocked off its hinges issued from Jake's console, followed by FBI agents shouting their identities and ordering everyone to the ground.

A helpless spectator, Jake saw nothing but heard protests and guards arguing the interruption of a bona fide CIA operation.

But the FBI had overpowering numbers and a warrant, and with a whimper, the standoff ended.

Wearing an FBI jacket and flanked by two of his officers, Jennings appeared before the screen Linda had ducked from. He almost smiled. "It's over, Jake. Your wife's safe. Make your fleet stand down."

His throat tight, Jake protested. "Show me my wife!"

Jennings looked away, gestured towards himself, and ushered Linda to the computer.

Her face was a mix of horror and relief. "Is it really over?"

Tears welled in Jake's eyes. "Yes, honey. It is. That's Mike Jennings, my Naval Academy classmate. You can trust him."

"I already do. He just saved my life." Surprising the FBI man, she hugged him.

Wrestling Linda aside gently, Jennings nudged his face to the display and interrupted the reunion. "Stop your fleet, Jake!"

"Give me thirty seconds!" Jake shifted windows about his screen and issued an immediate ceasefire and surfacing of all his ships. "Done. Let the Navy know that we're standing down and will comply with the United States Navy and the Turkish Navy in releasing the *Preveze*."

"I'll make that call now."

An FBI jacket across her back, Ariella appeared. "Thank you, Jake. You did well. Is Terry okay?"

"We haven't talked in a while, but I just ordered him to surface. I'll have him call you on his satellite phone."

Lowering his phone from his ear, Jennings interrupted yet another reunion. "My boss has confirmation that the *Lincoln* battle group acknowledges your fleet's intention to return to Toulon without hostility."

"That's great!"

"There are stipulations."

"Aren't there always?"

"You need to remain surfaced throughout the entire transit, you need to allow naval observer parties on each ship to assure your compliance, and you need to follow an escort ship that will take you directly to Toulon."

Jake sighed. "Fine. None of those are deal-breakers."

"They'd already thought this through. You really have turned that fleet into a thorn in many people's foot. I suggest you comply."

Jake considered the conditions for two seconds. "Agreed. What about the *Preveze*, though?"

"Get rid of that dangling torpedo and send the submarine home just like you ordered Sutton to do. Our navy will allow the transit if you head straight north to Turkish waters.

"Done. The *Goliath* will have to partially submerge to get the torpedo off its back and then the *Preveze* will have to command-inert it to sink it. Can you arrange for that? I don't want a hidden American submarine to destroy my ship and the *Preveze* based upon a misunderstanding."

"Hold off on the maneuver until I can confirm it, but it shouldn't be a problem.

"And what about Olivia?"

Jennings snorted. "The CIA is working with us, now that we have a warrant and can share what we know. She'll have a lot of explaining to do."

While the world righted itself, Jake looked to Commander Laurent. "You've been quiet."

"I've had nothing to say. But now, I must say that watching you was like watching a younger Pierre. He chose his replacement wisely."

"I'm not his replacement. I command a submarine. This was an accident."

The Frenchman smirked. "We shall see."

Surfaced, Danielle hailed Jake, and he accepted. "Danielle! It's over."

"What's over?"

"Everything except clean up. The FBI just stormed the hotel and has everyone's family safe."

"You haven't broadcast that yet."

"Shit! One moment." Jake typed a status about the safe families and then sent it.

She smirked. "I see it. That's better."

"Things got dicey here. Thanks for reminding me."

"I have another question. May I share our ruse with the *Rahab* with Commander Dogan. He's asked out of curiosity."

"You've developed quite a relationship with him?"

She gave her polite smile. "Of sorts."

"Why not? The Turks would eventually figure it out anyway."

"Also, he has a message for you."

"For me?"

"Maybe. Or maybe for Pierre. Depends who's in charge."

"What is it?"

"He says he knows you recruit wounded animals as commanding officers, even people you've fought against, like Dmitry Volkov."

Jake grunted. "There's some truth to that."

"He insists that he is neither wounded nor job-hunting, and he asks that we never call upon him again."

CHAPTER 23

A month later, Dmitry Volkov's lungs heaved as he approached the high plateau shy of the summit of Mont Sainte Victoire, the peak Jake had ranted incessantly about as having been glorified by the post-impressionist, Paul Cézanne.

Volkov considered Jake's favoring of French impressionists a side effect of studying the culture while learning the language. As he reconsidered the low place of his native Russian artists in history's rankings, he conceded the art argument to his American colleague.

As uneven and jagged stones slowed his steps, an updraft from the valley lifted the scent of lilac and lavender to his nostrils, distracting him from thoughts of art.

Looking upward, he reminded himself that summiting the mountain was his favorite teambuilding exercise, and he enjoyed being part of the team, especially with its latest addition.

To his elation and trepidation, the fleet's newest commander had agreed to accompany him on the climb.

In flannel hiking garb, Danielle labored through steps below him.

Volkov resisted the temptation to extend a helping hand. Wanting the human contact, he feared she'd see the gesture as an accusation of her weakness, or—worse—see it for what it was.

His yearning.

Instead of burdening the moment with unrealistic expectations, he sought the conservative approach of encouragement. "You doing great!"

He considered himself a buffoon when her polite, dismissive smile comprised her entire response.

A group of worshipers returning from a pilgrimage to the

summit strolled in the opposite direction, and, relieved nobody spoke French to him, he waved at a dozen descending hikers.

Danielle reached Volkov's side. "They must have started early."

"Yes. Real early. Our group lazy. Start late. Most people on way down already. We earn it though. This our vacation."

She gulped from her water bottle and then rested her hands on her hips while scanning the environs of Provence. "It's beautiful."

Yes, you are beautiful. Wait. Don't be an idiot. And hurry up and learn more English, you fool! "Of course. Every time. Always very beautiful view up here."

"I could get used to this."

"The effort makes the top valued."

She chuckled the polite gesture she'd repeated a dozen times during the ascent after his linguistic errors. "I think you mean the journey makes the summit worth the climb."

"Yes. I mean this."

Overpowering the November chill, her sincere smile warmed him. "Your English is very good. I know it's hard. I tried Spanish in school, and I can barely say 'good morning'."

As movement at a lower switchback caught his eye, Volkov frowned. "Bodyguards with Pierre."

The aging Frenchman arrived with the final pair of ten protectors he'd employed for assuring his growing team's safety. Renard labored, but his face showed strong color as he called out in English. "Hello there! How wonderful to see two of my commanding officers enjoying the climb."

Danielle checked her watch and responded. "Good morning, Pierre. Barely."

"Ah, it's almost noon, is it not? I know I slow the team's advance, but I will climb this mountain until I no longer can."

Volkov risked English in front of his boss and the object of his desires. "You climb forever. I say this is Pierre's mountain."

Unwilling to yield his momentum, Renard escorted the

husky guards past the commanding officers. "I appreciate the vote of confidence. Don't linger too long. This is the last of our party."

Lamenting the addition of extra protective services, Volkov accepted his lot as a high-risk personality. Guards, hiding, and security boundaries were in his future. "My fault. Danielle very patient with my bad English."

As Renard and his bodyguards rounded a turn, the *Goliath's* former temporary commander stuck her water bottle into her backpack. "Ready?"

"Maybe we let Pierre go ahead. Don't catch him yet."

"Ah. Good idea. Let's keep the boss happy. Make it look like we had to hurry to catch him." She took several strides and then squatted with her back against an escarpment.

Volkov moved before her. "We going to make great partners."

"Um, okay. I'm not sure if your English is off a bit there. What are you trying to say?"

He raised defensive palms. "No. No. I mean, you on *Xerses*. Me on *Wraith*. We are assigned pair. Not sure of home port yet. Pierre say maybe Singapore. Pacific or Indian Ocean. Don't know."

She cast a demure stare at the ground. "I misunderstood you. No, you're absolutely right. We will make a good team."

"Still very impressed with you on *Goliath*. What you did. Everyone still talking."

"Given the company, I was just passing a job interview. I assume I passed, given that Pierre hasn't kicked me off the team."

"No. You do very well. We each score one submarine–you, me, and Terry. No credit for me on *Preveze*. Let get away. My first big mistake in fleet."

"You were forced to hurry. You had little choice."

"You very kind."

"From what I understand, you still have earned credit for the most submarines removed from action. You caught and surpassed Jake long ago, and now you just added one more to your lead with the *Sakarya*."

He understood half of the words in her compliment but enjoyed them all. "I am glad you stay."

"I think taking care of the *Preveze* was exactly what I needed. A little luck was part of it, for sure, but it helped me prove myself to the fleet, and to myself."

Volkov recognized the Turkish submarine's name. "Ah, and you first commander to score a submarine without using weapon."

Looking away, she processed the comment. "Huh. I guess I hadn't thought of that." She wriggled her weight over her thighs and extended her arm. "Help me up."

Like a child, he beamed with joy at the opportunity to hold her hand for fleeting seconds. "Okay."

She stood and faced the looming climb. "Let's go."

"*Da*! You lead."

After speechless, rigorous climbing he rounded a turn, and a wooden chapel came into view. He crossed the doorstep and smelled stale oak. Except for a statue of Christ and a few rows of pews, the chapel was bare with a worn floor.

Volkov knelt, crossed himself, and uttered a quick prayer.

Behind him, Danielle questioned his actions. "You're religious?"

"I am... called I think, Orthodox." He hoped it wasn't a problem from her perspective.

"I'm Anglican, supposedly. I don't practice much."

He shifted his focus back to his colleague. "Come on. I show you great view."

In the grassy yard outside the chapel, he led her to a glass wall that blocked people from falling down the southern escarpment. The green plain spanned the horizon.

She beheld the panorama. "It's amazing."

"Jake tells me much greener until fire long time ago."

"That's sad."

He felt like an idiot struggling with English. "No, no. It's okay. It's nature."

She was kind with his linguistic vulnerability. "I understand.

I like the view a lot. You can see so far in every direction."

Careful to avoid touching her, he moved close and smelled her hair while pointing. "Toulon over there. Our ships in a dry dock. Barely see the town from here." Mesmerized by her scent, he enjoyed it for a moment and then backed away.

Following his lead, she trailed him into a building that resembled a misplaced barn and served as a gathering place for climbers resting below the summit.

Inside, a mix of French, Australian, and Russian sailors of the mercenary fleet worked through language barriers to lob volleys of taller and taller tales of heroism.

Letting Danielle mingle with the others, Volkov smelled dampness, aged wood, and vodka while he strolled to his crewmen. Finding the dolphin trainer and his proper executive officer, he sat on a creaky bench. Speaking his native Russian relaxed him. "What's for lunch?"

Sergeui extended a wrapped sandwich. "I grabbed a roast beef for you. I didn't have much choice, since you're the last to arrive."

"It was worth the delay."

Vasily chided him. "You're spending quality time with the fleet's latest rising star."

Volkov sighed. "I'm afraid it's a fool's hope."

"Bullshit, Dmitry. I know women."

Sergeui chuckled. "We're all still debating that."

"If we compare notes, I will put you to shame like a virgin." Vasily returned his focus to his commanding officer. "I was watching carefully when she entered the room. There's a glow about her, for sure. Some of it's the excitement from her success and her acceptance into the family. But there's a little extra something. It could be her reaction to being around you."

Sergeui countered. "Don't give him false hopes. Stick to your dolphins. Speaking of which, you got any ideas on how to make them useful again?"

"Yes, yes. I'm happy it's getting easier to pick them up when we lose them, but I'm tired of losing them. It took two days to charter a boat this time. I'm going to try some new communication techniques with them and also with the Persian females. I have hope for them, too. Maybe we can deploy dolphin pairs on each submarine."

Sergeui nodded. "That would be excellent."

As Volkov swallowed a mouthful of beef, Renard stood at the front of the room and addressed the two dozen sailors. "English should be fine for everyone except for our Russian friends. I'm going to speak slowly anyway."

Volkov's translator marched to the trio he'd abandoned. "Sorry. I'll help when needed, but I'm afraid you're slowly outgrowing your need for me."

With the interpreter filling in blanks, Volkov listened to his boss.

Renard was reserved compared to his normal boasting. "I feel like I abandoned you before this mission, but trust me, I considered it a difficult sacrifice for the better good. And who can argue with the results of our hero who led us. Take a bow, Jake."

The American bent forward and then straightened his back. "Do I get one, Pierre? You promised."

"Fine. Just one. Everyone, I promised the bible college student one philosophical riddle for our entertainment. Uh... please bear with him, and my apologies if it's excruciatingly boring."

Jake raised his voice. "Here's the riddle. At least I think it's a riddle. Science can't define what gives the human consciousness life. Therefore, it can't define what gives the human consciousness death. Therefore, all the evidence available to science cannot prove or disprove that the human consciousness survives death. Therefore, an afterlife must be considered possible."

Silence.

Renard frowned. "Huh. That's actually thought-provoking."

"Do I get another?"

"Why not? But only one. People want to see the summit."

Jake launched his next brainteaser. "Each human is capable of infinite thoughts but has only a finite number of synapses.

Therefore, human thoughts exist beyond the natural human body. Therefore, human thought is supernatural. Therefore, each of us is supernatural, and supernatural elements must be considered when answering philosophical questions."

Renard glared at him. "If I don't restrain you now, you'll drive my fleet mad with your riddles. Enough."

Smiling, Jake waved off his boss and sat next to his wife, the newlywed Cahill with his bride, and the Walkers.

Renard concluded. "Finally, let's welcome our latest addition to the team, Danielle Sutton. I think we can all agree she's passed the audition!"

Standing, she was radiant as the momentary center of the fleet's attention, and she was stunning as the enduring center of Volkov's fantasies.

The lovesick Russian lingered as the others flowed out the barn and towards the summit. Finding his way to Danielle, he requested a reunion. "Not far now. You want to join me?"

Her smile melted him. "Sure."

After a difficult incline and a steep turn around a final corner, Volkov saw the mountain's top. Visitors were standing and seated on rocks around the six-meter cross that graced the peak.

"Not the highest point." He lifted his arm in front of her. "Highest point over there. But this best spot. View all directions."

"I like it. It's an incredible view."

Butterflies ransacking his stomach, he made his move. "Jake pick out restaurant they speak good English and great food. You join me? Make big appetite with mountain climb."

"Oh, now you have Jake helping you?"

"I need all help I can get."

She crossed her arms and kicked a rock across the rubble. "I've been hurt before."

As Volkov drew confidence with her confession, a gooey feeling overcame him. Afraid to recoil into silence, he blurted what came to mind. "I don't hurt people. Help people. Ask Vasily, Anatoly, or Sergeui. I help all be better people."

"I know." Tightening her body in subconscious defense, she released a coy smile. "Sergeui likes you a lot."

"You ask him about me?"

Wrapping herself tighter in her hug, she shrugged. "Maybe."

Hope rose within Volkov. "Do I have chance get to know you, Danielle?"

She studied her boots and then gave him a sideways glance. "If you treat me right, Dmitry, you have every chance in the world."

THE END

ABOUT THE AUTHOR

After graduating from the Naval Academy in 1991, John Monteith served on a nuclear ballistic missile submarine and as a top-rated instructor of combat tactics at the U.S. Naval Submarine School. He now works as an engineer when not writing.

Join the Rogue Submarine fleet to get news, freebies, discounts, and your FREE Rogue Avenger bonus content!

ROGUE SUBMARINE SERIES:

ROGUE AVENGER (2005)
ROGUE BETRAYER (2007)
ROGUE CRUSADER (2010)
ROGUE DEFENDER (2013)
ROGUE ENFORCER (2014)
ROGUE FORTRESS (2015)
ROGUE GOLIATH (2015)
ROGUE HUNTER (2016)
ROGUE INVADER (2017)
ROGUE JUSTICE (2017)
ROGUE KINGDOM (2018)
ROGUE LIBERATOR (2018)
ROGUE MERCENARY (2019)

WRAITH HUNTER CHRONICLES:

PROPHECY OF ASHES (2018)
PROPHECY OF BLOOD (2018)
PROPHECY OF CHAOS (2018)
PROPHECY OF DUST (2018)
PROPHECY OF EDEN (2019)

John Monteith recommends:

Graham Brown, author of The Gods of War.

Jeff Edwards, author of Sword of Shiva.

Thomas Mays, author of A Sword into Darkness.

Kevin Miller, author of Raven One.

Ted Nulty, author of Gone Feral.

ROGUE MERCENARY

Braveship Books

www.braveshipbooks.com

The tactics described in this book do not represent actual U.S. Navy or NATO tactics past or present. Also, many of the code words and some of the equipment have been altered to prevent unauthorized disclosure of classified material.

ISBN-13: 978-1-64062-100-8
Published in the United States of America

Made in the USA
Columbia, SC
09 December 2019